The Death Of Time

Byron Grush

Published in the United States by Broadhorn Publishing, Delavan, WI

ISBN: 978-0-9985454-3-1

Part One

The Coddiwomplers

Preface to Part One:
The Coddiwomplers

Coddiwomple: to travel purposefully toward an
as-yet-unknown destination
—English slang

According to Wikipedia (if it is on the internet, it must be true), TIME is "the indefinite continued progress of existence and events that occur in apparently irreversible succession from the past through the present to the future." Well, that's a mouthful! Human life is like the gnomon on the sundial, casting shadows on a dais which has been marked off in minute life spans to count the hours and days and months and years in arbitrary measurement. Irreversible succession. Aristotle was not so sure about that. He said that "time is not composed of indivisible nows any more than any other magnitude is composed of indivisibles." According to Judeo-Christian philosophy, time is linear and points along a vector stretching from the creation of the universe by God, and ending at the "end time," when God is done putting up with the human race. Other ancient cultures saw time as circular: wheels of time where events happened over and over. The Kabbalah said that time was a paradox, an illusion, wherein past and present co-existed in the moment. Then along came Newton, followed two centuries later by Einstein.

What if we could travel back and forward in time? What would we do? Who would we most like to meet? If a poet, would you like to meet Milton or perhaps Ovid? If an author, perhaps Hemingway or Shakespeare or Chaucer? If an artist, would you travel to the time of Van Gogh or Michelangelo? If a scientist, how wonderful to chat with Galileo or William of Ockham! Are you religious? Would you wish to witness the life of Jesus, of Moses, of the Buddha, of

Mohamad? Would you travel to the time of the extinction of the dinosaurs? Or would you dare to seek out the future?

And what if you could change history? Those of my generation, many I imagine, would elect to stop the assassinations of the Kennedys and Martin Luther King. We could stop 9-11 from happening. Maybe we could stop Donald Trump's father from having intercourse. The options for altering history are endless—as are the consequences. In 1963, in his treatise, "The Predictability of Hydrodynamic Flow," scientist Edward Lorenz stated that it was possible that "one flap of a seagull's wings would be enough to alter the course of the weather forever." A dozen years earlier, Ray Bradbury wrote a science fiction story called "A Sound of Thunder," that gave rise to the term "the butterfly effect." A single butterfly, flapping its wings creates an event so small as to be deemed insignificant. But could it change the course of history? Is the butterfly cognoscente of its role in the causal nexus? Is the butterfly like a tiny god-thing? Or is the butterfly, as Zhuang Zhu suggests, dreaming it is a man?

1

Alchemist's Room

The shelf was heavy oak of an uncertain age, etched with cracks and fragmented into splinters at the ends. It was supported against the stone wall with brackets of iron where cobweb spiders spun homes with filaments of delicate silvery thread, invisible except when struck by sunlight—sunlight chronically absent in the chamber. Upon the shelf balanced glass orbs and bottles and long-necked containers of various sizes. These contained the congregant sampling of universal elements in symbolic form: a medley of tokens from earth, air, water, and fire. Their arrangement was according to the four colorings: black (nigredo), white (albedo), yellow (citrinitas), and purple (rudedo).

A long table sat in a sea of dust in the center of the dark chamber. Retorts bubbled over flaming wicks of twisted flax infused with oil. Near the edge of the table sat a stoppered bottle containing an Acherontia atropos, a large moth with narrow wings and a bulbous body upon which were markings strongly resembling a human skull. This was a hawk moth or sphinx moth, commonly called a death's head moth. It was exhausted from its futile flappings to escape its glass prison; it no longer emitted the loud squeaking it made by forcing air through its proboscis.

In one corner of the room there was a cylindrical stone stove.

Cinders glowed inside of this, the remnants of virgin timber which had flamed through the previous evening heating an iron caldron to a rolling boil. Its contents had been transferred to a series of glass vials where it had been diluted with nigredo in the form of coal dust, aldedo in the form of chalk, citrinitas in the form of powered sulfur, or rudedo in the form of red clay—all elements of Earth. The results of this process had been disappointingly mundane. Sludge.

Outside, Teige, the alchemist's Irish wolfhound, was creating a racket. The alchemist had forgotten to tie the dog up and now he was chasing something near the edge of the forest, barking furiously. It was irritating and distracting and caused the alchemist's hand to shake slightly as he poured an elixir of heated mercury onto the lump of a compound of sulfur, saltpeter, and dried foxglove. The mercury spilled onto the table where it sat in a shining puddle, reflecting the flickering tongues of flame beneath the retorts and casting an eerie constellation of dancing shapes against the walls and ceiling of the room.

The four elements were merely different stages of the Divine Light of Universal Creation: earth was just condensed water, water was condensed air, and air was nothing more than condensed and uncouth fire. The regions of separation of those elements and the transmutations of each to the other…ah, that was the mystery whose understanding was the goal of the alchemist.

This was the real, observable world where physical substances could be seen and touched. But there were other worlds in the alchemist's imagination. The Kingdom of God, of course…Heaven and Hell and all that went with them. And many possible worlds in between; some angelic, some demonic, some banal. But just as the physical elements were all made of the same material, simply vibrating at different wave lengths (the concept of wave vibration wasn't yet thought of by the alchemist but he sensed this), the different worlds were also strata of a continuum.

One just couldn't see into those other worlds, but, according to the best philosophy the alchemist could muster, because all things were part of a universal system, because correspondence was the law of the universe, those worlds must exist! Was there a philosopher's stone to transmute common reality to the sublime? As above, so below, as within, so without, as the universe, so the soul—those were the words of the Thrice Great, Hermes Trismegistus, the grandson of

Adam, the builder of the pyramids, the author of the Hermetica. What had he said about the transmutation of the soul?

The Alchemist often studied the 42 texts of the Hermetica, those remaining tomes not destroyed in the burning of the library at Alexandria. As he thought over the essential problems of alchemical science, he was reminded of tablet ten of the Emerald Tablets, the one called "The Key of Time." Therein Hermes had stated that "mystery is only mystery when it is knowledge unknown to man." He had said that "TIME is the secret whereby ye may be free of this space." In particular, the alchemist was intrigued by the stanza:

Time changes not,
but all things change in time.
For time is the force
that holds events separate,
each in its own proper place.
Time is not in motion,
but ye move through time
as your consciousness
moves from one event to another.
...
Then sought I to solve the mystery of time.
Found I that time moves through strange angles.
Yet only by curves could I hope to attain the key
that would give me access to the time-space.
Found I that only by moving upward
and yet again by moving to right-ward
could I be free from the time of the movement.
Forth I came from out of my body,
moved in the movements that changed me in time.
Strange were the sights I saw in my journeys,
many the mysteries that opened to view.

Before he had studied this passage, the alchemist had thought of time as a straight line, a static, never varying vector that humankind followed mindlessly from cradle to grave...and beyond? Now he saw time more as a meandering river, winding through eternity, carrying along with it the events of man. Hermes had moved upward, then right-ward, and freed himself from time. And freed himself from the commonplace plane of existence that was the knowable world. He had been there and had returned to tell the tale. But how?

This year was 1573. The alchemist had a copy of Tycho Brahe's *De nova et nullius aevi memoria prius visa stella* (Concerning the star, new and never before seen in the life or memory of anyone), in which the astronomer and fellow alchemist had described in detail his observations of the appearance in the previous year of a new star in the Milky Way. What he had seen had been the afterglow of a supernova—the death, not the birth of a star. The event had challenged the common belief that the heavens were unchangeable. Tycho countered criticism of his discovery by writing, "Oh thick wits. Oh blind watchers of the sky...." The publication was the newest of the many books the alchemist had in his library. Tycho's assertion that the Aristotelian world-view was becoming obsolete helped to reassure the alchemist in his quest for truth.

Included in the alchemist's library were John Dee's *Monas Hieroglyphica*, Sir Henry Billingsley's translation from the Greek of the *Elements of Euclid* (with Dee's preface and supplementary material), Roger Bacon's *Speculum Alchimae (the Mirror of Alchemy)*, John Pontanus' *Epistola de Igne Philosophorum (Epistle concerning the Philosophic Fire)*, and an original copy of George Ripley's *Cantilena Riplaei* (the scroll called *The Compound of Alchemy, or the Twelve Gates leading to the Discovery of the Philosopher's Stone*).

A great assortment of books such as these was piled against one wall, their reddish-brown bindings fading toward darker brown, their gilt embellishments scratched or missing. On top of these sat a large, long-haired gray cat with a notched right ear, lazily licking its paws and brushing its whiskers. Its yellow eyes surveyed the room, watching the alchemist as he finished yet another failed experiment. A field mouse ran across the floor; the cat ignored it.

The alchemist sighed. Perhaps chemical means were not the sole requirement for piercing the veil between worlds. He went to the stack of books, picked up and placed the cat on floor saying, "there you go kitty," (the cat had no name which was known to the human) and rummaged through the books until he found his copy of Euclid. This he tucked under his arm as he continued to rummage. Now he retracted from the pile a new addition of *The History of Herodotus*. There was something lurking, not totally identified, in the back of his mind...an irking feeling that the answer was here, that he had read something, stored it away and forgotten it in that gloomy corner of the brain where one sweeps the overflow, the not-quite-trash of the day's studying.

The alchemist placed a dish of milk on the floor for the cat with no name and left the chamber with his books. Later, after a briskly consumed meal, he settled into a comfortable chair in his living quarters on the floor above and opened the Euclid. In John Dee's preface he found:

All thinges which are, & haue beyng, are found vnder a triple diuersitie generall. For, either, they are demed Supernaturall, Naturall, or, of a third being. Thinges Supernaturall, are immateriall, simple, indiuisible, incorruptible, & vnchangeable....

We before termed of a third being: which, by a peculier name also, are called Thynges Mathematicall. For, these, beyng (in a maner) middle, betwene thinges supernaturall and naturall: are not so absolute and excellent, as thinges supernatural: Nor yet so base and grosse, as things naturall: But are thinges immateriall: and neuerthelesse, by materiall things hable somewhat to be signified....

Of my former wordes, easy it is to be gathered, that Number hath a treble state: One, in the Creator: an other in euery Creature (in respect of his complete constitution:) and the third, in Spirituall and Angelicall Myndes, and in the Soule of mã. In the first and third state, Number, is termed Number Numbryng. But in all Creatures, otherwise, Number, is termed Nũber Numbred. And in our Soule, Nũber beareth such a swaye, and hath such an affinitie therwith: that some of the old Philosophers taught, Mans Soule, to be a Number mouyng it selfe.

He pondered the meaning of these words of wisdom. What had Dee meant, that man's soul was a number? He read on:

Of Astrologie, here I make an Arte, seuerall from Astronomie: not by new deuise, but by good reason and authoritie: for, Astrologie, is an Arte Mathematicall, which reasonably demonstrateth the operations and effectes, of the naturall beames, of light, and secrete influence: of the Sterres and Planets: in euery element and elementall body... and we, also, daily may perceaue, That mans body, and all other Elementall bodies, are altered, disposed, ordred, pleasured, and displeasured, by the Influentiall working of the Sunne, Mone, and the other Sterres and Planets.

Was this so? What implications had the effect of the sun, the moon, the stars, and the planets for the transmutation of the soul to other realms? He further studied in great length certain passages: the dissertation upon horometrie (*"Which demonstrateth, how, at all times appointed, the precise, vsuall denomination of time, may be knowen, for any place assigned."*), and the paragraphs on Thaumaturgike (*"Which geueth certaine order to make straunge workes, of the sense to be perceiued: and of men greatly to be wondred at."*), and lastly the explanation of Archemastrie (*"Which teacheth to bring to actuall experience sensible, all worthy conclusions, by all the Artes Mathematicall purposed: and by true Naturall philosophie, concluded… with helpe of the forsayd Artes, to the performance of complete Experiences…"*)—and yet the alchemist was not illuminated toward an understanding of how mathematics could be instrumental in his quest.

Now he turned his attention to Herodotus, especially to the histories and descriptions of Egypt and its environs. All things had come from the Egyptians: great thinking, great art, great architecture, and the seeds of all other religions. He lingered over Herodotus' analysis of the pyramids. The Great Pyramid of Cheops sat on a perfect square, Herodotus said, with each side measuring eight hundred feet, and the height was the same. Each side was equal in area to the others. There was a footnote to the translation relating to more recent attempts at measurements of the pyramid. Here the alchemist learned that the height was 480 feet, the sides were each approximately 756 feet in length, the perimeter was 3023 feet, and the angles of the corners were 90 degrees. The slope of the sides was 51.5 degrees. They all faced either north, south, east, or west. And the apex pointed toward the heavens, towards the sun, the moon, the stars and the planets.

And Hermes Trismegistus had designed the pyramids, or so it was said. Had Hermes pierced the veil by means of geometry? The alchemist soon found he was becoming obsessed with the idea. He took a parchment and a quill pen and ink from a drawer and began to sketch. He made a rough drawing of the pyramid and labeled its sides with the values he had learned. Now, because of his study of Euclid, he realized that if one dropped an imaginary line straight down from the apex to the ground, and then turned the line sharply toward one of the corners, the two lines with the addition of the side formed a right triangle. Using the Pythagorean theorem so ably proved by

Euclid in the *Elements*, he could calculate the length of the sides. Taking the values he thus computed and placing them over the values for the length of the base, he created a ratio which he could apply to a pyramid of any size.

The following morning the alchemist took himself to the woods surrounding his house and cut some young saplings of poplar. These he stripped of bark. He cut four of these to equal lengths for the sloping sides, and then applying the ratio he had derived, cut four more in the appropriate lengths for the base lines. He repaired to his chamber to assemble the model. The gray cat with no name was waiting for him, a limp mouse hanging from her jaws.

"Well, kitty," he said, "it looks as if you have finally earned your keep." Another dish of milk was her reward. This the alchemist absentmindedly placed on the experiment table among the vials and retorts. Kitty jumped up.

He had sent to Paris for a protractor some months before. This he found in a box where he had stored various measuring devices. It was made of brass and etched with abstract designs and delineated in degrees and seconds of degrees to an accuracy that was the best that could be achieved in that era. He also extracted from the box a compass. Laying out the poplar sticks that were to function as the base lines, he consulted the compass and adjusted the positioning until the base lines were at right angles to the cardinal points. He propped the sides against the corners of the square thus formed and attached their other ends with wire to form an apex. Now he checked angles with the protractor, made slight adjustments, and, satisfied, stepped back to admire his work.

Now what? The pyramid model was about 4 feet tall. The alchemist stooped and crawled into it, sitting cross-legged directly in the center. Nothing. He waited. Still nothing. Perhaps using wood was the mistake; he should have built it from metal. Or there was an additional element needed: some chemical compound that produced fumes, or a crystal amulet, or the chanting of priests, or other such nonsense. But as he sat mulling it over he came to realize that his error was that he had built the model indoors. It must have to communicate directly with the sky, with the sun, the moon, the stars, and the planets.

Tomorrow he would reconstruct it outside. But tonight…he was exhausted. He needed his easy chair and a good book. Even the cat was stretched out on the experiment table, snoring. The alchemist exited the pyramid, picked the dead mouse up from the floor where kitty had left it, placed it in a jar, collected his much perused copy of *The Secret Book of Artephius,* extinguished the flames under the retorts, and left the chamber.

Kitty yawned and rolled over, her feet engaging the side of a glass jar filled with some noxious substance that glowed in the half light. Annoyed that this silly jar was taking up room on the table where she was meant to stretch, she batted at it. It tipped and rolled off the table top smashing on the floor. The contents of the broken jar flowed across the stone floor in the direction of the pyramid. It seeped under stick that formed the base line and coated the square floor of the interior of the model where it stayed, glowing faintly.

Now kitty noticed the bell jar in which the death's head moth had been placed. The moth was nearly dead but it quivered and raised its wings in a last futile effort to escape. This interested the cat. Again and again she batted at this glass container that held such an intriguing prize. Slowly the jar inched toward the edge of the table. Finally it fell, and like the jar before it, smashed into fragments. This released the moth which flapped and flew erratically around the chamber. Kitty followed it with hungry eyes. When it landed, she jumped.

The moth had landed inside the pyramid model and was stuck in the liquid that congealed there. In the next instant the cat landed next to it. There was a barely perceivable flicker of light. The faintest of shudders shook the air in the room. There was a sound like the click of a door closing. And the moth and the cat had disappeared.

2

The Alchemist's Apprentice

Ireland in the sixteenth century was recovering from the Reformation; Henry VIII had been recognized as the King of Ireland in 1541 and had proceeded to confiscate Catholic Church properties and the lands belonging to Irish rebels. Queen Mary of Scotts rose to power in Scotland and tried to restore Roman Catholicism there; this rallied many of the Irish people opposed to Protestantism. There were rebellions. The O'Neill battled against the government at Dublin but was ultimately defeated and murdered. In the 1560s Queen Elizabeth I asserted her authority, replacing certain government officials with people loyal to herself. The Gaelic chieftains were to be controlled by selling cheap land to English and Scotch immigrants. There was no peace in the land; two main grievances occupied Irish social and political life: religion and English rule.

Riordan Éamon Ó Ciardha came from a small village called Innishannon in the County Cork by the River Bandon. It was a stopping over place for travelers on the road to Cork who fancied a mug of ale or a decent meal. Riordan had grown up on his Uncle Ultán Alastar Ó Ciardha's farm, working long hours building stone fences to corral the sheep that otherwise might wander off to be claimed by a neighbor as their own. His father and mother could not afford to send him to school and so relied on the uncle to tutor the boy during evenings. His education, therefore, was limited to animal husbandry and religion (Catholic, despite the ill effects of the Reformation upon County Cork).

The boy had a hunger for knowledge beyond what was proffered. Thus, when he achieved his 15th year he thanked his uncle for his kindness and walked the twenty-some miles to Cork. The walled city hadn't changed much since its early days as a medieval monastic settlement—save that the abbeys and monasteries that sat outside the walls had been dismantled or destroyed by agents of Henry VIII. Although many of the bishops of the First church of Ireland in Cork remained attached to the rites and pageantry of Roman Catholicism, Protestantism prevailed itself upon the unwilling citizens of Cork.

Riordan entered the city by the South Gate Bridge which spanned the River Lee. He had never seen a large city before; Cork had a population of nearly 800—before the Black Death of 1349, over 2,000 souls had lived within the walls. Its mercantile establishments were distributed along a single main street. Clusters of houses lined the central quay. There were two churches inside the walls: Christ Church and Saint Peter's, the first controlled by the British Crown, the latter of conflicted loyalties. Riordan wandered, somewhat aimlessly at first. He applied himself to locating a position in some trade. It was going to be difficult.

The wealthy were extremely wealthy, and the poor were extremely poor. Only about a dozen families controlled commerce in the city, exporting hides, wool, and timber, and importing grain and other foodstuffs which the city could not provide in sufficient quantities to feed its inhabitants. Riordan eventually found employment with a firm owned by the family of Roger Skiddy, the one-time Bishop of Cork and now the Warden of Youghal. Here he heaved bundles of hides and bales of wool onto wagons bound for the harbor. His pay barely kept him from starving, but he was allowed to sleep in the companies stable, out of the rain and away from the boisterous underbelly of night-time Cork—its taverns and gambling houses and brothels.

The church, of course, could offer him the semblance of an education, but Riordan had had enough of religion. He was curious about the universe...the sun, the moon, the stars, and the planets. One day he overheard some gossip about a peculiar individual who had an estate not far from town. This man was suspected to be a sorcerer, or at the very least, involved in devilish practices that were frowned upon by the clergy. The term "alchemy" was bandied about. To Riordan this sounded very scientific, and if the church opposed the man...that was all the more reason to seek him out.

After many inquiries he managed to get directions: "Go ye along the Lee...upstream...until ye attend a gradual rise leading to a stand of wood on a hillside. Beyond you will encounter an old castle made over now for the sorcerer's vile purposes. Beware! Surely you will be turned into a toad...or worse!" The admonishment only added to the youth's determination to meet the maligned alchemist. It would be several months before Riordan could save enough from his meager salary to outfit himself with a good pair of brogues to protect his feet for the journey.

It was 1572, the year that the new star appeared in the heavens. It was the year of the St. Bartholomew's Day Massacre in Paris, when Catherine de'Medici arranged the murder of Protestant leader Gaspard de Coligny and the blood of many thousands of Huguenots ran like a crimson river through the streets. It was the year that the Martyrs of Gorkum, 19 Roman Catholic clerics and friars were hung by Calvinists opposed to Spanish rule in the Netherlands. It was the second year of the Desmond Rebellion when James FitzMaurice FitzGerald and the Irish clans, after attacking an English colony south of Cork were forced to retreat into the mountains of Kerry. They would be back. More blood would spill.

It wasn't much of a hill as hills go. Sheep spotted it, the tree line defined it. The castle, if that was what it had been, was deep in the woods toward the down slope on the other side...the side you couldn't spy from the road. As close as it was to the city, its isolation was assured by the thick undergrowth of the small forest. Riordan saw a hawk on the wing riding updrafts as it prowled the skies with a sharp lookout for rodents. He skirted the tree line looking for a path. He found it at the extreme edge of the hilltop where a rocky overhang prevented further passage and his only recourse was to enter the woods.

The path was overgrown with brush that hid jagged rocks and twisted roots. The going was not easy and he was thankful for his sturdy new footwear. As he neared the castle a furious barking ensued causing him to stop his advance. Suddenly a large, furry shape bounded into the woods in front of him. A huge hound! It stopped short of the youth, ceased its fervor, sat and waged its tale eagerly. "Well, hello, boy," said Riordan. "What's your name?"

"That's Teige," said a voice. "Teige is my most excellent watch dog. And who might you be?"

If Riordan had expected to see a stooped old man with a long beard, dressed in a flowing robe decorated with signs of the zodiac and wearing a peaked hat, he was disappointed. Before him stood a man of thirty years at most, a lock of hair dangling over one eye, dressed in the usual ankle-length leine (linen died a brilliant saffron color and bloused over a leather belt, with wide cuffed sleeves), and a brat of wool with a heavy fringe draped over his shoulders. He lacked the inar jacket which should have completed his costume, but his skin-tight trius pants were of the checkered variety that distinguished him as a true Irishman, not apt to adopt the English style to appease London. He held a leash in his hand, one end of which he now tied to Teige's collar.

"My name is Riordan Ó Ciardha, sir," he answered.

"And what might you be doing in my woods?"

Riordan attempted to tell his story without stammering. His nervousness was apparent, and his explanation that he was seeking an education elicited a chuckle from the alchemist.

"Have you numbers?"

"I do. I can count, which I often needed for minding the sheep. And I can add…three and two equals five."

"Very good. Can you read and write?"

"A little. My uncle taught me the first chapters of the Bible. 'And God said, let there be light, and there was light. And God created man in his own image. And…' "

"And you believe all this?"

"I think there must be more to it than what it says in the Bible. That is why I wish to learn about the planets and the solar system and the universe."

"And you are not afraid that people will ridicule you for seeking the truth? You know what they say about me?"

"I heard you were a sorcerer, casting evil spells. They blame you if a sheep dies or their crops fail. I know that isn't true. It couldn't be."

"Hmm," mutter the alchemist. "You wish me to teach you about the planets? I could use some help around here. If you aren't afraid of hard work, you may stay here and do chores for me. If I have any free time...which is doubtful...I may instruct you on one or two pieces of useful knowledge. By the way, my name is Lorcan Mac Conmara. You may call me, 'Master.' "

Riordan's duties included carrying water from the well, feeding Teige (but not kitty as the alchemist liked to do that himself), sweeping the laboratory (but not unless the alchemist requested the cleaning—some experiments were not to be disturbed), filling the oil lamps, peeling potatoes, and washing clothes (but only once every two weeks as necessary). None of this seemed to the youth to be hard work. He was not allowed to watch the alchemist at work. He was not allowed to ask questions while the alchemist studied his books or wrote in his journal. However, Mac Conmara took time to work with Riordan whenever possible.

Riordan learned the symbols used in alchemical texts and their meanings: the crescent moon, circle, and inverted cross that represented mercury, which meant "mind"; the triangle and cross that stood for sulfur, which meant "spirit"; the seven metals that were under the influence of the seven planets—lead, tin, iron, gold, copper, and quicksilver, which were associated in turn with Saturn, Jupiter, Mars, the Sun, Venus, and Mercury. He learned that the sun, moon, and earth were spheres and that the moon and the sun revolved around the earth (this according to Tycho Brahe).

Slowly the alchemist revealed things about the processes used in chemical exploration. The primary of these were distillation and fermentation. Others were called incineration, fixation, congelation, and calcination. They were indicated by the signs of the zodiac: Virgo, Capricorn, Sagittarius, Taurus, and Aries. Essential to Riordan's education was the Belgian first edition of *Theatrum Orbis Terrarum*, the "Theater of the World" by Abraham Ortelius, a collection of world maps by contemporary cartographers. Riordan loved studying these colorful charts and one day he asked the alchemist, "Where are Heaven and Hell located?"

"There have been many attempts to diagram the cosmos to include Heaven in the firmament and Hell...well, these men make the mistake of believing there is only this world and therefore Heaven and Hell must be part of it. No. I believe there are other worlds next to ours but not overlapping. If we could enter these…"

"We would find Heaven."

"Or Hell."

"Is this the work you do? To seek other worlds?"

"You are wise beyond your years, and curious…a dangerous propensity. Someday you may learn to help me more closely. For now, be patient."

Often when the alchemist was occupied with his experiments and Riordan was left to his own devises he would explore the castle, poking his curious nose into those rooms that were closed up and not used. There was no obvious reason for this closure other than that the alchemist only needed a minimum of space for his living area. These unused spaces offered the youth an experience of much dust and cobwebs and some very large spiders. Some of the rooms still had artifacts from the days when the castle was occupied by a baron: picture frames without pictures in them, candle sticks of tarnished metal, furniture covered with rotting cloths which in turn were covered with dust and cobwebs and some very large spiders.

Sometimes the alchemist would send Riordan into the village for supplies. He would take Teige with him so that the dog would have some exercise—which consisted of running after rabbits or the occasional deer that crossed their path. The village shopkeepers would look askance at Riordan; understandably as he was known as the alchemist's apprentice and therefore guilty by association (of what they weren't sure). Still, the exchange of coins for staples would go politely and on a rare occasion, Riordan would be rewarded with a kind smile.

There was no one of Riordan's age with whom he could form a friendship. There were young men and women who worked on the farms but he had no interaction with these. His world of acquaintances consisted of the alchemist, Teige, and the cat with no name. He buried himself in his studies and was making enough headway that the questions he asked the alchemist impressed the man with his innate intelligence. Gradually, the alchemist brought the youth into the laboratory to assist him.

The alchemist introduced Riordan to the use of the shrewstone.

The shrewstone was used for scrying, the evocation of visions through gazing in a relaxed state at its reflective surface. Although a device more related to mysticism than to alchemy, it had come to Lorcan Mac Conmara's attention through his familiarity with the Englishman, John Dee, Queen Elizabeth's astrologer. Dee used a shrewstone in a search for angels and other spirits. Ancient cultures such as the Greeks and the Mayans had employed crystals or mirrors in a similar manner for divination or other types of ceremonial magic. The seer, Nostradamus, stared into a bowl of water in order to see the future. Mac Conmara felt the stone might aid him in his search for other worlds.

This particular shrewstone was a disk of polished obsidian, imported from the Aztecan realm in Central Mexico; its black surface was mirror-like without unduly reflecting the distracting room it was in. The alchemist set it on a round wax tablet incised with alchemical symbols. Near the shrewstone he placed a single candle made of black wax. It would be the only light source in the room. This he lit and cautioned Riordan to sit where he could not see his own image or the image of the candle in the stone.

"You must relax your mind...be calm and unconcerned with me or the room or any thoughts which might occupy you. Gaze into the stone and slowly soften your vision, letting your eyes search deeply within the surface. Try not to blink your eyes. Let the visions come to you. Now I leave you."

As Riordan relaxed his mind and his vision, a mist seemed to form on the surface of the shrewstone. Shapes solidified from the mist: indistinct shapes like clouds billowing across a darkened sky, ever changing through metamorphosis into animals or faces. Now these sharpened and became objects the likes of which the youth had never before seen—nor could he identify their purpose. Metallic boxes on wheels had scurried along great white ribbons like chariots pulled by invisible hoses. Behind these rose impossibly tall towers that gleamed in the sunlight as if they were made of crystal and silver. Across the sky flew birds also made from metal—their wings were not flapping. He reeled with astonishment and not a little fear.

He told the alchemist of the phenomenon he had just experienced. "It is possible," said the man, "that you have been privileged to witness some aspect of another world such as I have postulated exists. Or it may have been the effect of a bad piece of cheese. We will never know until we have successfully reached that or another such world in our physicality."

"It didn't seem to be Heaven," said Riordan. "So it must have been Hell!"

Riordan had returned to his daily routine of chores, study, chores, study, and chores. He had been with the alchemist for over a year now and it was not unnatural that the chores were boring and the studies were tedious—he yearned for more of the hands-on assisting with the alchemist's work—assisting that he so rarely was allowed.

One morning the alchemist had indicated that there was a great mess in the laboratory that required cleaning up. He warned Riordan not to touch the pyramid model while he was cleaning, and to see if he could locate the cat which had apparently disappeared. Riordan complied quite willingly as it was a chance to explore the laboratory more closely and perhaps to examine some of the apparatus there without the oversight of the alchemist. The vision of the strange world that appeared in the shrewstone was still on his mind; it had seemed so real and yet so fantastic. If the opportunity should present itself to try gazing into the shrewstone again…

The broom was waiting for him in a corner of the chamber. He saw the shards of glass on the floor and the congealed liquid that had spilled there, still glowing and giving off a putrid odor. First I'll look for the cat, he thought, and see what I can see. He saw the bottles and vials of chemicals all neatly labeled with alchemical symbols. He found a feather duster and gave these a good cleaning. He saw the oven; its open door revealing ashes and charred wood that had cooled—he swept these into a bucket he used for trash. He did not see the shrewstone anywhere in the chamber. He did not see the cat.

Now he turned his attention to the broken glass. This he swept up with broom and small shovel. The pieces he placed with the ashes in the bucket. It was nearly full so he took the bucket outside and emptied it into an old dried up well he used as a trash dump. Back in the chamber he pondered how to clean the spilled chemical. He knew some things were caustic and he might be burned. He would get a mop soaking with water and swab it up. His hands would not touch it. There was a small problem: the liquid had run under the wooden pyramid model which he was not supposed to touch. He shouldn't move it out of the way of his cleaning, but…

But he would. He would return it to its place after the floor was clean. It was fragile so he would creep beneath the wooden struts in order to lift it from the underside. As he stooped to enter the pyramid he thought he saw something: a thickening of the air not unlike the mist that had formed on the shrewstone. In he went. It felt…larger on the inside than seemed possible. He could stand. But he could no longer see the room outside of the pyramid. The mist completely filled his vision. It brightened. He felt a slight vibration and a numbing sensation. There was a sound like a distant clap of thunder. Then he was somewhere else.

In his place, under the frame of the pyramid, in the chamber of the alchemist, sat someone else. A man, dressed, not in the leine, brat, and inar of a sixteenth century man, but in loose-fitting khaki shorts and a colorful Hawaiian Aloha shirt decorated with palm trees and hibiscus blooms. A look of astonishment was on the man's face, for he was not where he had been a few seconds ago. Not in the place…or the time where he had just been.

Byron Grush

3

The Man from Oak Ridge

The calutron is a type of sector mass spectrometer, an instrument in which a sample is ionized and then accelerated by electric fields and deflected by magnetic fields. The ions ultimately collide with a plate and produce a measurable electric current. Since the ions of the different isotopes have the same electric charge but different masses, the heavier isotopes are deflected less by the magnetic field, causing the beam of particles to separate out into several beams by mass, striking the plate at different locations....During World War II, calutrons were developed to use this principle to obtain substantial quantities of high-purity uranium-235, by taking advantage of the small mass difference between uranium isotopes....the calutron was first operated on 2 December 1941, just days before the Japanese attack on Pearl Harbor brought the United States into World War II.

——————Wikipedia.org

Around the turn of the twentieth century, in a rural area not far from Knoxville, Tennessee, a man named John Hendrix, who was an ascetic, a wanderer of the ridges and valleys of that place, and a self-proclaimed prophet, found himself standing before a group of locals in a country store near his home. Apprehensive at first, then gradually gaining confidence in his firm belief of the vision he had during one of his meditative hikes, he related to the people assembled there the following (as described in *The Oak Ridge story; the saga of a people who*

21

share in history, 1950, by George O. Robinson, Jr):

"In the woods, as I lay on the ground and looked up into the sky, there came to me a voice as loud and as sharp as thunder. The voice told me to sleep with my head on the ground for 40 nights and I would be shown visions of what the future holds for this land.... And I tell you, Bear Creek Valley someday will be filled with great buildings and factories, and they will help toward winning the greatest war that ever will be. And there will be a city on Black Oak Ridge and the center of authority will be on a spot middle-way between Sevier Tadlock's farm and Joe Pyatt's Place. A railroad spur will branch off the main L&N line, run down toward Robertsville and then branch off and turn toward Scarborough. Big engines will dig big ditches, and thousands of people will be running to and fro. They will be building things, and there will be great noise and confusion and the earth will shake. I've seen it. It's coming."

Most laughed, knowing that Hendrix was considered to be eccentric and a dreamer. But less than 40 years later, the prophesy was to come true. As early as 1939 an Austrian physicist, Lise Meitner, and a German chemist, Otto Hahn, conceived of the idea that atoms could be split into smaller atoms and would therefore release staggering amounts of energy. Albert Einstein wrote to American President Franklin D. Roosevelt to warn him that Germany might develop an atom bomb. Roosevelt authorized the Manhattan Project in 1942 and assembled a group of prominent scientists including Felix Bloch, Enrico Fermi, and Bruno Rossi to work on it.

On December 2 of that year, Enrico Fermi, Leó Szilárd, George Weil and the Chicago Pile Team achieved the world's first controlled release of nuclear energy under the stadium of an old squash court at the University of Chicago. Material for the tests had been supplied by a converted cyclotron (now dubbed the calutron) at Berkeley. Further development of the technology and the training for supplying the rare isotope uranium-235 was initiated at the Oak Ridge, Tennessee, facility which went into operation in July of 1943, as an official military district. The town that grew up along the Black Oak Ridge was at first a military secret although by 1945 it supported nearly 75,000 people. Local residents were evicted from their homes as land was cleared and three large plants were built.

A temporary town took shape designed by John Merrill of the

firm of Skidmore, Owens, and Merrill. It featured ten schools, seven theaters, seventeen restaurants, thirteen supermarkets, a library, a sporting facility, a symphony orchestra, seventeen churches, and a Fuller Brush man. The prefabricated housing was constructed of cemesto, which was an amalgamation of cement and asbestos. None of the workers (mostly women) that ran the control panels for the long arrays of calutrons called "racetracks" knew they were producing material for the atomic bombs that would devastate Hiroshima and Nagasaki.

Two years after World War II ended, Oak Ridge became Oak Ridge National Laboratory under the civilian direction of the Atomic Energy Commission. Three of the calutron racetracks survived a cleaning out of equipment deemed obsolete and these were put to good use for various experiments. A greatly reduced workforce remained to assist the scientists as it was no longer the singular commitment of the lab to produce fissionable nuclear material.

Francis Delaney had been one of the women that had worked on the Manhattan Project at Oak Ridge. She had sat at a panel in a long room full of such panels and such women, monitoring gauges and adjusting dials as the racetracks accelerated particles through a series of calutrons, ultimately to break apart into usable stuff for the Devil's own weapon. Francis lived in the prefab community with her son, Wayland. Like many of the women now stranded in Oak Ridge after V-E Day, her husband had died in the war.

The son, Wayland, had been thirteen when Francis Delaney arrived at Oak Ridge in 1943 to devote herself to the war effort. The trip from their home in the tiny mountain community of Pigeon Forge had been difficult due to their lack of money and the isolation of the town. The closest train station was at Sevierville some 11 miles away, and they had had to cross the Pigeon River at a ford since there were no bridges. Wayland dutifully carried the two valises that held their worldly possessions as they walked the dirt paths that served as roads in that area. At Sevierville they boarded a train for Knoxville with the last of their funds.

The Oak Ridge facility, at that time, was surrounded by a tall fence and guard towers. Access to the plant from the prefab town was through one of seven closely guarded gates and employees wore badges with their pictures and ID numbers on them. As a boy, Wayland wasn't allowed into the compound, but he could wander through the valley or climb Black Oak Ridge. He could fish the Clinch River. The school he attended was strictly segregated and would remain so until the mid-fifties.

Although there were Black laborers at the plant, mostly scrub women, there had yet to have been constructed a separate "colored" neighborhood. Blacks were housed along side whites in the rows of apartments at the far end of the town. During summers Wayland would play stickball with Black friends he had made despite the segregated schools. Years later in 1952, when he applied to the newly opened Oak Ridge School of Reactor Technology at Oak Ridge National Laboratory, these friendships nearly resulted in his rejection. However, his performance on the entrance exam was stellar and his school grades indicated he was a serious student; he had attended the University of Tennessee at Knoxville and completed a Bachelor of Science degree, specializing in physics. He was awarded a scholarship and began a twelve-month program in Reactor Hazards Analysis at ORNL.

There were still secret areas at the lab. Research into anything with a remote relationship to a military application was kept under wraps. As part of his studies in Reactor Hazards Analysis Wayland was apprenticed to Dr. Madison McGinley, a veteran scientist from the Manhattan Project who was undertaking independent research into the application of quantum theory. Whether this research would ever result in a new type of weapon was unclear, but the Atomic Energy Commission higher-ups weren't taking any chances— according to Senator McCarthy of Wisconsin, there were Reds in every crevice of the government. Dr. McGinley's research was highly classified and so Wayland Delaney underwent a security clearance.

Again, his friendship with Blacks came into question. There was nothing, however, to suggest he was not patriotic, nor that he could be compromised or blackmailed by a foreign power. His security rating was upgraded, the color of his ID badge changed to indicate his new access, and he reported to Dr. McGinley in an obscure area of the huge building designated as Y-12.

Dr. McGinley had a build that suggested his love of rich food. One would not say he was portly, but pleasantly ample. He sported bushy mutton-chop side burns and often had a pair of half glasses perched on the end of his nose. During the Christmas season he would be drafted to play Santa Claus at the Youth Center. He had only one flamboyant aspect: he loved colorful shirts and sent away to the territory of Hawaii for silk examples of the Aloha shirt that GIs had begun to popularize at the end of World War II. Wayland showed an interest in the shirts his mentor wore and soon was wearing one. The other scientists in the building laughingly referred to their attire as the "McGinley Uniform."

At their first meeting, Dr. McGinley quizzed Wayland on his knowledge. "How much do you know about quantum theory?" he asked.

"Well, from Einstein we know that time is relative to the observer. For example, say a man takes a spaceship and flies out into space at nearly the speed of light. He takes with him a clock. This clock moves at the same rate as a similar clock that has remained on Earth. One second measures one second on each, and so forth. When the man returns, however, it is many years into the future."

"Very good. Time is important. What else?"

"There is Schrödinger's cat. The thought experiment in which he suggests placing a cat in a sealed box along with a flask of poison gas and a Geiger counter and in which there is a small amount of radioactive material. If the Geiger counter detects the emission of radiation, a hammer is released which smashes the flask and therefore kills the cat. There is no way to know if or when this will happen. Now, at any time without opening the box, the question is: is the cat alive or dead?"

"Well?"

"It is both dead *and* alive because both possible states exist simultaneously. If you open the box and become an observer, the dual states collapse, and the cat becomes one or the other."

"Are you familiar with the Many Worlds Theory?"

"I've never heard of it. The Schrödinger's cat experiment suggests this?"

"You haven't heard of it because it hasn't been published just yet. My colleague, Hugh Everett, and I have discussed this at great length. He suggests that once the box is opened, the cat still exists in the dual state. Then the reality of observation splits off into two different branches: an observer looking at a live cat *and* an observer looking at a dead cat. There can be no interaction between them because the two states of the cat are decoherent, that is, their former coherence has decayed because of the observer. However…

"We define a 'world' as the totality of a macrocosm…people, buildings, trees, rivers, etc. There can be no superimpositions of dual states in any given world according to Everett. But probability demands that there is a dead cat world *and* a live cat world."

"And many other possible worlds," said Wayland. "I understand. It is like one of those very vivid dreams you have where you construct a whole city filled with people that can't possibly exist but when you wake you are struck by the degree of detail you remember that you can't possibly have imagined. Another world somnombulistically glimpsed."

"That's a good analogy, but not quite accurate. And there is no such word as 'somnombulistically.' Think, though, about four-dimensional space. Length, width, depth, and time. If there are multiple worlds with their own unique dimensions, why should not time exist with multiple possibilities? And if there are multiple possible dimensions, why should not some of them overlap or touch?"

"And so, we are searching for those possible connections between multiple worlds?"

"You've hit the nail on the head, my boy. Congratulations. And now I have something to show you." Dr. McGinley led Wayland to a locked cabinet which he opened from a key on a ring attached to his belt. Inside were a series of drawers. One of these he pulled open revealing several small objects laid out on a piece of cotton cloth.

"This," he said, pointing to a silver coin, "is a Roman sesterius depicting Marcus Aurelius. It was used around 200 BC."

"But it is so shiny! It looks like it is in mint condition. I've only seen old coins in pictures, but they are usually in a very used condition, pitted and tarnished."

"I have had it carbon dated. It is, within a small margin of error, only 2 years old."

"Then it is a reproduction. Why show me this?"

"Because, my boy, we retrieved this from the past and we believe it to be genuine. Now look at this object," he said, pointing to a flaked piece of flint with a sharpened point at one end. "This is one of the most perfect examples of a Clovis point ever found. They date from around 13,000 years ago."

"Let me guess…it's new."

"Carbon dated as five years old. Again, we retrieved it from the past. It is not a fake. And here is the most remarkable artifact we have retrieved."

Dr. McGinley closed the drawer and pulled open the drawer just beneath it. There, on a piece of cotton cloth sat the most unusual object Wayland had ever seen. It was a flat, round cylinder with striations around its rim and two very thin filaments of wire extending from one side. Wayland saw that it was made from some kind of semi-transparent material like plastic…but not plastic."

"It appears to be similar to a very high grade of aluminum. Yet you can see through it and it does not conduct electricity. It is resistant to solvents, heat, and drilling."

"It is from the future?"

"That is our best guess. We haven't been able to target specific areas of space-time as yet. Nor can we bring back artifacts of a larger size or of organic material, much less anything alive. We do believe, however, that these things are from our own world and not from an alternate universe of some kind. We think we have penetrated time itself!"

Wayland thought of it as a Time Machine, but he did not dare call it that in front of McGinley or any of the other scientists. H. G. Wells was not considered an appropriate area of study for an apprentice and anyway, no one had taken a trip through time in it…yet. It was not a big box made of iron nor was it any other kind of enclosure. It resembled a sort of electronic trellis with metal struts—six of them arranged in a circle and joined at the top—and covered with all manner of wires, tubes, and coils. It was open on all six sides. They had scavenged, Dr. McGinley had told him, parts from the disassembled calutrons. It was somehow attached to one of the remaining racetracks where particles could be accelerated and bombarded. Its exact workings were classified, of course.

It was large enough for a man to stand up inside. Wayland wondered why only small objects had been brought from the remote past or future. When he asked about this he was told that it was a matter of the amount of energy which could be applied to the machine without melting it down to a puddle of molten metal and glass. They were bringing in some unique refrigeration units that had been used in Werner von Braun's rocket experiments. Perhaps that would solve the problem.

One day, as Wayland was coming out of the laboratory, he noticed a young Black man in the hallway engaged with a mop and a pail. As he approached the man he suddenly recognized him as one of his old stickball fellows. He knew him only by his nickname, Judo. Judo was large for his age, as Wayland remembered, and a little clumsy, but he could hit the ball so far down the street where they played that it sometimes got lost. "Hey, Judo," he called, "is that you?"

"Hey, Wank. Wha's happenin'?" responded Judo, using Wayland's nickname (which he had hoped had been forgotten).

As the days passed, the two young men could be seen together in the cafeteria—an odd couple, considering the climate of racial intolerance in Tennessee at the time, and further, of the unequal status between the two men. Characteristically independent, Wayland was unconcerned with the reproachful glances he got from other whites in the room. This was an old friend, and he hadn't had many, so Judo's companionship was to be cultivated not shunned. The friendship seemed innocent enough. It had not yet been brought to the attention of the security staff, but it would be.

It was the day after the cat came through the time machine. It was alive (at least in the version that quantum mechanics had provided). There was, however, a very dead moth hitchhiking with the cat. Everyone had been elated. Wayland was so excited he broke the rules and told Judo about it. Judo had never outwardly asked about the secret project and so it did not occur to Wayland that this infraction would have any consequences. After all, Judo couldn't be a spy, could he? Then Judo asked to see the time machine.

Wayland would later say he didn't remember pointing out the off-and-on switch to Judo. (Actually, it was much more complicated than just a single switch.) But somehow the time machine was up and running. When he saw an object materializing under the struts he absent mindedly reached into the machine to retrieve it. At the amount of energy it took to bring forth what was a small ring or bracelet, there would not have been much danger. But things changed rapidly and the machine began to tremble and surge. Sparks ran up and down the struts. A thick fog was forming that seemed to blot out the rest of the big room. Wayland felt a strong suction pulling him into the machine.

The next thing he knew he was in a dark chamber. The walls and floor were made of stone. He was sitting under a wooden frame shaped roughly like a miniature pyramid. He wasn't in the same place he had just been. Or in the same time.

Byron Grush

4

McGinley's Cat

Dr. Madison James McGinley lived in a comfortable bungalow on Chariot Lane just off of Pennsylvania Avenue. He was a bachelor and fastidious in his habits. At precisely four o'clock in the afternoon, provided that his attendance wasn't required for some experiment, he settled down in his favorite chair, an antique rocker he had inherited from an aunt, opened the extra edition of the Knoxville Sentinel, or thumbed though a favorite book (Robert Louis Stevenson's *Treasure Island,* or perhaps Jack London's *Call of the Wild*), and cautiously sipped a steaming cup of oolong tea. Today, the time-traveling cat with no name was curled up on his lap. The book he had selected was *The Rubáiyát of Omar Khayyam* in the translation by Edward Fitzgerald. His gaze lingered on quatrain LXXI:

> *The Moving Finger writes; and, having writ,*
> *Moves on: nor all your Piety nor Wit*
> *Shall lure it back to cancel half a Line,*
> *Nor all your Tears wash out a Word of it.*

That's what you think, Omar, old sport, he thought to himself. Kitty still did not have a name although McGinley was considering calling her Scheherazade, after the sultan's wife in *The Arabian Nights.*

31

She had been brought home by the scientist after she had appeared in the time machine the day before; he hadn't thought of himself as a cat person but he warmed to her immediately. Something about those yellow eyes behind all that gray fur intrigued him. It was as if she knew something humans could not know…and she wasn't telling.

Someone was knocking at the door. McGinley bounced Scheherazade off his lap and crossed the braided rug. Looking through the leaded glass window in the front door he saw that his visitor was Dr. Frederick Duban, another scientist at Oak Ridge. The best of friends, he and Dr. Duban often debated aspects of the quantum theory project, an exercise which stimulated their thought processes. Perhaps he had come to examine the cat.

"Hello, Freddie," said McGinley. "Have you come for tea, or would you like something a little stronger? I've a bottle of Mr. Daniels' excellent sour mash concoction."

"Nothing for me Madison. I've just come from the lab. There has been an accident. The Star Chamber has been destroyed!"

Although Wayland Delaney thought of the device as a time machine, the scientists had derived a suitable acronym for it: Space-Time Accelerating Reciprocitor, or STAR. McGinley of course, liked to reverse the words to form: RATS. Duban explained that an alarm had summoned them to the Star Chamber where they discovered the device going up in smoke. Someone had apparently turned the energy accumulator up to full power.

"We think it was sabotage. Your apprentice, Wayland Delaney and that Negro custodian he hangs out with are missing," said Duban.

"Wayland wouldn't do anything like that. Why would you think that he did?"

"Security has been watching them. Someone saw them go into the lab shortly before the fire. They will be found eventually…they can run but they can't hide."

"Is the machine completely destroyed?"

"Completely. And I doubt whether there will be further funding available to rebuild it. Just as well. Time travel isn't practical."

"You don't know that, Freddie. It was just a matter of time…if you will forgive the pun…before we could send a human back."

"Think about the paradox, Madison. If time travel was to be invented, then certainly someone from the future would have visited us or to a time in the past."

"Perhaps they have. They would be cautious not to reveal themselves or change anything. The grandfather syndrome, you know. Killing your own grandfather and all that. Or perhaps…perhaps it was someone from the future who destroyed the RATS chamber."

"Now you are really dreaming. Give it up, Madison. We'll get ourselves a nice contract from Monsanto or somebody to do weapons research. It's much more doable. Oh, and by the way," he said, pointing at an inert gray shape on the rug, "I think your cat is dead!"

High on a ridge overlooking the valley was an old settler's cabin. Gaps between the wall boards and missing shingles on the roof made it uninhabitable, but it served as a temporary hiding place for the two runaways. Riordan Ó Ciardha, the alchemist's apprentice, was catching his breath, trying to balance on a broken chair that wobbled and creaked under his weight. Judo paced.

"They's aft' us fo' sure," he was saying. "I dint mean fo' the thing to 'splode! It was an accident. An' po' Wank! He dade for sure! I donno where yo' come from, but they arrest yo' too. Yo' best stay with me."

Who was Wank? What had 'sploded? Where…and when…was he? Riordan suspected…no feared…that the alchemist had somehow sent him into one of those other worlds he talked about. How and why, Riordan didn't know. This dark-skinned man might be a Moor or an African. Yes, he must be in Africa…or a parallel world like Africa. But the buildings in the valley below! That great metal and glass castle they had run away from…he had never seen anything like that.

"An' those clothes yo' wearin'? Yo' goin' to a costume party or sumpin? My name is Raymond P. Washington but they calls me Judo. What's yours?"

"Riordan Ó Ciardha, from County Cork. Where is this place?"

"Huh? This Tennessee. Way down south. Yo' a little confused?"

"Is this part of Africa?"

"Wha? No, man. Are you making fun of me? I don' hold wit no bad-mouth comments."

"I meant no disrespect, Judo. It's only…I haven't seen many…I mean…in County Cork we have no Moors or Africans, so naturally I just assumed…"

"You assumed. Where exactly is this Cork?"

"Why, in Ireland, of course."

"Well, Roy, in Tennessee we got no Irish. Lot of Africans, though. And an awful lotta red necks."

"The year? What is the year?"

"It 1952."

"The Gregorian calendar?"

"No, stupid…the one wit Marilyn Monroe. Whad yo' think?"

No, thought Riordan, I'm not going to tell him I thought it was 1573. I'm having a hard enough time believing this myself. He will think I'm crazy…and maybe I am!

Judo was standing at the door, watching the approach to the cabin when he saw a pickup truck climbing the road. "Oh Lordy," he said, "They's sendin' the Klan after us!"

At approximately the same time (in a parallel time-world in 1573), Wayland Delaney, still a bit dazed, sat beneath the wooden pyramid in the alchemist's room and considered: it was obvious that the time machine had worked and had sent him…somewhere…and sometime. But where, and when? He looked around the room at the table filled with glass retorts and jars, the shelf with its oddities, the stack of old books, the empty dish which was just the size one might use to feed a cat—had he traded places with the cat? There was only one way to find out what his true circumstances might be: venture outside and find someone to ask.

Pain slowed him down; he had not fared well during the time-traveling. There were bruises on his arms and legs and his back felt as if it had been wrenched and twisted. He would have to remember to describe this in his report…if ever he got to make one in his own time period. Exit to the chamber was up a circular flight of stone stairs and through a heavy wooden door that swung on iron hinges. Certainly, he was in a distant past. He looked back at the edifice he had just left: a castle! Would there be knights in shining armor and damsels in distress? He hoped for the damsels at least.

A thickly wooded area faced him. He started to circle around the castle to find a better route when a loud barking startled him. The wolf hound, Teige, bounded from the woods and ran toward him.

Wayland froze. The dog stopped just short of him and sat. Apparently it was not going to rip his flesh and tear him to pieces! "Good boy," Wayland said. "Who's a good boy?"

The barking had alerted the alchemist that a visitor was present. Upon seeing the manner of dress of the man, Mac Conmara was dumbfounded. The Aloha shirt was something far from the alchemist's experience or imagination. The shorts—this man was in his undergarments!

Wayland, for his part, saw the clothing of the alchemist not as an anomaly, but as confirmation of his theory that he had traveled back into the past. He must be somewhere in Europe, he thought. He ventured to speak in English, hoping he would be understood. He only knew a few words of French and less of German. If this was Scandinavia he would be hopelessly lost—or was it Russia, or...?

"Greetings," he managed to say, his voice squeaking from apprehension. He held out his hand, a gesture he knew was an ages old sign of friendship: the hand that held no weapon was not to be feared.

"What manner of man are you, and why are you not dressed properly?" asked the alchemist.

"I am a traveler. This is my native costume. My name is Wayland Delaney, from America. I'm a bit lost. Could you tell me where I am?"

"America? You aren't Spanish, you are too pale. You speak more like an Englishman, but I cannot place the accent. You must explain. Please come into my home so we can speak in comfort."

Wayland turned the man's words over in his mind as they entered the castle through a different door than the one he had used to leave the dark chamber. The British had not colonized the Americas until 1620. This man would have thought him English if the current date was later than that. The Spanish had arrived to colonize Florida around 1560. The man assumed an American would be Spanish. Wayland therefore placed himself in the late sixteenth century. And realizing that the man spoke with a heavy Irish or Scotch accent, he decided that he must be somewhere in the British Isles.

The man noticed the bruises on Wayland's arms and legs. "Let me attend to those," he said. From a cabinet in the corner of the room they had entered he brought forth a stone mortar and pestle and a cloth bag. He placed a handful of dried leaves from the bag into the pestle and began to pound these. Another trip to the cabinet produced a vial of some purplish liquid which the alchemist poured into the pestle. The resulting concoction was applied to Wayland's bruises. Instantly his pain subsided.

Introductions and an offered flask of mead which Wayland declined were followed by a discussion of professions. Upon learning that Lorcan Mac Conmara pursued various areas of study, including cosmology, Hermetic theory, pharmaceutical and herbal remedies, occultism, and alchemy, Wayland could not resist revealing that he too was a scientist. This was a mistake on his part for as the alchemist began to expound upon about various theories of the transmutation of metals, Wayland was forced to blurt out:

"You can't turn lead into gold, you know. It doesn't work that way." As soon as he spoke he realized his faux pas. In trying to back track he succeeded in making things worse: "There are complex materials you can synthesize or compound, and those you can reduce to their base elements, but most elements are unique," he said.

The alchemist was not pleased. Here was this young rogue telling him his business. "Who have you read?" he demanded.

Wayland tried to remember the dates lived by early scientific thinkers: Robert Fludd? No, he probably wasn't born yet. Roger Bacon? Probably not current enough to impress the alchemist. Robert Boyle? Again…wrong century. Newton, Descartes, Pascal—all seventeenth or eighteenth century. William of Ockham? Fourteenth century, but…

"Parsimony, as put forth by William of Ockham, says that natural philosophers should never postulate unnecessary entities. One should always explain things in the simplest terms without hypotheticals. Entia non sunt multiplicanda sine necessitate—this is called Ockham's Razor." Wayland watched to see what effect this might have on Mac Conmara.

The alchemist was silent for a moment and seemed to be studying the corbels holding up the ceiling beams. Then he smiled. "I have also studied Ockham and his natural philosophy. In reasoning, he alludes to two forms: the intuitive and the abstract. With intuitive reasoning one has the necessity of having a real object…or a non-existent one if the theory demands it, while in abstract reasoning the object itself is removed from the equation. Ockham also criticized Aristotle for filling in the gaps in his logic with suppositions. I don't know, however, what you mean by the term, razor."

"What I'm getting at," Wayland then offered, "is that you mistakenly begin with an assumption that all elements are different variations of a single form. Therefore, the idea of transmutation makes sense. However, the premise is false. You will learn this in time."

"In America has science progressed so far that it negates all that has come before it? And tell me, how is it you come from this far continent but show no attributes of the Spanish who inhabit that land? There must be an interesting story to explain this."

Wayland couldn't think of one that was plausible. So he said, "I was born there."

"What? You are no aborigine. I have seen the renderings of those natives. And certainly, they are not capable of reading Ockham!"

"What I mean to say is…I *will* be born there. In about 350 years."

Meanwhile, in 1952, Doctors Madison James McGinley and Frederick Duban sat in McGinley's living room and debated the status of Scheherazade, the time-traveling cat. Duban stated unequivocally that the cat was dead; McGinley was just as adamant that it was alive. They had not moved to actually examine the cat closely, that would have spoiled the exercise.

"We are both experiencing a unique branch of reality due to our observations of a common phenomenon. But as Everett maintains, there can be no overlap, no interaction. Why, then, are we conscious of each other's worlds?" asked McGinley.

As if in answer to the question, Scheherazade stretched and gave out a loud meow. The two men laughed. "I might have some of that Jack Daniels you offered earlier," said Duban.

Later that afternoon, Dr. McGinley hastened to the STAR lab to examine the remains of the device. The walls of the room were charred. There was a pile of twisted and melted metal where the STAR Chamber had been, and a white ash was everywhere. There didn't seem to be any hope that they could rebuild the device unless they could get funding to do so. Without any substantial successes to give them legitimacy, this didn't seem likely.

As McGinley stood looking with dismay at the wrecked time machine a mist began to form. This thickened until it obscured most of the room. That's curious, thought the scientist. Not a breeze in here so it isn't the ash being stirred up. It must be some sort of a hallucination. Gases left over from the melted equipment. And yet…

He wondered whether there was some residual effect from the massive surge of energy that had caused the explosion. An atmospheric effect? Or could it indicate a temporal rift? A fracture between parallel time worlds? That was just too far fetched. McGinley stepped closer to the densest part of the mist.

He felt a tingling sensation. Suddenly he was disoriented as if he were falling or weightless. He blacked out. When he regained consciousness he found himself lying on a cold hard floor made of stone. Above him was a wooden framework, a sort of pyramid. A glance around the chamber told him he had traveled through the rift. Where and when were yet to be determined. He picked himself up and, after examining the chamber, left by the circular stairs and soon found himself outside the castle where earlier Wayland had encountered the dog, Teige.

As the castle was obviously inhabited, McGinley shouted a hearty series of hallos, but to no avail. Thus he entered the castle through the main entrance. Now Teige had sensed him and ran to him, barking his usual greeting for strangers he did not consider to be a danger. On his heels came the alchemist and Wayland. When the alchemist saw the Aloha shirt McGinley wore he started to laugh. "Another American, I presume," he said.

The three spent most of the afternoon discussing each other's recent adventures, the future, the past, and various theories that might explain their present situation. The alchemist was astounded but at the same time, entranced. McGinley explained that the surge of energy at the point of their time experiment had no doubt opened a rift in space-time. The machine was no longer a necessary vehicle for bridging the rift, which was obvious since it had been utterly destroyed. Mac Conmara was anxious to visit his laboratory to see the rift for himself. McGinley told him that he and Wayland should return to their own time as their presence in the past was dangerous—the frightening syndrome of "what if you killed your own-grandfather?"

Mac Conmara said he could not pass up the opportunity to accompany them to the twentieth century. McGinley wasn't sure this was a good idea. However, the three scientists repaired to the alchemist's laboratory with Teige trailing close behind. There they saw the thick mist hanging over the wooden pyramid.

"I don't think your pyramid has anything to do with the anomaly," said McGinley. "The mist you see conceals the rift itself. We simply walk into it…and come out in 1952 at Oak Ridge."

McGinley stepped forward and disappeared into the mist. Wayland hesitated and considered the opportunities for a man from the future in this time period. But then, logic and good common sense prevailed, and he stepped into the mist. And disappeared. Mac Conmara did not hesitate. Here was his life's ambition available to him for a mere step in the right direction. He took that step and into the mist he went. And disappeared. Teige leaped after him.

One by one the three scientists and the dog emerged from the mist. As they looked around they saw trees and a small pond. There was playground equipment on an adjacent grassy area, but no children were present.

"We're outside the compound," said Wayland.

"No," said McGinley. "This isn't Oak Ridge. I know where it is. We're in Central Park, in New York City!"

"But how? Does the rift connect more than one space-time, do you think?"

"Obviously it does, my boy. The question is not where we are, but when we are!"

Byron Grush

5

The Girl in the Rusty Red Pickup

The pedigree of the truck was dubious. The front end was a 1941 Ford half-ton with its characteristic pointed hood and vee-shaped grill, once cherry red but now speckled with rust spots. The head lights were mounted flush on the front of the fenders and probably didn't work. Under the hood was a rebuilt flathead six-cylinder engine from the late forties which had found its way to the patchwork vehicle from the same junk yard as the front end. It did work. The chassis and bed of the truck were from a 1948 Chevrolet pickup. The front bumper was missing. On a windy day like today, a cloud of black smoke preceded the truck up the road.

The driver was a 19 year-old girl named Melanie Langford. Melanie had a head of curly hair the color of the rust on the sides of the truck. She wore blue jeans she had shrunk to fit by wearing them in the shower. Her plaid cotton shirt was unbuttoned just enough to show the tops of her breasts, pushed up by a pink bra. An unfiltered camel cigarette was clenched between her lips and a half full bottle of coke balanced precariously on the bench seat beside her. She was maintaining a speed (some would say much too fast) which allowed the truck to glide across the washboard ruts on the old gravel road without shaking her bones. She had climbed the road nearly to the top of the ridge where an old settler's cabin was perched. She would stop there to finish the coke and chain smoke more cigarettes.

It was late in the afternoon and soon the sun would set on the horizon beyond the ridge. Melanie liked to come to this spot to watch the fall of night and search the stars for familiar constellations: Orion, Ursa Major, Canis Major, or Cassiopeia, depending on the season. Tonight she would look for the bright stars in Sagittarius known as the Teapot, near the center of the Milky Way. She had been fascinated by stars since she was a small child, inspired by her father who was an amateur astronomer. Dad had let his young daughter look through his telescope. He was gone now, a victim of the polio epidemic. The telescope was gone too, in the first garage sale orchestrated by her mother soon after her father's death.

She was bitter about what she perceived as her mother's callousness. It was one way of dealing with her loss. There were others. High school parties at the roller skating rink which led to after-party rendezvous in the parking lot with boys who had cars, for instance. She learned to drink beer before she could conjugate regular verbs in French class. She learned to smoke cigarettes before she could solve an algebra equation in math class. She learned to carry condoms in her purse.

She wasn't pleased when she found two young men in the cabin—her cabin—her private sanctum sanctorum. Men only wanted one thing. Which was okay when she was in the mood, but this was her place to be alone and think about stars and the universe. One was Black and the other, although he had red hair like herself, was dressed like an Arab. It just wouldn't do.

"What y'all doin' up here?" she quizzed. "This is private property." (Technically not her private property, but none the less…)

"Please Miss, we hidin' from the Klan…they's aft' us," Judo responded.

"Nonsense. The Klan isn't active here. You're just paranoid."

"Oh they here all right. You don' know. I seen 'em before. They's nasty, they is."

"Well, anyway, I wish you would leave."

"We caint go nowhere, Missy. We hunted."

"What did you do? Drink from the wrong water fountain? Sit in the front of the bus?"

"We burned up the laboratory down in the valley."

Melanie laughed. "Oh, well, that's all right then. Can I give you boys a lift somewhere?" She gave it a moment of thought—a short moment. This, to her adventurous mind, was getting to be intriguing. Escaped arsonists! Much better than star gazing.

"We caint go into town," said Judo.

"I've always had a hankerin' to see Nashville. You game?"

"Well, we caint stay here. I guess we comin'."

"You two ride in the back. If we go through some small towns you hunker down so no one sees you. Okay?"

Judo and Riordan climbed onto the bed of the pickup. Melanie revved the truck up to the speed that would take the road a few inches above the gravel—at least that was what it was supposed to feel like. However, the boys, as she called them, felt every bounce and bump. Riordan couldn't help thinking about the vision he had seen on the surface of the shrewstone: the metal boxes with wheels that traveled along the white ribbon of a road without the aid of horse or mule, the towers of silver and glass—like the huge castle they had run from not so long ago.

Melanie drove down the old Oak Ridge Turnpike to pick up US Highway 70. It was over 170 miles to Nashville and would take them about 4 hours to make the drive. It was going to be dark soon and the headlights didn't work.

At the town of Sparta, just as they came to the Calfkiller River which flowed north through the town, Melanie pulled over. Coming around to the bed of the truck she was somewhat surprised to see that the two escapees hadn't fallen out along the way. "Hey," she yelled at them, "either of you two jokers got any money? We're almost out of gas."

Judo shook his head. Riordan reached for the purse that was hanging from a leather belt that cinched up his linen leine and brought forth a handful of coins. He offered these to Melanie.

"Wait a minute," she said, "what's all this? Old coins? We can't spend these."

Judo looked at the coins. He knew just enough about coin collecting to realize that these weren't just old...they were *valuable* old. "What's this one say?" he asked, turning around a copper coin which had printing around the edge. "Looks like 'ELIZABETH D G AN FR ET HIBER RE.' What do you suppose that means?"

Riordan still hadn't revealed his true origin to Judo. Now he realized the proverbial cat was out the bag...or out of his purse at any rate. "It means," he said, 'Elizabeth by the grace of God, Queen of England, France, and Ireland.' On the other side it says 'I have made God my helper.' "

"What's it worth?" Melanie wanted to know.

"It's a penny," replied Riordan.

"A penny! And the rest? All pennies? How are we going to buy anything with that handful of nothing?"

"Now wait," said Judo. "What is the date of those coins?"

"Hm…probably 1570, give or take a year."

"British coins from the sixteenth century! These should be worth a lot to a collector. Do you think we could find an antique shop around here?"

Now Melanie's interest was piqued. They drove around town until they found a second hand shop. There was a sign in the window that said, "We buy old gold." Well, copper…not gold. But maybe…. Later they were back on the road having acquired the sum of $30.00 for the coins.

"At least we can buy some gas and get a good meal at Nashville," said Melanie. "We'll have enough left over for a motel. And I want to go to the Grand Ole Opry. Did you know that Lester Flatt of the Foggy Mountain Boys was from this town of Sparta?"

Judo was giving Riordan some curious looks. "Yo' goin' to have to come clean wit me. They don' still use dem old coppers in Ireland. Who are you?" he asked.

"You won't believe it if I tell you."

"Try me."

"My name is Riordan Éamon Ó Ciardha from County Cork in Ireland. I was born in the year of our Lord, 1557. I was apprenticed to the alchemist, Lorcan Mac Conmara. He found a way to pierce the veil between different worlds and different times. Somehow, I traveled from my own time of 1573 to yours. I don't know how to get back."

"Um…okay. Sure. Why not? Time traveler. And I'm the Easter bunny."

"I told you that you wouldn't believe me."

"Don' mention it to the Missy or she cut us loose."

Nashville, Tennessee: Music City, U. S. A.; the Athens of the South; the buckle of the Bible Belt; the cradle of the Lost Cause of the Confederacy. And home to the Mother Church of Country Music, the Ryman Auditorium, where the Grand Ole Opry was broadcast by station WSM and heard in over 30 states. Where Bluegrass music was king as performed by Bill Monroe and his Blue Grass Boys, Lester Flatt and Earl Scruggs and the Foggy Mountain Boys, the Stanley Brothers, the Osborn Brothers, Mac Wiseman, Carl Story, Jim and Jesse, the Country Gentlemen, and many others. It was Old Time Music, Hillbilly Music—it was Bluegrass Music.

In 1894 the National Association of the Daughters of the Confederacy, later called United Daughters of the Confederacy, was founded in Nashville. Its mission was to promote the erection of monuments which would memorialize the Confederacy, to retell the story of "the glorious fight against the greatest odds" as a Holy War for Christianity, chivalry and honor, and for a glorious dying culture (where slaves were happy and were well treated), and to support the ideology of The Lost Cause, which represented a view of white supremacy that would last for another 150 years…and then some.

Melanie had left her charges in the truck while she arranged for a room at the Golden Spur Motel on the outskirts of Nashville. Traveling with a Black person, and particularly cohabiting with one, was not something she wanted known by the desk clerk who was thumbing through an old copy of the Confederate Veteran Magazine when she entered the office. There were twin beds and a roll-a-way in the room. There was a coin-operated vibration box on one bed, a built-in radio (tuned to WSM) on the wall, and a black and white television set on a metal stand in the corner. Deluxe.

She had gone for pizza and returned with a steaming hot cheese and sausage. Riordan sat on the roll-a-way staring at the TV set which hadn't been turned on. Judo noticed his vacant stare and gave him a soft punch on the shoulder. "Hey Cuz, wake up and smell the pizza."

Riordan pointed at the TV. "I can't evoke anything from your shrewstone," he said.

"Huh? No, it's a Zenith. Ya gotta turn it on, ya dope." Which Judo now did.

They ate their slices of pizza and watched the news—Riordan, of course, having no concept of television, believed it to be a modern day shrewstone. He watched the static and the rolling frames which settled into a somewhat stable image as Judo adjusted the rabbit ears. He was already living in the future, and now would be privy to seeing even farther into it! But the newscast was giving details of a fire which had consumed an experimental lab at Oak Ridge. Arson was suspected. A fuzzy picture of Wayland Delaney appeared on the screen as the announcer said that the man was wanted for questioning about the incident. He might be traveling with a colored man, the announcer said.

"That my buddy, Wank!" said Judo.

"You weren't kidding about burning up the lab," said Melanie. "But that isn't a picture of Roy."

"No, Roy ain't got nothin' to do wit it. That Wank, who got kilt in the fire."

"Roy," said Melanie, looking critically at Riordan's costume, "are you an Arab or something?"

"No, I'm from County Cork."

"He from way in the past," offered Judo. "Queen Elizabeth the *Furst*. That what he say, anyway."

"Tomorrow we will get you some normal clothing, Roy. There's a Wally's Western Wear across the highway. You look conspicuous. And you, Judo, there's a Negro district over on Jefferson. I think you'd be safe there. I don't want to just dump you, but we three are going to attract a lot of attention from the wrong sort of people."

"Yes," answered Judo. "Like the Klan!"

"You boys stay here while I go out and find me a nice honkytonk over at the District. I need a tall cool one."

"Thought they all dry in these parts," said Judo.

"They are…except when they serve booze, which is always."

Once Melanie had left, Riordan asked, "Why does she refer to us as 'boys'? We're not boys."

"They white folk always calls us nigras 'boys,' even when we ain't. Specially when we ain't. It ain't no term of endearment. Yo' want that last piece of pizza?"

It was three o'clock in the morning before Melanie returned to the Golden Spur Motel. Riordan was awake, watching static on the television. All the stations had signed off hours ago and now the room was illuminated by the dull blinking of the set. Judo was snoring away in his bed, drowning out the soft hiss of white noise the television gave out. The flickering of a neon sign outside cast alternating hues of red and green against the window shade.

Riordan was now evoking images from the modern electronic shrewstone. On it he saw his mother and father back in Innishannon; she was bending over a bubbling kettle which hung in the hearth over a lively wood fire, the mutton and vegetables in it slowly cooking to perfection; he was sharpening an axe against a whetstone and humming an old tune. He saw his uncle, Ultán Ó Ciardha, shearing a sheep which brayed and struggled aimlessly while ravens circled in the sky above the meadow. He saw Lorcan Mac Conmara in his saffron-colored leine and fringed wool brat—but the alchemist wasn't in his chamber surrounded by bubbling retorts—he was with two strange men in a wooded area where machines like the rusty red truck, but smoother and shinier as if they were made from quick silver, were approaching them in what appeared to be a menacing manner.

This last image frightened Riordan. He saw that the dog, Teige, was there and was barking at the machines. He saw that the men were trying to run from them but had no place to hide. Then the image faded. There was some commotion outside at the door to the room. Riordan rose and went to the door. Before opening it, he listened to the voices that came from outside. One of these he recognized as Melanie's. She sounded distressed.

Melanie had been drinking all night at Jimmy Hyde's Unique Club, a honkytonk on Printer's Alley. She had attracted the attentions of several men whose advances she had expertly repelled. But soon she was slipping off the bar stool and so inebriated she could hardly stand, much less wobble to the street where her rusty red pickup was parked. A group of the men she had earlier rejected observed her fragile state and proceeded to flip a coin to determine which of them would act the chivalrous knight and come to the damsel's rescue. The honor fell to one whose nickname was 'Slim,' although his ample girth seemed to contradict that ironic appellation.

Slim had driven Melanie to the motel in his own car. They now stood at the door to the room arguing. "Why won't you invite me in? You owe me," Slim insisted.

"It's late. And my...mother is sleeping inside. I don't want to wake her."

"That's a lame excuse. Give me a kiss at least."

Slim grabbed her and held her close, trying to force his lips against hers. Melanie struggled and cried out. That was enough for

Riordan who had heard the entire exchange. He threw open the door and pushed at Slim, who staggered back, releasing his grip on the girl.

"Oh, this must be your mother," said Slim. "I like her evening dress. Come on, mom. Push me again."

Riordan was enraged and glared at the big man. He pulled Melanie into the room and was about to slam the door shut when Slim pushed his way in. He swung at Riordan and connected with his jaw. The blow knocked Riordan to the floor where he lay, momentarily dazed. Then he passed out. Melonie screamed again but Slim put his hand over her mouth and pushed her down on the bed.

The fighting had awakened Judo who now entered the fray, ripping at Slim's heavy body which was pressed against the girl's on the bed. The jostling somehow switched on the vibration box and the bed began to vibrate beneath the three as they rolled and tumbled, each trying to dislodge the others. Slim's bulk had the advance over Judo. Despite what his nickname implied, Judo was not a fighter. Soon he was sprawled on the floor in a semiconscious state. Slim turned his attention to disrobing Melanie and tore open her blouse.

Melonie shut her eyes tightly and turned her head to avoid the hot, alcoholic breath that came at her from the ugly face that pressed down against her own. Her arms were pinned under her or she would have run her nails across that face, digging the deepest of furrows she could manage and marking the man for life. Slim's hands now pulled at the tight jeans. She tried kicking, but the man's weight pressed her into the vibrating mattress. She was going to be raped. She knew it. She cried out. Suddenly, the man stopped moving and seemed to sink more heavily down on her. Like a dead weight.

Riordan had regained consciousness. Seeing Judo on the floor and the big man forcing himself against Melanie, he did the only thing he knew to do. He reached for the shearing knife that hung from his belt. With an accuracy that came from slaughtering sheep and pigs on his uncle's farm, he plunged the knife into the man's back, piercing his heart. He then rolled the man off the girl and onto the floor. He shook Judo to wakefulness while Melanie sat up, began breathing heavily, and started sobbing.

After what seemed like an eternity in which the three companions sat in shock and disbelief, Melanie managed to calm herself and evaluate their situation. People had seen her leave the honkytonk with Slim. The room was registered in her name. They would have to run. Her pickup was still parked near Printer's Alley. She ruffled through the dead man's pockets and found his car keys.

"Hey Judo," she said, "you know how to drive stick? We've gotta get the fuck out of here!"

Byron Grush

6

Tempus Non Fugit

Central Park, New York City, had not changed much in the 200 years since Dr. McGinley had last seen it. Except that there were no people present. And except for the very tall silver pinnacle that rose above the trees and seemed to disappear into the clouds.

"What is that?" asked Wayland.

"Some sort of monument, I suppose. Or it could be a building. This obviously is not 1952!" answered McGinley.

"Nor is it 1573," added Mac Conmara. "Where are the people?"

By way of an unexpected, and unwanted answer, vehicles came at them from all sides. Shaped like elongated eggs with mirror-like surfaces and no apparent wheels or other moving parts, six of them floated across the ground toward the three scientists at a slow but steady speed.

"We'd better go back through the time rift," yeller McGinley. "And hurry!"

But when they turned to where the rift had been, it had disappeared, and with it, their only hope for escape. The egg-vehicles closed in, forming a tight circle around them, and stopped. On one of the vehicles a door opened. The surface had not shown any outline or indication of the door, but indeed, an opening appeared. A man stepped out.

"Well, at least he is human," said Wayland.

"I wouldn't jump to any hasty conclusions," said McGinley.

The man was tall, slender, and hairless on his head and face. His clothing was skin-tight and without buttons or zippers. It was made of some silver material than looked like metal or shiny plastic but was soft and pliant and did not bunch up as the man walked toward them. His expression was bland and his manner and intent could not be interpreted from it. When McGinley held out both hands in a gesture of friendly submission, the man gave no reaction.

Teige the dog, however, was off in the bushes barking and growling at the strange shiny shapes that surrounded his master. A door opened in another egg and two men, similarly hairless and sheathed in silver like the first man, came out carrying a web-like net. They approached Teige cautiously. The dog, never afraid of humans, stopped barking and sat down wagging his tail. The net came down over him and the men dragged him back to their egg and thrust him into it.

The man approaching the three scientists from the past held a small silver tube in his hand. At first, McGinley thought it was a pencil or pen. The man pointed it at him and that was the last thing he saw before he plunged into oblivion. Mac Conmara and Wayland also succumbed to the weapon.

When they awoke they were confused and disoriented. There was nothing in the large room to give them any indication of their location. Certainly, they had been transported to a building somewhere…but where? There were no windows and the only door was a solid piece of opaque material without knob or handle. The only furniture, if one could call it that, consisted of three throw rugs without a discernible design or pattern, upon which they were lying.

"Did you notice anything unusual about those men?" asked McGinley. He was sitting cross-legged on his rug, like a Buddha.

"They looked like clones of each other," answered Wayland. "Do you think we been have transported to some alien world?"

"I don't think so. The rift is only one of time. If it were a space-time rift we could very well materialize inside of a star or out in empty space. No, I think this is earth…just at some future time."

"Until we were attacked," said the alchemist, "I thought we might have reached Heaven. Those men didn't act like angels, however. If this is a future time, I don't think I care for it very much."

"My, but how time flies when you're having fun," Wayland said, trying to interject some humor into their situation. "Tempus fugit and all that."

"I think the actual quote is, 'sed fugit interea, fugit inreparabile tempus,' ...'but time is lost, which never will renew.' Or possibly, 'fast flies meanwhile the irreparable hour.' Virgil, from *Georgics*."

" 'Time is not composed of indivisible nows.' Aristotle said that," added Mac Conmara.

" 'The arrow of time often falls short of the mark.' I said that," answered McGinley.

"Oh, I have one," Wayland said. "Shakespeare. From Hamlet's 'To be or not to be' speech. We memorized it in high school and I've never forgotten it. He talks of 'the slings and arrows of outrageous fortune' and asks 'who would bear the whips and scorns of time?' Maybe it is *time* for us to take arms against our own sea of troubles."

"And by opposing, end them. Yes, but how?" McGinley walked to the knobless door and ran his hands over it. "Nothing here to show how to open it. I guess we wait. Time is not on our side."

"And one hopes that this is not 'the last syllable of recorded time.' Sorry, I just switched to Macbeth," joked Wayland.

"I know of this Macbeth," said Mac Conmara. He was king of the Scots. A little before my time. It is unfortunate that we cannot control which time we step into, or we could visit some of these famous figures."

"Wayland," said McGinley, "if that were possible, to control the time period we step into, to when would you go?"

"I would...I would go pre-Nazi Germany and kill Hitler before he rose to power," Wayland answered.

"But suppose in doing so, you inadvertently changed other things that resulted in equally bad circumstances? Suppose, for instance, that Einstein never left Germany since the Jews were not being prosecuted. But he still contributed to developing the atom bomb...and Germany dropped it on America?"

"These people and times you speak of," Mac Conmara said, "they suggest a terrible world that lies ahead of my former present. Could it be that the world simply gets worse and worse as 'time flies?' Our current present may be the dreadful result of such an evolution."

"I think I prefer to believe," said Wayland, "that we are on an alien planet. One that mimics an alternate version of our own."

The door opened. McGinley had been leaning against it and almost fell out of the room but caught himself in time. One of the silver clad men stood outside and beckoned for McGinley to follow him. McGinley shrugged and did follow the man. The door swung shut before the others could get to it.

"Now what?" asked Wayland.

"Now we wait," said Mac Conmara.

Time passed, but neither man could think of any more quotations or wise sayings. Two hours later, McGinley returned. He threw himself down on his rug, brought his knees up to his chest and hugged his legs, rocking slowly. The others waited while he composed himself to the extent that he could talk. He was noticeably shaken. He had been taken to an interrogation room, he said, and questioned by three of the hairless men. He hadn't let on that he and his companions were unwilling visitors from the past, maintaining, instead, that they had mistakenly wandered onto the island and had become lost. He made up a story about living across the river in what had been New Jersey, in an isolated community that knew nothing about Manhattan. He asked his own questions and was surprised that his interrogators were willing to answer.

"What I learned," McGinley said, "is this. The dominant inhabitants of what used to be Manhattan Island are an inbred group of hairless whites who have mastered the use of advanced technology yet have no expertise in developing new ideas or theories. Hence, they are at an impasse with evolution, both physically and intellectually. Emotionally they have suppressed feelings of joy, happiness, love, hate, anger, and fear to the point where they react dispassionately to any given situation, relying on habit instead of reasoning to adapt or to solve problems."

"You got all this just from questioning them?" asked Wayland.

"They were fairly transparent in their manner of discussing their own social and political situation. They are the absolute rulers of New York City, and there are no longer elections. Power descends through families."

"Just like in my time," commented Mac Conmara."

McGinley continued: "Buildings in the city include examples of fantastic architecture erected years ago by talented and far-thinking individuals now deceased. The city had been rebuilt after an environmental devastation in the late 21st century. Because of unchecked human use of fossil fuels, the ozone layer was destroyed, the climate heated up, and the polar ice caps melted. Rising sea levels that took away major portions of shore line reduced Manhattan considerably in area. Skyscrapers now stand on stilts and rise higher than ever before.

"A second group of people, some descendants of the original New Yorkers, live in the older parts of the city where the buildings are crumbling and infested with rodents and insects and feral dogs and cats. These disenfranchised denizens have little power to influence the political and social affairs of the city. Splinter groups of radicals have arisen to confront the hairless aristocracy but have had small impact against them. The city rulers do, however, worry about outlying bands of dissidents who may soon organize and attack. That is why they picked us up in the park."

"Amazing," said Mac Conmara. "But what do they plan on doing with us? They think we were here to attack them?"

"They had to be sure. You see, they have a protocol for everything. Encounter strangers, arrest them and interrogate them. If they are the enemy, kill them. If not, let them go. They have no pity for insurgents and little concern about inconveniencing those who are innocent."

"And which are we?"

"We will learn that in due time."

They came next for the alchemist and took him to the interrogation room where he sat before the silver tribunal. Their main questions focused on his unusual clothing, a type they had never encountered. He explained that he was a scholar specializing in the study of ancient cultures. This was the costume of a man from the British Isles in the sixteenth century. He wore this as part of a reenactment of those times in which he and his fellow scholars engaged to better understand their topic.

"What have you done with my dog?" Mac Conmara asked.

Teige, they told him, was a stray mongrel and was not allowed in the city proper. It was scheduled to be destroyed in a few days. When the alchemist insisted that the dog be reunited with him, the three inquisitors were incredulous. No one had ever demanded anything from them. And no one had any use for a dog, except, perhaps, for food. It was an unreasonable request. As unorthodox as the man's clothing. Incongruous and eccentric.

Wayland Delaney was the next to be brought before the three interrogators. Was he also a scholar studying ancient cultures? Was that explanation for the brightly decorated shirt he wore? Wayland was unaware of the alchemist's lie and therefore did not substantiate it. Instead, without thinking things through, he told them that he, and the others, were scientists engaged in research into quantum mechanics. These silver men, being from his future, would certainly know all about particle acceleration and time displacement and dead-alive cats and so forth. His slip in almost revealing the real nature of the time-travelers did have one positive outcome: it saved them from immediately joining Teige in the execution chamber.

Spies and ingrates were disposable. Scientists capable of original thinking were to be prized—and exploited. The men in this city had no concept of quantum theory. They knew how to turn the machines that kept things running on and off; that was all. But they understood that progress was at a standstill and it behooved them to prime the pump a little here and there. New developments were always welcome if it meant implementing things with a minimum of intellectual output. Laziness, in this day and age, was close to Godliness. As there had once been slaves to do the manual labor, now there were slaves to do scientific development. Therefore McGinley, Wayland and Mac Conmara were added to the sparse company of scientific thinkers kept on tap by the rulers of the city.

The lab was on what had been the 86th floor of the Empire State Building, one of few ancient buildings that had survived the years of rising flood waters. The 86th floor was now only twenty or so stories above the ocean's surface. It was connected by transportation tubes through which the egg-shaped vehicles could pass to a modern building situated behind the dikes which surrounded upper Manhattan.

McGinley was missing his old familiar Aloha shirt; they had been given modern clothing to wear of the same material the silver men wore but of a drab green hue. It reminded McGinley of the green cotton scrubs that doctors wore back in the twentieth century. Except these scrubs were skin tight and seemed to maintain an even body temperature regardless of being in a hot or cold environment. They had rooms two floors down from the lab where there was also a cafeteria in which the scientists ate and a lounge in which they could relax. The accommodations were more than adequate, save that they were virtual prisoners.

Mac Conmara had managed to negotiate the return of his dog. Teige was allowed to roam through the vacant floors of the building while the alchemist was occupied in the lab above. The windows of the lowest of these floors had been sealed against the rising waters. The stairwell and the old elevator shaft had likewise been barricaded. The dog found little of interest beyond the occasional river rat nest which he demolished in a search for its rodent occupant. The rats were elusive but provided a great game for the dog.

On the first day of their servitude they were introduced to the other scientists housed and working in the Empire State Building. Arnold Wolfe would have had gray hair, if he had had hair, and was spry for his 70-some years. He spent most of his time when in the lab writing in a spiral-bound notebook with an antique fountain pen; an anachronism, as the others used electronic tablets. By contrast, Winston Cooper was young and energetic, constantly moving about the lab to check on experiments, and one of those talkative types that McGinley found interesting, but that Wayland and Mac Conmara found tiresome. McGinley would compare notes with Cooper in the days to come, and often came close to revealing the truth to him about himself and his fellows.

Two others, Leith Carlyle and Albert Breckinridge, were not from the population of the city proper, had hair on their heads, and were of a much shorter stature. McGinley asked about their backgrounds but encountered a reluctance to discuss their origins. All that he could discover was that they had been born and raised in the city's ghetto but had been educated at the Manhattan Institute of Technology under a pilot program begun during a short-lived era of progressive liberalism—a program designed to expand the city's scientific community, but which soon dissolved as conservative attitudes again prevailed.

The experiments these four scientists carried on did not amount to much: old tried and true chemical reactions and various ways of generating electricity to run motors. Even the alchemist knew considerably more about chemistry than what was represented here. McGinley wondered, had so much scientific knowledge been lost? The level of technology in the daily lives of the citizens of this modern New York would argue against that theory. Perhaps it was taboo to engage in certain activities, especially those involving atomic energy.

Wayland could not resist asking outright. After all, he was a youth, and hence might not be expected to know the history of science. He was in the lounge with Leith Carlyle and Albert Breckinridge, having a cup of herbal tea in which floated green flakes of an unidentifiable substance when he broached the subject of atomic energy. There was nothing to tell, explained Carlyle, and Breckinridge confirmed this. Atomic energy had been banned many years ago after the terrorist attacks by the Koreans and the subsequent cleansing of that peninsula with dirty bombs by the U.S. government. A world-wide ban had resulted, and all reactors and plants had been dismantled.

What about particle research? Forbidden. What about relativity theory? Quantum mechanics? No longer relevant. What then was the point of science? To stay alive and come up with a new soft drink or cleansing powder once in a while to please the city rulers. Was it possible that anyone could conduct such research uninhibited by the government? Impossible.

"What if I wanted to build a particle accelerator? Could I get the parts?" asked Wayland.

Carlyle was intrigued. "There is a committee that reviews our equipment requests. But…"

"But," Breckinridge completed the comment, "if we bundled the parts together with other things, and spread the requests out over a long period of time…"

"They wouldn't catch on! Why do you want to build a particle accelerator?" Carlyle asked.

"Well, it's the sort of research we should be doing, isn't it? Instead of developing a better toothpaste. It sounds like you would be interested."

"Just don't tell the others," said Breckinridge.

Later, when he had the opportunity to talk to McGinley and Mac Conmara alone, Wayland described his conversation with the two scientists.

"They would help us. Of course, I couldn't tell them the real reason…that we'd be building a time machine. And there is the problem of the energy source. There are no reactors here."

"We've got the best energy source there is," said Mac Conmara. "One we alchemists know all about: lightning."

"Of course," said McGinley. "And this building has a spire that rises to 103 stories. There is still a lightning rod attached to it, I'll wager. There is a huge empty space between this floor and the upper deck. We can build it there, out of sight."

"Say," said Wayland, "did you ever see that old movie? About Frankenstein's bride? They send the monster up to the top of the castle to get struck by lightning. Oh boy! Mr. Alchemist, you are brilliant!"

"Of course I am. Just born at the wrong time. Irrelevant now, as it appears."

7

Sweet Home Chicago

A black '49 Hudson Hornet was parked on Church Street next to a fire hydrant. The Nashville police had ticketed the car and called for a wrecker to tow it away. The wrecker was busy elsewhere and so the Hudson sat for two days before anyone noticed the fowl stench emanating from its truck. The Davidson County's Sheriff was summoned, and a crowbar was swiftly applied to the vehicle's trunk, resulting in the discovery of the body of the man who was called Slim. The person or persons unknown who had perpetrated the crime had left no finger prints or other clues so the police were temporarily stymied. When Slim's immediate acquaintances were questioned it was learned that he had been last seen in the company of a very drunk young woman with red hair. No one knew her name.

The rusty red pickup had rolled into the City of Big Shoulders carrying the three fugitives who were still in a state of near panic. They had driven all day and all night and finally reached Chicago in the early hours of the morning when the urban bustling began in earnest. Along Fulton Boulevard the market had been throbbing with activity since before the dull red sun had pierced the heavy haze. Men in dirty aprons pushed carts piled high with vegetables and fruits. In the harbor near the old Navy Pier fishing boats pulled away from shore. Sailors untangled and repaired fishing nets as gulls circled expectantly overhead. Along Kinzie Street men wearing hats made from folded newspaper hurried to their jobs at the printing presses where "all the news that's fit to print" would roll in a continuous, rumbling ribbon of paper smelling of fresh ink and machine oil. Soon, the commuter trains would arrive from the suburbs. Men wearing fedoras and shiny shoes would fill the sidewalks of the Loop.

At the International Amphitheatre on Halstead at 42nd Street, next to the Union Stock Yards, preparations were getting underway for the 1952 Democratic National Convention where a presidential ticket would be chosen. U.S. Senator Estes Kefauver of Tennessee, Governor Adlai E. Stevenson II, of Illinois, Senator Richard Russell of Georgia, and Averell Harriman of New York were the front runners. Ten days earlier, in the same art deco building, the Republican National Convention had met and chosen General Dwight David Eisenhower, a popular war hero, for president, and for vice president, Richard M. Nixon, the Senator from California, who was a principle on the House Un-American Activities Committee, and an inspiration for Senator Joseph McCarthy and his Communist "witch hunts." The smell from the stock yards had crept into the amphitheater and blended imperceptibly with the odor of politics.

The rusty red pickup was parked downtown on Wells Street. Bars of light and shadow filtered from the overhead elevated tracks, partially illuminating the colorless gloom of the cavernous street. Occasionally a train would pass, causing the light to flicker, and echoing a clatter, a screech, and a roar that deafened the walkers below; walkers who struggled against the fierce winds that blew around corners and down the street and sucked papers from the windows of the second story offices. The three that had ridden in the pickup now joined those walkers in a wind-blown ritual of dodging the paper jetsam, the air-borne cigarette butts and candy wrappers that swirled across the gritty pavement, the scores of pigeons that danced through the dust, and now and then, a drunk or a panhandler who stumbled down the sidewalk. Cars drifted slowly through the street like metal sharks.

Riordan now had on twentieth-century clothing: khaki slacks and a blue polo shirt with an embroidered kangaroo on it. Melanie had found a haberdashery where she picked out an outfit for him that would allow him to blend in with the crowd. The proprietor had been interested in Riordan's sixteenth-century costume and traded for it offering a pair of penny loafers and a pair of argyle socks. Riordan felt uncomfortable in the socks and so he wore the loafers without them, stuffing them into his back pocket. His purse and his knife could not be displayed on the street. These he wrapped in a paper bag from the store and carried under his arm.

Judo followed Melanie and Riordan a few paces back. Chicago had a large Black population and there were no water fountains marked for whites or blacks only, yet the separation of the races was evident in the looks white people gave him. No sense tempting fate.

Riordan was trying to keep up with the pace Melanie had set—a pace consistent with the moving crowd of pedestrians. "This future is much too noisy and dirty," he complained. "And people walk too fast."

"Better get used to it," replied Melanie. "You're in the big city now. You really must be from the country like you told us."

"I want to go home to my own time. Is there any place here where the alchemists gather?"

"Chemists? Well, I suppose one of the universities. Why do you ask?"

"Could we go to one of the universities? I would talk to the alchemists about my desire to return home."

"How about I find you a travel agent? Oh well, I guess we could find us some scientists somewhere. Kind of a crazy idea, but I will humor you since you basically saved me from a fate worse than death. I'll ask directions and we'll see."

The photographer pulled the black cloth over his head and stared at the ground glass of his 8-by-10 Deardorff view camera. As he worked the bellows back and forth, the upside-down image of a group of men and one woman, standing in front of the arched doorway of Bernard Albert Eckhart Hall came slowly into focus. It was an appropriate setting for a document of this second reunion of atomic scientists since here, on the campus of the University of Chicago, under the west stands of Stagg field in an abandoned squash court, the first controlled nuclear fission chain reaction had taken place on December 2, 1942.

Among the group of scientists were Eugene Wigner, Leona Libby, James Franck, Leo Szilard, and Enrico Fermi. Franck had won the Nobel Prize in Physics in 1925 and had been director of the chemistry division of the university's Metallurgical Laboratory where research was conducted into the structures of plutonium and uranium during the beginning of the Manhattan Project. He had recently published dire warnings about the dangers of a world-wide nuclear arms race. Szilard had left Nazi Germany in 1933 with a group of Jewish and Hungarian scientists that included Edward Teller, John von Neumann, and Eugene Wigner. Fermi had similarly escaped from Fascist Italy in 1938 when accepting his Nobel Prize for Physics in Sweden. Fermi and Szilard were the leaders in the construction of the reactor, Chicago Pile-1, and together with the others, had fathered the Birth of the Atomic Age.

The lone woman posing that afternoon was Leona Marshall Libby. She had been the only woman present when CP-1 went critical. The others had tried to discourage her from an involvement in the potentially dangerous research, but she had persisted. She had later followed Enrico Fermi to Argonne National Laboratory when the reactor was moved there, working while pregnant with her first child. She defended the dropping of the bombs on Hiroshima and Nagasaki. She was famously quoted as asking, immediately after that first sustained chain reaction at the squash court, "When do we become scared?"

The photographs taken, the negative holders packed, and the tripod collapsed, the photographer carried his equipment back to his truck. The entourage of twenty-plus scientists and technicians broke up into smaller groups. The more prominent of them clustered together waiting for the others to disperse. A plan was put forth to migrate up the street and across the campus to the Quadrangle Club where they could relax over food, and beer, wine, or fruit juice as each might desire.

Fermi, Libby, Szilard, Franck, and Wigner ambled up University Avenue toward 57th Street, chattering about old times and new. They had walked up about half of the block when a rusty red pickup pulled along side of them. A red-haired young woman yelled out the window at them:

"Hey, any of you folks know where we can find a scientist?"

James Franck, laughing, approached the truck. "What do you want with a scientist?" he asked.

Riordan and Judo popped up like jacks-in-the-box from the bed of the truck where they had been keeping out of sight.

"My buddy here needs to go back to his home in the sixteenth," said Judo.

"Sixteenth Street? Sixteenth Ward? What do you mean?"

"I means the sixteenth century."

"It's true," said Riordan. "I have traveled through time and now I need to go back. I need to find an alchemist to help me."

Now the laughter from the group of scientists ceased. Why were they talking to this crazy person on the street when there was food and liquor waiting? Wigner tried to pull Franck back, worried that a misadventure was at hand, but Franck shook him off.

"There is something interesting here," said Franck. "I want to talk to this fellow."

"We'll be waiting at the Quadrangle, Jim," said Wigner. "You come along when you're ready."

But now, Enrico Fermi stepped up with a suggestion. "Gene," he said, "let's bring the lad with us. It may prove to be an entertaining afternoon." And to Riordan he said: "We are all scientists, although sadly ignorant of alchemy. We study atoms. We wish to invite you to a late lunch so we may compare our twentieth century science with what you know of your own century. Will you come?" It was difficult for Fermi to conceal his mirth. He went on: "I'm afraid your companions would not be welcome at the club. You see, it is members only and young women and Blacks..."

"You go ahead, Roy," said Melanie. "We'll be waiting around here somewhere if I don't get a parking ticket."

Leona Libby, the only woman present at the world's first sustained chain reaction, was now the only woman present in the lounge of the Quadrangle Club. It was only recently that women had been allowed membership. Few applied. The group of scientists and the young man from another century sat around a large round table. The only actual club member of the group was James Franck, but he was allowed to bring guests for a meal or libations, especially when those guests were as auspicious as Enrico Fermi and the others.

Fermi and Leo Szilard were arguing. They hadn't worked together since the early Manhattan Project and differed greatly on procedure and the role of the scientist. Fermi felt Szilard was too eager to hand off tasks to subordinates; Szilard thought Fermi was arrogant.

"You don't like to get your hands dirty, Leo," said Fermi. "But you miss out on essential aspects...you can't get a true understanding of the process without getting deeply into it."

"You love to take the credit, Enrico," answered Szilard. "That's why you're always sticking your nose into everything."

"Gentlemen…gentlemen!" Wigner insisted. "Let us turn our attention to our young guest. He may be able to enlighten you about the origin of the universe." He chuckled.

Leona Libby was the only person not silently laughing at Riordan. While the others bickered, she had been conversing with Riordan, quizzing him about his background, testing his authenticity. She got him talking about alchemy and his role as an apprentice. She had been interested in the history of science for years and had studied about practitioners of the arcane arts and their search for the philosopher's stone. She had read Carl Gustav Jung's comments about the Chinese alchemical text, *The Secret of the Golden Flower*, and its relationship to what he called the process of individualization. She knew all about Albertus Magnus and Roger Bacon, about Robert Boyle, Mary Anne Atwood, Ethan Allen Hitchcock, Robert Fludd, the Rosicrucians, Comte de Saint-Germain, Count Alessandro di Cagliostro, and other famous alchemists. She knew which of their beliefs had led to later scientific processes and discoveries, and which were part and parcel of what Phineas T. Barnum called "The Humbugs of the World." And the more that Riordan spoke of his own world, the more convinced she became that he was being truthful. Was he a time traveler? That she could hardly believe…and yet…

"Enrico," she said when she had hustled the scientist off to the bar to order drinks, "you know those experiments we talked about at Argonne, the ones concerning quantum theory?" He nodded, wondering where this was going. "Well, I have been talking to our young friend about alchemy and time traveling, which he maintains explains his presence in our century."

"And you believe him?"

"I don't. But he had some insights, because of…however he obtained such a vast knowledge of alchemy. I would like to have him around as a sort of…consultant…bizarre as that might seem. Could we get him a pass to the lab at Argonne? He appears to be homeless. He could stay with me."

"You are serious. I would have to think about this. Our reputations…"

"It may come to nothing. But you of all people should know when to take chances. Remember that first slip of the control rod and the noise it made? I was terrified we'd blow up the whole city. But you continued the experiment."

"And then we blew up two cities."

"Not us personally. But it ended the war. Saved more lives than it took."

"An alchemist's apprentice, you say? If nothing else, it might be a welcome distraction. And who knows? Maybe he *is* from the sixteenth century."

Chicago Pile-1, the reactor Enrico Fermi and his crew used in their experiments, was originally to be built at the Metallurgical Lab's isolated Site A, a facility being built in the Red Gate Woods section of the Argonne Forest of the Cook County Forest Preserve near Palos Hills, but labor strikes forced construction of the pile to be moved to the stadium at the University of Chicago. Once it was concluded that pile CP-1, now famous for that first sustained chain reaction, was too dangerous to be located in the city, it was moved to Site A and rebuilt as CP-2. A second reactor, CP-3 was quickly built at the facility, now called Argonne Laboratory, and nicknamed "The Country Club" after the Palos Park Golf Course that had once been located there. But Site A was painfully small and on land deeded to be for recreational purposes.

By the early '50s, CP-2 and CP-3 had become obsolete and were decommissioned. The reactors were dismantled, and their radioactive fuel and heavy water coolant were removed and shipped to Oak Ridge. Parts of the reactors were encased in concrete and buried 40 feet deep on the spot.

Argonne moved 40 miles southwest to a 1,700-acre unincorporated area in DuPage County near Lemont. The new lab with its series of specialized buildings was surround by an idyllic natural landscape called Waterfall Glen, a wooded area where white-tailed deer roamed freely—and assured, by their very presence, that no lethal atomic radiation was leaking from the lab. The lab was heavily guarded and surrounded by a barbed-wire fence. It could only be entered through check points where a photo ID badge and pass were required.

Riordan was wearing his badge pinned to his polo shirt as he strolled through the woods outside of the lab complex. The badge was a frame made of tin with the words, "Argonne National Laboratory," and the letters, "AEC," for Atomic Energy Commission, pressed into it. His picture was slipped into the frame. The back of the badge consisted of a film packet covered partly with a cadmium filter. It would be inspected as he entered or exited the lab for any evidence of radiation contamination. In the early experiments at Site A, two scientists had been stricken; one having his skin severely blistered, and another finding his white blood cell count had plummeted. Better precautions were now part of daily routine.

On his own, Riordan followed a path through a stand of black walnut and white oak. It was early fall and the leaves were just beginning to turn. He saw honeysuckle vines invading the underbrush; the flash of an iridescent humming bird sampling the last of the season's blossoms had attracted his attention. He plucked one of the lacey yellow blooms and popped it into his mouth. He was rewarded with a sweet honey-like flavor. He knew, however, to avoid the vine's poisonous black berries. He came upon the Sawmill Creek and followed it through a ravine to a rushing waterfall where slabs of limestone formed a simple dam over which sheets of fresh water fell, glistening in the afternoon sun. He watched a fan-tailed hawk circling overhead. He heard the cooing of morning doves and the chippering of brown squirrels. He thought of home.

He sat for a while by the waterfall. Above the falls was a smooth placid pond where water had backed up. No ripple betrayed the next phase of that water's travels. At the edge of the limestone dam the creek seemed to hesitate and swirl in eddies of reluctance. Then leaving the security of the pond, it leaped over each stepped plateau of white rock, arching and splashing down and making a joyful sound. At the bottom of the falls it pushed against previous arrivals of fluid and foam, boiled briefly, then raced down the long and lonely river toward its next adventure. How like life, thought Riordan.

How, indeed. His life now—he considered himself again an apprentice, although this was not strictly true—living with Leona and her husband and small child, he was inundated with books filled with symbols he did not yet understand. His visiting the great laboratory where his new masters worked—but only occasionally. The endless discussions with Leona about the alchemical arts. He was learning about modern day science from Libby, she learned from him. At least he did not have to sweep the floor or carry out the trash. Yet he was no closer to going home.

Byron Grush

8

A Fearless Symmetry

Simultaneity: events separated by space but occurring at the same time—a concept that entered the thought experiments of Einstein and others and gave rise to a mathematical model of space-time in special relativity: it is impossible to say whether events separated by space do exist at the same *time* because this is relative to the *position* of the observer. And a single observer who is in *motion* will observe the *simultaneous* events as if they happened at different times.

The inability of humans to understand the totality of the universe is perhaps due to our sense of space as existing in three dimensions and our sense of moment as *now*. We cannot see time any more than we can see the wind. Yet we experience wind by *observing* its effect upon real objects—the rustling of leaves in a tree or the ripples of water on a pond. We experience time by measuring it with clocks or drawing our initials in wet cement. Our *now* carries with it the idea of past and present, although we cannot exist in all those time-frames simultaneously. Or can we?

If we could move along a time-line without changing our position in three-dimensional space, what would we be able to observe? If we could move along that time-line and also move through the space associated with that particular *point* in time, would we not be time travelers? Can we not then propose the simultaneity of space? Could

71

not two distinct coordinates of space exist at the same time? If so, then space would be relative to the time of the observer, and an observer in motion would be able to enter a space which existed in a different time. Remembering the words of Hermes Trismegistus:

> *Found I that only by moving upward*
> *and yet again by moving to right-ward*
> *could I be free from the time of the movement.*
> *Forth I came from out of my body,*
> *moved in the movements that changed me in time.*

New York, 2152

The three time travelers were having a private conference in the break room. On the table before them sat three cups of the strange tea, as yet untouched. There was something about the ominous green *things* that floated in the cups that was off-putting. Through the windows, mold-coated on the outside, they could barely see the route of gulls in flight; white winged shapes cutting through an inbound fog. Off in the distance, the tip of the Statue of Liberty's torch still stood as a sentinel against the pounding waves, yet Lady Liberty was mostly submerged, unable now to coax the tired, the poor, the huddled masses, the wretched refuse, from other teeming shores.

"Doctor McGinley," said Wayland, "you told me that the rift is only a time rift, not a space-time rift. Why is it then, that we did not end up back at Oakridge? How did we get to Ireland and now to New York?"

McGinley swirled his tea, trying to sink the green things. He gave this some thought.

"We tend to think of time as being strictly linear," answered McGinley. "As if we are moving along a wooden ruler laid on a flat surface. But I suggest that time itself is like a piece of string, flexible and wrapped around itself, like a big ball of twine. Normally, we, and the space in which we exist, move along the twine…either inward or outward within the ball…I don't know which. Always in one direction however. What we have done by creating a time rift, is to move at right angles to the outer circumference of the ball, thereby ending at different points along that twine. Like all things in the universe, the ball of twine is also in in motion, probably rotating. Hence there is a bit of slippage as we move."

"That is an interesting concept," interjected Lorcan Mac Conmara. "Suppose also, that the ball is not tightly wound. The twine can move or wiggle within a certain confined space. One traveling obliquely through the ball could miss parts of his time stream and therefore find himself in some unusual space...like this one!"

"And here's another thought," added Wayland. "Suppose there are multiple strands of twine in the same ball. Perhaps even short fragments and loops that are endless. If you landed on one of those..."

"You'd live your life over and over and never be aware of it. Gentlemen, I think it is time to bring Carlyle and Breckinridge into our confidence. We need all the minds we can safely muster on this project. Perhaps there is a way to pin-point the time and space to which we travel. But Wayland, do not think of the murder of Hitler or Napoleon or any other. We must not meddle with events that have already taken place."

"Of course not," said Wayland. But inwardly he thought about the possibilities.

Argonne National laboratory, 1952

Riordan Ó Ciardha paced outside the lab, annoyed that he had been excluded from what he perceived to be an important meeting. Behind the closed door, Leona Libby and Enrico Fermi were entertaining a visitor from the Oakridge National Laboratory, Dr. Frederick Duban. Dr. Duban was an old friend and recently had been in contact with Fermi concerning the disappearance of his colleague at Oakridge, Dr. Madison McGinley.

Fermi and Libby, having listened, albeit with a grain of skepticism, to Riodan's story, and then to Duban's, began to think that the disappearance of McGinley and the sudden and simultaneous appearance of O' Ciardha were just a bit too coincidental. Was there a correlation? They asked Duban to meet with them at Argonne.

McGinley's absence was noticed shortly after the fire in the STAR lab. Duban was one of the few people at ONL who was aware of the specific kind of research McGinley conducted, and although he discounted the idea, the ever-so-very-slight possibility that McGinley had stepped into the STAR chamber and disappeared into time, this gave Duban grave pause. Now he was being told about the mysterious young man who claimed to be from another century, and so his doubt that time travel was possible was being seriously challenged.

"Did he leave any notes?" asked Fermi. "What did the STAR chamber consist of? How about the power source?"

"His notes were destroyed in the fire. All we would have to go on is what I remember from our conversations. These were not detailed enough that I could do much more than give a slim outline of his approach. But perhaps, since you have been experimenting in that same direction…"

"We have made some progress in the theorical area but haven't tested our theorems with any practical experiments. However…"

"However," said Libby, interrupting Fermi, "we have the boy. And if what he claims is true, then some kind of overlap between his space-time and ours must have happened. Is it possible that a window in time was opened by Dr McGinley's apparatus and that Ó Ciardha stepped through it at the same instant that McGinley did?"

"That would suggest," said Duban, "that McGinley is now in 16th century Ireland. You know, there was this cat that he thought came through the STAR chamber. We joked about it."

Riordan had been listening as best he could with his ear up against the door. When he heard mention of a cat that had possibly made the same trip in time as he had, he could no longer restrain himself. He began pounding on the door. "Let me in," he shouted. "I know about the cat!"

The door swung open. "You know about what cat?" asked Duban.

"If it was a long-haired gray cat with a notch out of its right ear, then it was the alchemist's cat. That cat disappeared the day before I walked into the mist," maintained Riordan.

Country road near Chicago, 1952

Autumn was doing its utmost to drape the landscape with the blush of burnt orange and rosy red, and the bruise of rusty ochre, brilliant yellow, and pale sepia. Fallen leaves swirled across the open road hurriedly as the rusty red pickup forged its way away from the metropolis sometimes known as the "Hog Butcher of the World." Melanie tossed an empty coke bottle out of the window. Beside her on the bench seat of the old truck, Judo leaned against the door frame, humming the melody of a blues tune once sung by Bessie Smith, *Careless Love Blues*.

"Say Judo," Melanie said, "you ever make it with a white chick?"

Judo flushed. He stammered, "Ah...I...no, Missy. I nev..."

"You a virgin then? We'll have to do something about that cherry."

"I...I promised my mamma..."

"Oh? A momma's boy! Well, we'll take it slow and easy. Meanwhile, we're almost out of gas and money. See that gas station up the road? Tell you what you do. I'll let you out right here and you stay back out of sight. You watch. I'll get gas and then do something to distract the attendant."

"What you do?"

"I'll think of something. When you see me get him into a back room or someplace, you come quick and empty the cash register. Once you're done, honk the truck's horn once and go on up the road as far as you can. I'll pick you up."

Judo was nervous waiting in a clump of bushes. He watched while the attendant filled the pickup's tank with gasoline. He saw Melanie talking with the man, then climbing out of the truck and following him into the station. Judo came closer and looked through the plate glass window just in time to see Melanie and the attendant disappear through a doorway. Then he followed through with something he had never done before: he slipped into the station in order to rob it.

The smell of oil pervaded the little office. An empty coffee cup with a dark brown ring inside sat on an old rolltop desk among crumpled candy bar wrappers. On a counter near the window he found the cash register. It was one of those old ornate uprights, silver colored and dusty. He pushed down the "no sale" key, being careful to hold the drawer so that it did not pop open with a loud "ding!" He grabbed the loose paper bills and scoped up the change which he stuffed into his pocket.

Melanie had forced a tear from her eyes when she told the

attendant she had no money to pay for the gas. Wasn't there some way she could make it up to him? Was there someplace out of sight of the road they could go and…talk?

He had led her into the station's bathroom and closed the door. Melanie ran her hands over his chest. "Oh, but I bet you're a big boy," she purred. Slowly she dropped to her knees and pulled at his zipper. "You *are* a big boy!" she exclaimed.

The horn honked. It must be a customer, thought the attendant. They can wait. When he and Melanie came out of the bathroom, there was no one waiting for gas in the drive. Melanie smiled. "Say," she said, "how about a free coke?"

Simultaneity, Spring, 1953/2153

The scientists were completing their preparations for the first trial of the new STAR chamber at Argonne and, in the loft room at the Empire State Building, 200 years into the future but on an adjacent time-stream, an equivalent device was being readied.

Argonne: Riordan watched as Enrico Fermi and Leona Libby ran their hands over all the switches and dials on the big control board, flipping and tapping, and smiling at each other as the results matched their expectations—it would be a "go."

New York: Wayland helped connect the big cable which ran down from the lightning rod on the Empire State Building's tower to the newly completed "time machine." Lorcan Mac Conmara consulted a dusty book he'd found in the library on Astrology. He was attempting to cast a horoscope for the device.

More fiddling and fussing and then…it was time. The scientists at Argonne put on dark-tinted goggles, expecting, perhaps, some blinding illumination from the machine that might injure their eyes. The scientists at the Empire State Building took themselves behind a barrier erected within the loft room. They too had concerns. Mac Conmara had finished his horoscope. "It is auspicious," he confirmed.

Simultaneously:

"Let me be the one that goes," said Wayland. "I am the least important of us. If things go wrong you will all be needed to fix it."

"I don't belong in this time," said Riordan. "I should be the one to step into the machine."

"Why don't we send the dog?" asked Carlyle. "No danger to humans."

"The dog won't be able to return to tell us anything," answered McGinley.

"Perhaps it makes sense to send the boy," said Libby. "But what assurances have we that he can return."

"I know what to do," said Riordan. "Walk into the mist."

"You may end up anywhere...anytime, Wayland. Remember we talked about the shift of location that happens when you change time-streams?"

"You will just step in, look around to determine when you are, then step back," insisted Fermi. "We need the data."

"I am ready," said Wayland.

"I am ready," said Riordan.

"The storm is intensifying outside," Breckinridge reported. "Soon we should get a lightning strike and then...the fun begins."

"The breeder reactor is brought up to full power," said Libby. "Do you want to have a countdown, or should we just throw the switch?"

100 miles out into the Atlantic Ocean, the warmth of the rising Gulf Stream had collided with the cold air masses of the Canadian jet stream. A cyclone had formed which was about to deliver a stinging nor'easter to the Atlantic seaboard. Northern New England was about to see snow in April. Intense winds began to buffet the island of Manhattan. Water spouts rode through the harbor and a tornado developed farther inland which moved erratically north and east. Bands of lightning streaked horizontally across the sky intermittently illuminating the dark clouds that obscured the sun.

McGinley was elated. Certainly the tower would be struck by lightning any minute now. Huge condensers were ready to absorb the energy from the bolt and feed it out to the device. Things were starting to crackle from static charges that leaped around the room like rabbits running from a hawk. Wayland was going to get his Frankenstein's laboratory. Only the monster was missing.

At Argonne there was an unexpected surge from the reactor which threatened to burn out the connections to the STAR chamber. Libby quickly adjusted the control rods. What could be causing the fluctuations? Hopefully the levels would stay even for the test. It reminded her once again of that first chain reaction which almost went wrong. But their knowledge and competence were far superior now…weren't they?

The next power surge occurred simultaneously (albeit two centuries earlier) with the first lightning strike on the Empire State Building's tower. It was followed by a second, even greater surge, and a second (lightning never strikes twice in the same place—but it did) bolt of pure electric fury. The effect of this doubling of energy at two adjacent poles of the time continuum was to open rifts in a chaotic and random fashion, not just at the sources of the disturbance, but here and there…and everywhere.

In 1965 Minneapolis, Minnesota, a woman was wheeling her grocery cart filled with paper bags of vegetables, paper-wrapped meats, cans of this and that, and sundries when, half way to her car in the parking lot, a thick mist formed in front of her. Her momentum carried her into the mist. She blinked. When the mist cleared she, and her grocery cart, were standing in an arena that resembled, because it was, a 14th century jousting tournament, complete with knights in full plate armor on horseback with long blunted lances, galloping at each other with intent to de-horse.

Sir John Beauchamp, mounted majestically on his colorfully cape-draped charger, found in front of him, not his opponent, but a heavy mist which he could not avoid. Exiting the mist, Sir Beauchamp reared up the horse just in time to be narrowly missed by a speeding Cooper Mini which was negotiating the traffic circle around the Arc de Triomphe in 1990 Paris. The driver of the mini also became enveloped in mist and was surprised to find that the road and the City of Light had disappeared to be replaced by a barren landscape and a red sky. As the car bogged down in loose sand, the unfortunate man and his automobile were battered by a rampaging triceratops.

And so it went. At the sources in 1953 Illinois and 2153 New York the rifts became vortexes, sucking in the scientists and depositing them over an array of times and spaces. Leith Carlyle and Albert Breckinridge had been standing the closest to the vortex when it opened. They were flung the furthest. Carlyle found himself tumbling down the rocky slope of a wilderness mountain, his descent arrested by the twisted trunk of a wind-blown cedar. He staggered to his feet and attempted to scramble back up the slope but was attacked by large brown bear. It was a mother bear and she was defending her cubs from the human who had rolled down the mountain toward them. She was not to be faulted for the rending of flesh that resulted. Breckinridge materialized inside of an underground cavern; it might have been Carlsbad in New Mexico many years before its discovery by humans. He wandered through the cold dark tunnels of dripping stalactites searching for an exit. He never found one.

Dr. Madison James McGinley, Lorcan Mac Conmara, and Wayland Delaney were hurled through space-time by the vortex, entering and exiting discontinuous eras in the manner of a stainless-steel ball traversing a pin-ball machine. At last they rested, somewhat shaken, on the edge of a cricket field in East Grinstead, in West Sussex, England, in 1840. A cricket match was underway.

At Argonne, Riordan Ó Ciardha saw Leona Libby and Enrico Fermi pulled into the vortex. He rushed forward, not knowing exactly what to do and was himself sucked in. The two scientists landed on a soft mound of grassy hill next to a rushing river and not far from a large city. Moments later, the alchemist's apprentice landed on top of them. They brushed themselves off and looked toward the town. They would discover that the river that swept by them was the Limmat, flowing out of Lake Zürich, and that the town was Zürich, Switzerland. And that the date was 1905.

Byron Grush

9

The Route 66 Bandits

Melanie Langford and Raymond "Judo" Washington were cruising along route 66 near Hydro, Oklahoma. A few hundred feet short of Lucille's Gas Station, Melanie pulled over to let Judo out. They were about to repeat the routine they had used successfully in a number of gas station robberies along the Mother Road. Melanie was gaining confidence in her ability to manipulate the male gas station attendants even without the fulfillment of a promised sexual act. She counted on Judo to be swift emptying the cash registers, an endeavor for which he was suited, at least in her jaundiced mind. She was a product of her environment, an environment tainted with prejudice, and although she accepted Judo as her equal—equal in crime—there was still that distance between them and that faint ghost of the time when they would have been master and slave.

Lucille Hamons, who owned the place with her husband, Carl, was tidying up one of the tourist cabins behind the two-story filling station when Melanie pulled up under the overhang where two shiny red gas pumps stood glistening with morning condensation. Carl was an independent trucker and out on a long cross-country haul, so Lucille was alone at Hamon's Court and Service Station that day. Hearing the pickup drive up, she hurried to attend to it, dropping the laundry basket of clean sheets on the floor.

Melonie's smile melted into a frown when she saw that the attendant was a woman. She would be unable to work her wiles on the lady—not that it wouldn't be interesting to try. She would need to invent some other ruse to get the woman away from the office where the cash register was located. Seeing the tourist cabins behind the station, she formulated a plan.

"Hello," said Melanie. "I would like to rent a cabin for the night. I'm very allergic to certain kinds of fabric, however. So do you think I could inspect your cabins before I commit to staying?"

"Why, certainly," answered Lucille. "You go 'round the back while I get the key from the office. Look at number 6. I just cleaned it."

Melanie walked toward the cabins as Lucille slipped through the side door into the station. She waited outside of number 6 for the woman to appear but she did not come immediately. After about fifteen minutes Melanie began to wonder if she should go jump in her truck and take off. There was Judo to consider. She could drive back down the road toward where he was hiding. But as she was thinking it over, a police cruiser appeared, barreling up the road with lights flashing and siren wailing. She panicked and ran to the truck.

Lucille had known about the other robberies. After all, the Mother Road was a tight community, highly communicative and friendly. She had heard that a young red-haired woman was seen on two different occasions on the same day and place of the robberies. She had immediately called the police.

Judo heard the siren, and also started running toward the pickup. Both of the bandits reached the pickup simultaneously with the arrival of the police cruiser. They were caught. Still, thought Melanie, there was no proof that they were guilty of anything…except running. This had been a bad idea, but in the heat of the moment, flight seemed the only option. "Let me do the talking," she said to Judo.

Officer Pepito "Peppy" Herrera had angled his cruiser to block the pickup. He walked slowly up to the driver's side of the truck where Melanie was applying lipstick, peering into the rear-view mirror which she had tilted toward herself. She smiled sweetly at the policeman. "Hello, Sargent," she said.

"*Officer* Herrera, Ma'am. Are you in some kind of a hurry? It looked like you were running when I pulled up."

"No…we were just getting a little exercise. I wanted to get a cabin, but the missy here didn't open it for me. So we decided to leave."

"I see. I must tell you, Ma'am, that you match the description of a woman that was observed at the scene of a robbery in Sapulpa last week."

"I've never been there. You don't think I could do anything like that, now do you, Officer Herrera?"

"I would like you to follow me into Weatherford, to the station house so we can take your picture and transmit it to the authorities in Sapulpa. It is just to eliminate you as a suspect. Will you do that willingly? Or do I have to take you in the cruiser?"

"Of course I will. Anything to help the police."

But as Herrera started down the road toward Weatherford, Melanie followed him only as far as the airport, where she saw a crossroad. It was too inviting, too tempting to turn onto the road. She slammed down on the gas pedal and took a few turns at speeds much too fast for safety, skidding and kicking up loose gravel from the shoulders as she fishtailed the truck. Officer Herrera had seen her do this in his rear view mirror; he was in pursuit but barely gaining on Melanie. She entered the small community of Dead Woman's Crossing, an unincorporated area named for the unsolved murder, in 1905, of Katie DeWitt James. The woman, estranged from her husband and filing for divorce, had left town with her infant baby, subsequently left the baby with a woman named Fannie Norton, an alleged prostitute, then disappeared. Mrs. James' remains were later found near Deer Creek, her head severed from her body. Mrs. Norton later committed suicide. It is possible that the psychic energy left at the scene influenced the event that was just about to happen, or maybe not.

As Melanie swerved around a curve in the road where a narrow bridge crossed the Deer Creek, a thick mist formed just ahead of her. She braked suddenly, but the pickup careened into the bank of the mist. Officer Herrera stopped just short of the mist and watched until it dissipated. To his amazement, there was no sign of the red pickup on the other side of the bridge.

Paris, August 24, 1572

The narrow bridge over Deer Creek had been just up the road in front of Melanie's pickup before she drove into the mist. Now another bridge occupied her field of view: an amazing and inexplicable sight rising before her in the presence of the Pont Notre-Dame, its arches spanning the Seine between the Île de la Cité and the right bank. The stone bridge held 68 brick houses above the busy river—identical multi-storied, gabled structures that to Melanie, resembled a picture in an old children's story book of a fairyland castle.

Of more immediate importance was the fact that the rusty red pickup hung precariously over the edge of the narrow roadway that ran parallel to the Seine and tipped gradually in the direction of that river. In a few seconds the vehicle would plunge into the water, taking its passengers with it. Melanie flung open her door and pulled Judo along with her, narrowly escaping the truck before it tumbled and splashed and sunk. Boatmen that swarmed like ducks along the Seine looked at the spot where now only bubbles remained, shook their heads and rowed on.

Something else was in the river. Many somethings that floated like pale logs. They resembled human forms but some lacked limbs or heads, and all were crimsoned with dark splotches of gore. Corpses—fresh ones. Men, women, and children. Melanie and Judo saw men dumping naked bodies into the river just upstream. These floated toward them, turning over and over in the current. Downstream a horde of people ran toward the river and started to jump into it. Up on the bridge there were soldiers armed with bow and arrow and throwing darts. They fired down at those who had jumped into the Seine. There was pandemonium as these unfortunates tried to escape the inevitable slaughter.

As Melanie and Judo stood at the edge of the river, aghast at the sight, a man wearing a white arm band and a hat on which was emblazoned a religious cross confronted them. He brandished a saber which was stained with blood. "Quel est le mot de passe?" he demanded.

"What?" answered Melanie. "We don't speak…what is that, French? Sorry."

"Quel est le mot de passe?" he repeated, raising his saber.

"Wait a minute," said Judo, "I have a hunch. Cross yourself…you know, like a Catholic."

"Catholic," said Melanie, and she crossed herself. Judo did likewise. The soldier just stared at them. Then he turned and moved away, muttering some words in French that Melanie was glad she did not understand, judging from his tone.

"I don't get it, Judo. What was that all about? And where are we, anyway?"

"We has time-traveled. You don' believe, I bet. But remember how Roy said he was from the past? We gone to his time. Only this ain't Ireland. More like it be France."

"Oh, Judo, that's just silly."

Only it wasn't silly. Earlier that morning, a group of King Charles IX's Swiss guards led by the Duke of Guise and encouraged by the king's mother, Catherine de Medici, dragged Admiral Gaspard de Coligny, leader of the French Huguenots from his bed, stabbed him, cut off his head, and threw his body out a window. It was said that school children had played kickball with the admiral's head in the streets that morning.

Tension between Protestants and Catholics had been compounding. Even Catherine's attempt to avert a crisis by marrying her (Catholic) daughter Margaret to a Protestant prince, Henry of Navarre, did nothing but pour more fuel on the impending fire. Shortly after the wedding a first attempt on Coligny's life was made as shots were fired from a window, wounding him. This riled the Huguenot population. Catherine and the court greatly feared the influence of the Colignys and so the fatal decision was made to thwart a suspected Protestant uprising: kill the leaders. Coligny was murdered. Two to three dozen Huguenot noblemen were congregated at the Louvre. The gates of the city were shut to prevent anyone from escaping. The Swiss guard descended upon the Louvre, expelled the Huguenots into the streets and methodically cut and hacked them to pieces. The king had given the order, "Qu'on les rue tous." And then things really got out of hand.

The ruthless slaughter that would come to be known as the Saint Bartholomew's Day Massacre would continue for four more days. Partly religious war, partly class war, ordinary Parisians took up arms against anyone they perceived as a Protestant, invariably anyone with position, wealth, or property. The atrocities would spread to Lyons,

Toulouse, Bordeaux, and Rouen.

Doors of Huguenot houses were bashed in and the helpless inhabitants dragged into the streets. Women and children were butchered. Streets were barricaded with heavy chains to corral the victims. Gutters ran red with blood and dismembered bodies were left to rot or were thrown unceremoniously into the Seine. Babies were thrown, alive and screaming, into that same river. The citizens of Arles, where the Rhône River had carried corpses from a simultaneous massacre in Lyon, could no longer drink the water. The death toll would be in the many thousands.

And Melanie and Judo had landed in the thick of it.

"We in deep shit, Missy!" said Judo. He had seen mob violence before, against Blacks. This was mob violence to the extreme. It was time to run.

The violence was everywhere. They ran across the Pont Notre-Dame bridge that led to the Île de la Cité, past the rows of houses, down a narrow street, and through an archway. Ahead of them stood a Gothic church, the Sainte-Chapelle. They ducked inside. A forest of colored glass rose above their heads, dazzling and brilliant like a jeweled box turned inside out. The height of the vaulted ceiling was dizzying. It was an impossibly beautiful space, overwhelming in its elegance, a glorious contrast to the blood and gore outside. They tried to catch their breath but the chapel was sucking it from them like an architectural vampire.

Neither had ever been in a large church before, certainly nothing like this one. They walked slowly around, in awe of the stain-glass windows and the sculptures. They nearly collided with a priest who was bowed in prayer in a small alcove off the main altar. The priest was startled to see a young Black man and a woman dressed in men's clothing. But having charity and benevolence, he greeted them—in French, of course.

"You don't happen to speak English, do you?" asked Melanie, not herself being gracious.

The priest might have avoided the perplexing situation that was about to occur had he simply shook his head in the negative. But he did speak English, as well as Spanish, Italian, and German, being a scholar and needing a certain competence in those languages to understand the texts that were his area of study, and his passion. Here were two persons, undoubtedly from the British Isles, he could practice speaking with in that other country's tongue.

"I do, my child" he answered. "Is this your first visit to our Holy Chapel? Are you devote? We have some famous relics here collected long ago by Saint Louis, including Christ's crown of thorns."

"Father," said Judo, using what he assumed was the proper address, "can you tell me the date?"

"Why, it is Saint Bartholomew's Day, the 24th of August. Are you not aware of this holiday?"

"No...no, I mean, what year is it?"

"Come, come now...are you that ignorant? It is the year of our Lord, 1572, of course. But it is sad day, is it not? With the mayhem in our streets. We here at Sainte-Chapelle cannot condone the murders taking place, even if it is of those that reject the Holy Father. You aren't Huguenots, are you?"

Both shook their heads vehemently. Not much of a lie since Melanie had never set foot in a church since she had been baptized, and Judo was a Baptist, which as far as he knew wasn't the same as a Huguenot.

"Then you have nothing to fear," said the priest.

"So this is Paris, huh? How do we get to the Eiffel Tower?" asked Melanie. Judo could have kicked her.

"I know nothing of this tower. What is it supposed to be for? Is it like your Tower of London?" The priest was becoming suspicious of his visitors. Perhaps they were Huguenot spies from the Netherlands, speaking English to confuse him. After all, their accents were peculiar.

Two men of the Swiss Guards had entered the vestibule and made their way straight toward Melanie and Judo and the priest. They questioned the time travelers abruptly, but getting shrugs instead of answers, began a dialog with the priest that was heated and threatening on both sides. The priest gestured angrily at them. Frustrated, the guards left the church but not without glaring menacingly at Melanie and Judo. Oh...oh, thought Judo. We in deep shit again.

"What was that all about?" asked Melanie.

"They believe you are Huguenots and they wanted me to turn you over to them. I told them that this chapel is a sanctuary and they had no business here. They could do their murdering in the streets, but not in the church."

"Well, thank you for that. I suppose we should leave. We don't want to get you in trouble. But…"

"But you had better wait until they are far afield from us. Come have a glass of wine with me. Or do you English prefer ale? Tell me about your travels and your impressions of France."

"Our impression is this is one hell of a bloody place! No, we'll leave. Is there a back door?"

The priest took them to a side entrance and told them to wait a few minutes before leaving, just to be sure the guards were gone. Then he went out the front door of the chapel where the guards were waiting. Their previous conversation had not been entirely antagonistic, in fact, the priest had suggested a plot to capture the suspected Huguenots. Now he told the guards where to find their quarry. Not being of subtle character, the two guards charged around the side of the building and ran at Melanie and Judo, waving sabers and shouting. This gave them enough warning to set their feet in motion.

Their flight took them past the Palais de la Cité, the former residence of the kings of France, and into the Jardin du Roi, a botanical herb garden enclosed by a low wall that sat just at the end of the island. At the end of the garden they found themselves staring into the brackish waters of the Seine. The guards were nearly upon them.

"This would be a really nice place for a bridge," said Judo."

They jumped. Struggling toward the bank where the quay ran along the side of the river was much more difficult than they might have imagined. For one thing, the current was swift. It eddied somewhat around the point of the island, but in midstream it tugged and pulled at them. Under normal circumstances they might have been rescued by a passing boatman. But today, Huguenots, even suspected ones, were not to be fished up like trout. They would more likely be battered with oars or struck by arrows from the bridges above. Their peril in the water was worse than it had been on land.

They floundered in the strong current, dodging floating corpses and struggling to get to shore. Then something miraculous happened: just downstream, in the direction they were being carried, a thick mist had formed and sat upon the surface of the river like frosting on a cake. Judo had another of his hunches.

"Missy," he called, "swim toward the mist bank. Hurry before it disappears."

Melanie had still not put two and two together concerning their travels in time and space. In fact, she believed she was home, asleep under a comforter, and dreaming it all. But she saw the wisdom of hiding in the mist which obscured everything behind it so completely. The two paddled toward the anomaly and into it, like strange fish caught in a stranger net. It swallowed them up and spit them out again, but this time onto dry land.

They had only inched along the twine of time. Backward and sideward. It was one year earlier. And a different place. The Seine had disappeared. A nearby small creek emptied into a larger body of water just over a hillock covered with tall grass—centuries later the creek would be named the Diascund and river would be called the Chickahominy. The peninsula upon which they had been dumped, still soaking wet, would one day be known as Virginia. At this time it was the home of Algonquian-speaking Powhatans. And it was currently being invaded by Spanish missionaries.

10

A Miraculous Year in Zürich

Enrico Fermi, Leona Libby, and Riordan Ó Ciardha had been flung through time to the town of Zürich in Switzerland. They walked up the broad avenue called the Bahnhofstrasse, peering into shop windows. Clothing they saw behind the mullioned panes gave them a clue about the time they had entered: long, flaring women's day dresses with puffed sleeves and impossibly narrow waists, men's cut-away four-button suit coats in stripes and checks, ladies' shoes with pointed toes and substantial heels, buttoned high above the ankle in smooth, exotic leathers, men's suspenders, women's corsets....

"Turn of the century, do you think, Enrico?" asked Libby.

"Yes, and I think this is Zürich, Switzerland. Do you know what that means?"

"It means our theory is a little off. We've shifted in space as well as in time."

"It also means...if this is Zürich...there are important things going on at the university. Wilhelm Röntgen may be here. Werner and Kleiner and..."

"And Schrödiner?"

"Not yet, but who, of all those important scientists...who is the one you would most like to talk to?"

"Ah! Einstein! Albert Einstein studied here at the polytechnic and published his first ground-breaking theories! He was here off and on, I believe. I wonder what year this is."

"Let's find out."

They had walked several blocks to the Lindenhof, the historic city square where once had stood an ancient Roman castle and later, a Carolingian Kaiserpfalz, or palace, on a hill overlooking the Limmat River. Near an old fountain they found two elderly gentlemen playing chess on a home-made wooden board balanced upon their knees as they sat, one on a low stone wall and the other on a wooden box. Fermi tried conversing in Italian and then in English, but the men shook their heads. His German was miserably inadequate and his Swiss-German was nonexistent. Libby, however, had a smattering of German left over from her high school days in La Grange, Illinois, and managed to get answers to two important questions: what was the date, and where was the university? It was 1905. The Universität was just across the river; you could see the buildings from here.

1905! It was year that Einstein would publish his Annus Mirabilis papers in the *Annalen der Physik* scientific journal where he would propose his theories on photoelectric effects, Brownian movement, and the electrodynamics of moving bodies. Most importantly, he would lay the groundwork for his theory of special relativity. He would postulate the mater-energy equivalence that would change scientific thinking for the remainder of the century. It was the source from which all theoretical scientific blessings flowed.

Riordan was ignoring the excited exchange between the two scientists as they discussed Einstein and his theories. Instead, he concentrated on the chess game the two old men were playing. Riordan was unfamiliar with the rules of chess although he had seen it played in the taverns of Cork. One of the men seemed flummoxed at the position of his pieces on the board. Riordan studied it. He pointed to the man's bishop and traced a path in the air above it, showing how the piece could be moved into a better position. The man brightened and moved the bishop as Riordan had suggested. "Das schach!" he exclaimed. Das schach…check…and soon it would be das schachmatt.

As they crossed the bridge over the Limmat, Libby asked Riordan, "Are you a chess player?"

"No, not really. I don't know the rules."

"Then how did you know to show that man how to move his bishop?"

"I don't know. I just looked at the board and saw a kind of pattern. Empty spaces where I figured the pieces could move. Just lucky, I guess."

They were searching for the Polytechnikum, the polytechnic school where they felt they might find Einstein who was still a student, working on his thesis. They found the physics building, located on the Gloriastrasse. It was an impressive neoclassical structure with arched doorways on the ground level and windows above which repeated the arched shapes. It seemed massive to Riordan; a great palace in which the royalty of science could dwell. So massive, in fact, that discovering Einstein there seemed improbable at best.

They stopped a female student in the first floor hallway and asked if she knew Herr Einstein. She laughed. "Do I know him?" she replied. "I should think so…I married him!"

She was Mileva Marić, a woman physicist from Serbia who was the only woman studying at the Polytechnikum in Zürich at the time. She had been working on her thesis in 1901 when she became pregnant by Einstein. Their daughter, Liederi, died two years later from scarlet fever (or possibly was put up for adoption). Marić and Einstein were now married, with a second child, Hans Albert, and were living in Bern, Switzerland, while the two worked on their PhD degrees in Zürich. Fermi would remember the controversy in his own time in which it was suggested that Mileva Marić had collaborated with Einstein on his theories, even contributing crucial ideas that would lead to the special theory of relativity. Perhaps he would now find out the truth of the matter.

[Author's note: the conversations between the time travelers and the Einsteins where in German, with Libby translating into English for Fermi and Riordan. In order to spare the reader the resulting tedium of such an exchange, the dialogue from this point will be presented in English only.]

"Albert is in his cubbyhole, working on some ideas we have discussed," said Mileva. "He finally submitted his thesis to Professor Kleiner and it has been accepted. It is called 'A New Determination of Molecular Dimensions.' We are trying to expand upon the idea that the inertia of bodies is related to their energy content, both at rest and in motion. Are you scientists, by the way? You would find this most interesting, I think."

"We are," answered Libby. "We have come a long way to meet Herr Einstein."

"But how do you even know of him?"

"Oh, well, we read his paper on…on…"

"The one on capillary phenomena in the *Annalen der Physik*?"

"That's the one. Do you think it would be much of a bother if we…"

"I'm sure Albert would be delighted to take a break and converse with colleagues from…where did you say you were from?"

"America."

"And this must be your son. You are looking to enroll him in the Polytechnikum? I'm sure he would benefit greatly from the physics department here. Well, follow me and we'll go see Albert."

Soon they were in what Mileva Marić had called Albert's cubbyhole, a small office with a desk, an overstuffed armchair, and a blackboard that covered most of one wall. The blackboard was filled with numbers and letters and strange symbols that Riordan did not recognize. Nor could he fathom their meanings or purpose. He saw nothing that he remembered from his study of alchemy, but the sight of all that mysterious scribbling caused him to think back—back to those more comfortable days in the alchemist's room when life was simple and familiar.

His mind drifted as the conversation between the Einsteins and the two scientists from the future touched on mass-energy equivalence and light-bending gravitation forces. Fermi and Libby were being careful not to let Einstein discover that they already knew the theories he had yet to originate. Still, it was tempting to nudge him a little where he was stalled in his thinking. But they resisted and listened dutifully. Riordan couldn't had followed any of it anyway, so he reflected on what he did know: the *Hermetica* of Hermes Trismegistus. A favorite passage came to him:

> *Seek ye, O man, to learn the pathway*
> *that leads through the spaces*
> *that are formed forth in time.*
> *Forget not, O man, with all of thy seeking*
> *that Light is the goal ye shall seek to attain.*
> *Search ye for the Light on thy pathway*
> *and ever for thee the goal shall endure.*

Without thinking, Riordan repeated out loud the phrase, "Light is the goal ye seek." Einstein had just been explaining that his goal was the understanding of the kinematics of moving bodies. He had stated that the commonly held theory of a luminiferous aether was absurd. He pointed to an equation had had written on the blackboard: $E=M$.

"Energy and mass are equivalent," said Einstein. "But the equation is not complete. It lacks some constant to balance what we know of when a body gives off energy and its mass decreases."

Just at this moment, Riordan had blurted out the Hermatic quote about Light being the goal. Einstein asked Libby what the boy had said and she translated the phrase for him. Light. Of course! The speed of light…the most universal constant! Quickly Einstein when to the blackboard and, with a piece of chalk that squealed like a wounded bird, added the letter "C" so that the equation now read, $E=MC$. Energy equals mass times the speed of light.

But it wasn't quite right, and Einstein knew it.

Riordan gazed up at the blackboard when he heard the squeaking of the chalk. He saw the formula Einstein had written. He saw the empty space that followed it. It was that space, like the space on the chessboard that had prompted his action in the park, that compelled him to fill that space with something. He moved to the board and picked up a piece of chalk. Libby and Fermi gasped as he added another letter "C" to the equation. Now it read, E=MCC. Energy equals mass times the velocity of light squared. The Einsteins just stared at it for an uncomfortable moment, then Albert Einstein let out a hoot that sounded something like, "Erstaunlich!"

"Oh my God," said Libby to Fermi. "Have we just created a paradox?"

"He would have gotten it eventually," replied Fermi. "However, it is time for us to go before Riordan comes up with any other bright ideas."

East Grinstead, West Sussex, England, 1840

Dr. Madison James McGinley, Lorcan Mac Conmara, and Wayland Delaney had been hurled through space-time by the vortex. When they came to rest, somewhat shaken, they were on the edge of a cricket field where a cricket match was underway. There stood a batsman defending his wicket while twenty yards away a bowler warmed up for an overhand pitch. An enthusiastic crowd surrounded the field, cheering on their favorite team.

"What the deuce is this?" Wayland wanted to know. "A strange sort of baseball game...or is it hockey?"

"That," answered Mac Conmara, "is the national sport of the British Isles...cricket. See those sticks standing up behind the batter? Those are the wicket and the goal is for the bowler to knock them down. The batter can hit the ball or divert it away from the wicket. If he hits it he can make a run to the other end of the pitch and his mate, the batter at the other end does likewise. Or if one of the fielders catches the ball before it bounces, the batter is out."

"Sort of like baseball and bowling combined."

"What is baseball?"

The bowler took a few running steps and hurled the ball at the wicket. The batter took careful aim and swung, connecting with the ball with a sharp "wack!" Still carrying the flat bat he ran for the opposite end of the pitch. The crowd reacted with cheers. Even Wayland let out a whoop. But the ball arched up over the heads of the bowler and the first fielder only to be caught by the second fielder. The batter was out. The sides changed.

Just then, a heavy mist formed at one end of the field. Out of the mist came a thundering herd of huge bison-like creatures, their long horns flashing in the sunlight, their hooves raising dark clouds of dust. The players and the spectators scattered, screaming. The three time travelers stood their ground, not from bravery, but from fascination with the phenomenon.

"Didn't know they had buffalo in England," said Wayland.

"Those aren't buffalo," said McGinley. "Those are Bison antiquus. Indigenous to North America—and extinct! See their panic? They are being chased by something. Something I hope doesn't make it out of the rift!"

But it did. Close on the heels of the herd came a Smilodon: a saber-toothed tiger, extinct since the Pleistocene epoch, 10,000 years ago. The large, hunched, muscular body leaped with great speed after the bison, gnashing its long, pointed canine teeth and emitting a horrifying roar. It was gaining on the herd. But just in front of the galloping behemoths a second bank of mist formed. Into the mist went the herd, disappearing from 1840 into some other unknown time. The tiger, now on the heels of the last of the bison, leaped for the kill—but that last lucky beast entered the mist bank just as it closed, and the tiger found only empty space before him.

Confused, the tiger looked around for his game. The herd was nowhere to be seen. He saw the three men not far away and although he had never seen humans before, these looked easy to catch. And he was hungry. He began to slink slowly toward this new prey, sniffing the air cautiously. He was hoping to smell the fear which would encourage his inevitable charge.

The time travelers were still awe struck by the incident and although they were aware of their danger, they did not run. Instead, Wayland picked up an abandoned cricket bat and Mac Conmara appropriated one of the leather-covered cricket balls—inadequate weaponry, perhaps, but they might intimidate the tiger enough that he would leave them alone.

"I suppose this is all our fault," said Mac Conmara.

"Indeed it is," said McGinley.

"And I suppose it is our duty to fix it somehow."

"Somehow."

"Can't you cast a spell on it?" Wayland asked Mac Conmara. "Send it back to prehistoric times?"

"I'm an alchemist, not a magician," growled Mac Conmara. "And here he comes!"

The tiger was creeping closer and closer, gaining confidence as it came, but still waiting for its intended prey to flee. He stopped a few yards from them and crouched. Saliva dripped from his jaws. Wayland began waving the cricket bat out in front of him. "Here, kitty, kitty," he called.

"Wayland!" exclaimed McGinley. "If that thing comes after you, that little paddle isn't going to keep you from turning into minced meat!"

Apparently, the tiger thought so as well for he began to creep forward again. A terrible growl rumbled from the animal and seemed to shake the very ground upon which they stood. McGinley and Mac Conmara began to back away slowly, realizing that running would cause the tiger to pounce. Wayland, however, stepped toward it. "Here, kitty, kitty," he repeated.

The huge jaws opened wide and the tiger's long teeth looked like two sharp swords. Any minute now, the Tiger would be at Wayland's throat. Wayland swung the cricket bat with all his strength and connected with the tiger's nose. It yelped and turned and ran.

"Brilliant," said McGinley. "Now you've gotten him mad."

It was true. The tiger stopped and turned back toward them, this time coming at a fast pace. There was only one thing that could save them now, and that wasn't going to be a cricket bat. Remarkably, another time rift opened up just between the charging tiger and the time travers. The tiger disappeared into the mist. The mist dissipated. They were alone in the middle of a cricket field.

"I think," said McGinley, "if we see another bank of mist we had better avoid it. I don't want to end up where that tiger went."

"Agreed," said Mac Conmara. "Let us see if we can find the town."

"We don't know what era this is, and we are dressed in these futuristic outfits. My guess is that it is the 19th century, somewhere in England, but that is based only on the cricket player's uniforms. We could be anywhere. If we are to blend in we need a change of clothing."

"There are some houses over that hill," offered Wayland. "Maybe we can find one that has a clothes line and has hung out the washing."

"And that they are our sizes. Well, I've no better ideas," McGinley admitted, "so let's get going."

"What do we say if we are asked about the bison stampede?"

"Somebody put drugs into tea?" said Wayland.

11

Chesapeake Bay Blues

Chiskiack Village, February 1571

The Spanish called the new land Ajacán. The Powhatan, indigenous to the region, called it Tsenacommacah, the densely inhabited land. Thirty years later, the first English settlers of Jamestown would call it Virginia.

The many tribes of the Algonquin-speaking peoples were being organized by a Mamanatowick, or principle chief, named Wahunsunacawh, into a powerful nation, one that European whites would find fierce and competitive. Here, along the Chickahominy river, were a few scattered villages, each with their own Weroance, or leader, who paid tribute to the Mamanatock. At one of these, the Chiskiack Village, a tall, lean man named Paquiquineo stood at the edge of the circle of yehakins, the bark-cover huts that provided shelter during the harsh winter, and listened to the rising song of a nearby naantam—a brother wolf.

Not far from the village was the Ajacán Mission, St. Mary's. Set on a hammock of dry land surrounded by swampy ground, a small wooden chapel and a two-room structure had been built only last autumn by Spanish Jesuits: Father Juan Bautista de Segura and Father

Luis de Quirós, six Jesuit monks, and a young servant boy named Alonso de Olmos, whom they called Aloncito. The Spanish had been exploring the Chesapeake Bay region since 1561. Most of their attempts at colonization of the northeastern coast of North America had been dismal failures, due, in part, to the misconduct of garrison soldiers in their interaction with the indigenous people they encountered. Many outposts were destroyed in attacks by the natives. Trying a different approach, Father Segura had managed to obtain permission to establish his mission without the support of colonial troops—this would prove to be a fatal mistake.

Paquiquineo knew the Spanish missionaries well. On that first exploratory voyage in 1561, Captain Antonio Velázquez of the Santa Catalina, had captured two Native American boys. One of them, the son of a local chief, they named Paguiquino: little Francis. He would later be known as Paquiquineo. They took him to Seville, Córdoba, and Madrid where he was displayed to King Philip II of Spain as "the little savage prince." His next journey took him to Mexico City in New Spain. He was educated there by Jesuits and baptized Don Luís de Velasco, after Luis de Velasco, the Viceroy of New Spain.

When it was decided to establish the St. Mary's Mission at Ajacán, Don Luís was taken along to become an interpreter. Once back in his home land, he ran away in search of his former village. Now he was situated at Chiskiack, and very much opposed to the Spanish invasion of Tsenacommacah. He had a unique understanding of the Jesuits and although there were no soldiers at the mission, the priests' presence was disruptive for the Powhatan people. There had been a long period of drought and there was a shortage of food. When the priests bartered for food, tensions were raised to a dangerous level.

Paquiquineo listened as a second wolf added his voice to the poignant song. Inside one of the huts a baby cried; the young mother held her child to her breast so that the infant could hear her heartbeat. A light snow had fallen during the night. The temperature had dropped below freezing. The Chesapeake Bay wind picked up the dusting of snow and flung it at the Native American; icy crystals pecked at his face and bare arms. He wrapped his cloak more tightly around his body.

Already the hunters were abroad, hoping to catch an otter or an opossum. Larger game had been scarce this winter. The tribe had been relying on all the bay oysters and crabs they could gather. There were striped bass and flounder to net, but the great abundance of water birds had dwindled as geese and ducks and egrets left for warmer climes. The loons were still here, but illusive. The blue heron was impossible to catch, but its discarded feathers were a prize and graced the headdress of many a Chiskiack hunter.

Paquiquineo saw two of the hunters returning early. With them were a white woman and a Black man. Strange. He knew there were no women or Blacks with the Spanish missionaries, but here they were. As he was the only person in the village who could speak the Spaniard's language, he would be required to talk to these unwelcome visitors. Unwelcome, because of the lack of food. Unwelcome, because of the animosity that the tribe, and particularly Paquiquineo, felt toward the Spaniards.

"Hola," he greeted them. "Quién eres sú? Por qué estás aquí?"

"Oh shit!" said Melanie. "You speak any Spanish, Judo?"

"Only a few words I learned from the Mexican boys back in my neighborhood. But those words, my mother would slap me if I used them," he replied.

"I nearly flunked Spanish in high school. But I'll try." And to Paquiquineo she said one of the only phases she remembered: "Hola. Cómo está usted?"

Paquiquineo was getting frustrated with these new arrivals. Clearly, the girl didn't speak Spanish very well, and she was redheaded, uncharacteristic for a Spaniard. The clincher was when Melanie asked, "Habla usted Inglés?" Do you speak English? Were they now to be invaded by the English in addition to the Spanish? Yet there was something amiss here. The two were severely underdressed for the weather and they were shivering. Paquiquineo ordered the two men to take their captives to the long house where the women could watch them until the council met. If there were more English around…well, it would not be wise to injure them. And they might make good hostages.

The long house was constructed from saplings bent over to form arches and covered with bark. It was similar to the yehakin huts but much larger, capable of housing up to two dozen families. Here and there a hole had been patched with mud from the creek bank. Low wooden platforms that served as beds were arrayed around the periphery. Partitions divided the long house into separate rooms. Fish hung from the bent saplings on the ceiling to dry.

In the center of the long house a fire was built. Smoke rose and exited through a hole in the roof, yet the air was acrid and hazy. Melanie and Judo observed the women and children: the children were naked, their bodies heavily oiled against the cold; the women had close-shaven hair and were dressed in long, leather apron-like garments trimmed with fringe, an over-mantel of animal skin, and necklaces made of shells. At least a dozen women were in the long house, most tending to their children or weaving baskets or sleeping mats. They brought Melanie and Judo blankets of deer skin with which to wrap in against the cold. They brought them a warm drink brewed from boiled mussels and oysters and served in a clay bowl.

Melanie's high school Spanish proved useless in trying to communicate with the women. They shook their heads and replied in Algonquin, which confused the issue even more. Judo's total experience with Native Americans up to this point had come from a myriad of matinees of cowboy and Indian movies in which, of course, the Indians were the bad guys. His favorite cowboy was Gene Autrey, a father-figure he greatly wished were present to affect their rescue. From those movies, however, Judo had learned, or at least he believed, that you could talk to Indians using sign language. He began gesturing. Eventually, after enduring much laughter from the women, he managed to convey their names and their offer of friendship. One of the women responded by touching her chest and saying her own name: Keegsquaw. She was young, perhaps a teenager, and had a long lock of hair which fell from the back of her head in a braid.

In the days that followed, Keegsquaw would decide that Judo might make a good husband even though he was deemed inadequate by the other women since he was unable to fend for himself, and certainly had no bride-wealth to pay to her parents. But not much later she asked her father to bring the two of them before Nixkamich, the Weronace (the chief), who would bring the couple's hands together and break over them a long string of sea shells, making them husband and wife. Judo would not understand what the ceremony meant, not until Keegsquaw led him to a separate yehakin where she undressed him and anointed his skin with fresh oils and perfumes made from dried berries. He was beginning to get the idea, and was not displeased.

Meanwhile, Melanie would also be pursued by a member of the

opposite sex, a warrior/hunter named Megedagik. Unlike Judo, Melanie would construe the man's intentions immediately—and would not discourage him. Megedagik, like other warriors, had the right side of his head shaved so that his hair would not become entangled in his drawn bowstring. He had pierced ears from which hung strings of beads made from polished bone. He had a tattoo on his neck of a fierce-looking snake and another on his chest of a stag, reared up on its hind legs. His breechcloth did not hide his excitement when Melanie was near. Melanie shared his enthusiasm.

Two weeks had gone by. Melanie and Judo had been officially adopted by the Chiskiack villagers, by virtue of their apparent spousal relationships with Megedagik and Keegsquaw. They helped with the chores of the community; Judo accompanied the hunters on fire hunts for deer, building the ring of fire to trap the animals; Melanie sat with the other women weaving or making clay pots. This day a deer had been brought back by the hunters. The women had built a fire pit over which a platform of logs had been raised to hold the slaughtered carcass. Flames crackled and the aroma of cooking flesh filled the air. It was this day when two robed missionaries from St. Mary's arrived at the village to barter. Father Segura and Father Quirós were surprised to see a white woman tending the cooking fire.

Melanie overheard the missionaries in a heated argument with Paquiquineo, the one Spanish-speaking Powhatan. She only understood a word here and there, but she got the gist of the disagreement: the missionaries wanted the muchacha blanca to return with them to the mission. "Me quedo aqui," she called out to Paquiquineo: "I stay here." Father Segura grabbed Melanie by the arm and began to drag her away from the fire. He yelled at her in Spanish, but Melanie was unable to follow his ranting. The act was observed by another Native America: Megedagik leaped upon the missionary, knocking him down.

Father Segura was able to get up without being further accosted. Megedagik and Paquiquineo and the other Powhatans watched as the missionary dusted off his long black robe. When he turned back toward Melanie, to try to persuade her to leave the Indian camp, Megedagik came at him from behind. This time the warrior had a war club in his hand. The wooden handle had a sharp ball of stone attached with leather thongs at the end. Megedagik was furious. He swung the war club with blind anger at the missionary's head, splitting it open as surely as if he had been hacking apart a ripe melon with an axe.

Father Quirós, aghast at the brutal slaying of his companion, now started to run from the camp. Paquiquineo, aware of the retribution the Spaniards were capable of bringing upon his people, threw a dart at the fleeing priest. His aim was good. Two priests now lay dead on the dirt courtyard of the village.

The incident was brought before Nixkamich, who would decide what steps needed to be taken. Paquiquineo described his own treatment by the Spaniards, the humiliating parading of him as the "savage prince" before the king and court of Spain, the indoctrination by the Jesuit brothers who sought to deprive him of his own religious beliefs, the stories of massacres of native peoples by the Spanish armies. He offered to lead a war party against the mission. Nixkamich would agree.

At the mission of St. Mary's, Brother Miguel de Barcena stood on the crest of the hill just behind the common house and gazed out in the direction of the sea. Although he could not see it, the sea represented the vast distance between his home and himself. He often stood here thinking of Madrid, its seven hills, its plazas, its ancient walls. He would have to do penance later for this prideful nostalgia. Now his thoughts turned to Father Segura and Father Quirós who still had not returned from the campo de los Indios. This was worrisome. Below was a stand of oak and maple where the wind blew bare branches against each other. There was a rustling in the underbrush as well. Perhaps a deer or a brown bear…

The first arrow struck him in the back of his right shoulder, spinning him around. The second pierced his chest just below his heart, knocking him to the ground where he lay, his life's blood staining the dirt, his vision clouding. The last thing he saw was the stone war axe descending.

Two monks, Brother Rodrigo Jose Arbieto, and Brother Igacio Martín de Molina were preparing the late meal in the kitchen area of the common house. Brother Arbieto went to the door to call for the boy, Alonso de Olmos, to come and help. "Aloncito!" he called. "Ven aca, por favor." It was then that he saw the war party emerging from the woods. He called to Brother Molina to run with him to the chapel. The two monks had almost covered the distance before arrows and darts brought them down.

Alonso de Olmos was stacking fire wood when he heard his name being called out. He came up the hill toward the common house in time to see the two monks running toward the chapel. Arrows were flying through the air. The war cry of the Powhatans filled the boy with terror. As quickly as he could he ran to the chapel. He rushed into the tiny sanctuary where the other three monks were bowed in prayer before a statue of the Virgin which they had brought with them from Mexico City.

"Padres!" he cried. "Los Indios!"

Two of the monks, Brother Alonzo Pérez de la Puenta and Brother Joaquin Bustamante, closed the chapel's only door and pushed the heavy statue of the Virgin against it. The only window had already been shuttered against the cold. Its fasteners, however, were on the outside. It would be a brief matter of time before los Indios figured out how to open them. The third monk, Brother Francisco Alvarez, opened the heavy chest where the missionaries kept a weapon their superiors in Mexico City had insisted that they bring. This was an arquebus, a long musket with a matchlock mechanism. It was not loaded.

As the tips of arrows began to poke through the chapel door, Brother Alvarez poured powder into the barrel of the arquebus and tamped it down with a rod. He next dropped a lead pellet into the gun and pushed this against the powder. A paper wad followed to be tamped into place. There came a rattling at the window; los Indios were pulling at the shutters. Brother Alvarez tried to hurry, but this loading took time. He opened the flash pan cover and poured in a good amount of flash powder. He closed this and checked to see that the fuse was in the correct position. Now he lit the fuse and braced the heavy arquebus on the back of a chair. He aimed it at the window.

The shutters fell to the ground and the face of a Powhatan warrior appeared. He wore a crown-like headdress of turkey feathers. Crude lines of red and white paint streaked across his cheeks gave him a ferocious countenance. Brother Alvarez pulled the trigger which lowered the smoldering fuse into the priming flash pan. The powder ignited and sent the flash through the touch hole to ignite the gunpowder in the barrel. In a few seconds there was loud report. The arquebus jerked backwards, knocking Brother Alvaez to the floor. The Powhatan warrior's head seemed to explode as the lead pellet hit him squarely between the eyes.

There would be no second chance to reload. By now the Powhatans had pushed open the door despite the Virgin's best efforts to stop them. The brothers fought valiantly, but against the knives and the war clubs of the Native Americans, they were not to prevail. The only survivor of the massacre was the boy, Alonso de Olmos.

"Let the boy live," said Paquiquineo. "He can be a warning to his people that we will kill them if they come to our lands."

It would turn out to be a bad idea. The next spring, a supply ship arrived in Chesapeake Bay. The Powhatans dressed in the monks' black robes, paddled canoes out to the ship with the intention of attacking it. They were captured and interrogated. The ship's captain learned from them the details of the massacre and the fact that a boy had survived. The following year, a company of soldiers under Pedro Menéndez arrived from Florida to avenge the slaughter. In the first foray Menéndez took many captives. He managed to trade some of his hostages for Alonso de Olmos. He was unable to obtain the transfer of Paquiquineo, whom they knew as Don Luís de Velasco and whom they blamed for the revolt. Paquiquineo escaped. Menéndez went into the village with dire results for the Powhatans. Twenty of the Powhatans were baptized and then hanged. The Spanish would abandon the idea of colonizing the region, leaving it open for the British. In 1607, the colony of Jamestown would be established, not far from the former village of Chiskiack.

Before any of these events, back just after the attack on the mission, the village celebrated. Clothing, ornaments, and useful articles such as pots and pans had been brought back by the warriors. Chief Nixkamich took Alonso de Olmos into his own yehakin. A feast was planned, and hunters ventured off to trap and fish. As yet, Melanie and Judo were unaware of the massacre. But watching the funeral arrangements for the fallen warrior, the building of the wooden platform for the pyre, the gathering of firewood, the prayers to Ahone and Okeus, it occurred to them that something dreadful had happened. When Melanie had finally been able to talk to the boy, Aloncito, she learned that "Los Padres están muerto."

Melanie took Judo aside as the feat began. She told him what the boy had said. "He also told me the year: 1571. And that this is the New World. Somewhere in New England, I think. Before the Pilgrims landed. He thinks the Spanish will come to retaliate and probably kill all the Indians. I think we should go."

"Oh boy…we in deep shit again!"

12

Catch the Whirlwind

Chesapeake Bay Peninsula, February 1571

Melanie and Judo had left Ciskiack Village during the height of the celebration. Dances and songs were the order of the day; it would be some time before they were missed. They had slipped away from their apparent spouses, Megedagik and Keegsquaw, and had followed the frozen creek until it disappeared into a snow-covered hillock. They walked on the ice so that they would not leave tracks. The gray sky portended a coming storm. The dark shapes of turkey vultures circled above them; flitting shadows that warned and waited. Now they followed the tracks of a deer that led them away from the creek—away toward the unknown.

Megedagik had searched in vain throughout the village for Melanie. She was gone. So too was the dark-skinned one. Had they run away together? He expanded his search, filled with rage. Tracks led him to the creek and then stopped at its edge. They were following the creek, walking on the ice to elude him. He looped his bow over his shoulder and hung his war club from his belt. Cautiously he placed a foot on the ice. It held him. Now he followed the frozen trail. At the creek's end he saw their footprints in the snow. Now the tracking would be easier.

The snow had blown into deep drifts around the edges of the wooded area Melanie and Judo now approached. Judo broke a branch from a fir tree and brushed their footprints away (this would not deceive the Native American tracker, however). Through the woods they trudged. Squirrels scattered before them. Jays scolded them from the tree tops. The deer tracks they had followed had disappeared, but they forged onward hoping for an early exit to the woods and a friendly village on the other side. If there was such a thing as a friendly village.

When they did emerge from the woods into a shallow valley where another frozen stream meandered, they stopped to catch their breaths. Making their way through the forest had been taxing; there was no path to follow, no deer spore to lead them. They were unaware that Megedagik was close behind. And so they rested for a while and marveled at the beauty of their surroundings as the winter sun reached its zenith and cast a sparkling veil across the crystalline landscape. They watched as an opossum scurried up a tree with its babies clinging to its belly. They heard the lonesome call of a loon and the faraway cry of a fox. Then Megedagik came out of the woods, his bow drawn, an arrow notched.

East Grinstead, West Sussex, England, 1840

Nearly three-hundred years into the future—and at the very same time—Dr. Madison James McGinley, Lorcan Mac Conmara, and Wayland Delaney, stood at the edge of a cricket field and watched as a new temporal anomaly materialized. This time the disturbance was larger, and the mist swirled and boiled like a hurricane lifting sea water into a vast vortex that moved destructively across landfall. Within the mist they could see images, sometimes faint, sometimes vivid: people, animals, buildings, mountains, forests, all tumbling through the maelstrom in no apparent order or direction. Nothing had emerged from that mist…yet.

McGinley, always the analytical scientist, studied the vortex and came to a conclusion: "I believe our dilemma may have an answer," he voiced.

"How is that?" asked Mac Conmara.

"If you watch carefully, you can see images from different time periods in history. They come and go, but I believe it may offer an opportunity to select which time one goes to if you jump into the mist at the right time."

"It's sort of like watching one of those speeded-up movies of flowers growing," commented Wayland.

"Time lapse. Yes, somewhat. Tricky, though. If you step into the vortex and miss your destination…"

"Doctor McGinley," said Mac Conmara, "do you think we could go back to our own times and stop this from happening?"

"Possibly. If we intervened with ourselves somehow to prevent ourselves from following through with the experiments. But that presents a paradox. Would we meet ourselves? Would not that cause some other kind of rift?"

"And if we do change the course of history to prevent time travel from happening…why then, we would not be here now! I see your paradox."

"We would be doubled in our own time. Is that even possible?"

"Oh, man!" said Wayland. "You guys are making my brain hurt. Couldn't you go back before you were born and eliminate whatever knowledge is necessary for your future selves to develop your theories? You'd be stuck in time, but well before you would be born. No doppelgangers."

"But there would be no guarantee that we wouldn't still come up with the theory. Or that someone else would. Perhaps we could leave a message for ourselves not to do the experiments."

"No, I think the answer lies elsewhere," said Mac Conmara. "You are correct in thinking that knowledge is unstoppable. We have to learn how to control the time-rift process."

"Ironically, we need more time to consider our options. I say we avoid this current manifestation of the rift. It is too risky. Let us continue on with our former plan and seek out the town."

They moved away from the churning vortex with its moving pantheon of history past and future. Except for Wayland, who approached the anomaly more closely. Would he see that one period of history flash by that so intrigued him and gave him the notion of altering the past? Would a glimpse of Nazi Germany appear just long enough for him to leap? Just how would someone go about killing Hitler?

Zürich, Switzerland, 1905

Enrico Fermi, Leona Libby, and Riordan Ó Ciardha walked along the banks of the Limmat, still awe-struck from their meeting with Albert Einstein. To be present at the very moment when the genius realized his most famous equation—albeit with a little help from a sixteen-century alchemist's apprentice—it was an honor and yet an unnerving experience, knowing, as they did, all that was to come from those three simple letters of the alphabet: $E=mc^2$. Energy equals mass times the velocity of light squared.

Few boats were on the river. Periodically, fishermen's skiffs and small rafts toting coal or wood were poled along by rugged men wrapped in oily old rags. On the opposite bank tradesmen pulled carts laden with every imaginable article of humankind: pots and pans, broken furniture, dust bins and old clothing, vegetables, chickens in wire cages that squawked and fluttered futilely. On the sidewalk, the parade of clerks and shop girls heading out for lunch slowly enveloped the scientists. They were carried along quickly with the crowd and soon reached the bridge that would take them back to the Lindenhof Square.

At the square they stopped to consider their possibilities. There were not many of these. At last they decided to return to the place where the time rift had opened and deposited them in Zürich. There was a chance it would reappear and that they could enter it to travel to their own time. This theory depended upon the rift being a sort of doorway between space-time locations and that did not change. They would soon discover the fallacy of this theory.

It was there: a thickening of the atmosphere like a mist. It expanded and began to rotate. This was something new, something inexplicable and disturbing. Now and then glimpses of what unmistakably were other eras rolled into view and then were supplanted by some other distant time and space. The Egyptian pyramids superimposed over a battlefield of the Great War. A bird-like dinosaur rushing along the Champs-Élysées dodging omnibuses. It was a temporal crazy-quilt. It was a history book whose pages had been ripped out and thrown into the air to swirl like autumn leaves in a whirlwind.

The two scientists were not about to throw caution to the wind, especially this particular wind. They watched and waited, curious to see if the phenomenon would abate or mutate or…heaven forbid, if it would begin spitting out people and objects that belonged elsewhere and elsewhen, or if it would begin devouring the environment, swallowing up Zürich to fling it back or forward in time.

Riordan was also intrigued. He was witnessing images of the future mingled with those of past events that had only been known to him as stories told by the old people or related in rare books. Suddenly, something did emerge from the whirlwind of time: a large animal charged from the mist straight for Riordan. He had no time to react before the creature was upon him, its paws reaching his shoulders, its wet mouth lapping at his face. It was a dog. It was…

"Teige!" exclaimed Riordan as the alchemist's Irish wolfhound who had been marooned in future New York City ran a drooling tongue over his cheeks.

Chesapeake Bay Peninsula, February 1571

Megedagik, warrior and husband to the white girl with the red hair, stood with drawn bow at the edge of the wooded area from which he had just emerged. There in the clearing before him were Melanie and Judo, hand in hand. Outrage overtook him. Who to kill first? The Black who would certainly turn on him and fight. The girl would then run, but Megedagik was swift in the notching of arrows. He would soon be avenged.

Melanie and Judo turned and saw the warrior threatening them. Fear immobilized them. As frozen in place as the snow-covered ground beneath their feet, they could only wait for the arrows to fly. But just then they heard a sound like the roar of a rushing waterfall. They saw the warrior drop his bow. Saw him turn and bolt back into the woods with a cry. Again they turned around. The time rift was forming a few yards from where they stood. It swirled and flicked with sights of faraway places and distant epochs. They were mesmerized by its enormity and its spectacle of unraveling space-time.

Then Judo brightened. "Look there!" he exclaimed. "It's my

buddy, Wank!" The whirlwind had brought into their view a scene of a cricket field where two men stood next to the familiar figure of Wayland Delaney, Judo's friend who he called Wank. Impulsively, Judo rushed forward toward the image and was caught up in the mist, swallowed into the scene. Melanie was stunned by his disappearance. She did the only thing she could think of to do: she also leaped into the whirlwind. Judo was transported to 19th century West Sussex, England where he would meet his old friend once again.

Melanie, however, was stuck in the whirlwind with no destination presenting itself for her escape. Objects floated around her; a heavy and ornate dresser flew past her head nearly cold-cocking her. Oh wonderful, she thought. I'm up inside the cyclone from the Wizard of Oz! Next thing I know I'll see a witch going by, riding on her broomstick!

Judo stepped out of the rift and collided with Lorcan Mac Conmara, knocking the alchemist to the ground. Quickly he helped the old gentleman up. "I'm sorry, Sir," he blurted. "I saw my buddy Wank in the mist and I had to get to him. I didn't see you standing right there."

"That's all right, my lad. Do we know you?" asked the alchemist

"Judo!" said Wayland. "How…? Oh never mind, Nothing surprises me anymore."

"You know this fellow?" asked Mac Conmara.

"He sure do," said Judo. "An' I knows the professor. Howdy, Doctor McGinley. We back in Oakland?"

"I'm afraid not, Judo," said McGinley. And to Mac Conmara: "This is the fellow that worked in my lab back in the 1950s. Or should I say, *will* work in the lab once 1950 comes around."

"And professor? I'm awful sorry I burned down your lab. You see, I fiddled with your machine and must of turned the wrong dial."

"You did? Blast it! Do you remember which dial you turned? It might help us cope with this disaster if we understood it better."

"Sorry."

"Well, it's water over the dam…or it will be. I'll say again, we should get away from this whirlwind. Go into the town. Find out where we are and make a plan."

"But Doctor McGinley," said Wayland, "don't you see? If Judo picked the time and the place he wanted to go to, then we could do the same. Wait for Oakland to appear and then jump."

"He has a point," said the alchemist. "It might just work."

"And it might not. We could end up anywhere. Let us go now."

As the scientist walked away from the raging whirlwind with the alchemist in tow, Wayland pulled Judo aside. "Judo," he said, "let those fools go. I have a plan. You and I can do something…something monumental. Something that will change history for the better. I need your help."

"What? Oh no, Wank. This sound like trouble. Count me out."

"Listen, we can go anywhere in time. We can make changes. I want to go back to kill Hitler. Think about it!"

"Now you really crazy. How you even find the man, before he become what he become?"

"With this." Wayland took a small, thin, rectangular object from his pocket and showed it to Judo. Its flat surface suddenly brightened and images appeared on it, little square images that changed colors. "I borrowed this from one of the scientists when we were stranded in New York in the future. I forgot to return it…well, sort of on purpose. It's a kind of calculator. It hasn't any keys like an adding machine, but you can touch those little pictures in certain ways and make it do things. You can talk to it and it talks back! It can translate language and it can find things. It's like a little dictionary and an atlas combined. If it can't find Hitler for us, I'd be very surprised."

"But how you gonna know if you're seeing the right time and the right place in that mist? Seems pretty iffy to me."

"We wait and we watch. There are certain buildings in Berlin that disappeared just as Hitler came to power. This calculator thing told me the whole history of it. Hitler had just been appointed Chancellor of Germany, which was his first step toward taking over the government. A Communist agitator set fire to the Reichstag Building, which was where the German parliament met. Hitler used this to begin ending certain civil liberties which stood in the way of his ultimate dictatorship. The fire took place on…wait a minute…"

Wayland pressed one of the colored squares on the device. "When was the Reichstag fire?" he asked. A female voice answered: "February 27, 1933, in Berlin, Germany." Then Wayland asked, "Where was Adolph Hitler at that time?" The answer: "Having dinner with Joseph Goebbels at Goebbels' apartment. When he heard about the fire, he and Goebbels drove to the Reichstag

Building to see for themselves."

Wayland exhibited an obsessive passion about the historical incident that left Judo unnerved. Certainly, it was a delicious idea: killing Hitler. And here was the time and place all laid out for them by this futuristic device. But Judo was afraid. He was afraid of the risk to their lives at such an attempt, of course, but he was also afraid of the fury he found behind Wayland's eyes when he talked of it. "This is a very bad idea, Wank," he told him.

"Just think! We could save the lives of six million Jews, hundreds of thousands of GIs."

"Don't you think someone else would take Hitler's place and go on with the Holocaust? Maybe this Goebbels fellow?"

"So we kill him too. And all the rest of the fucking Nazis."

"Wank, you crazy."

Judo was having a difficult time processing the concept of time-traveling to Nazi Germany to kill Hitler. The place would be crawling with Brown Shirts and bodyguards. They had no weapons. It seemed futile and foolish. But…

"How we kill them, Wank. We got no guns, no knives, no bombs."

"We'll think of something. Good always prevails over evil."

Oh sure, thought Judo. The Nazis killed millions of Jews and intellectuals and homosexuals and the retarded and many non-Arian people and—oh my! What did they do to Negroes?

"Wank, I'm gonna be a bit conspicuous. I think I'll stay here with the Professor."

"Judo, I need you at my back. It will be dark. No one will notice you, or me either, if we do this thing right. I've been thinking about this for a long time. We wait until they leave the car to go look at the fire. Then…I don't know exactly. I'll strangle him with my bare hands if need be."

Obsession, thought Judo, is the mother of stupidity. But it was also a good motivator. Wank was going to go through with his plan. How could he, Judo, not be at his back? And so they waited, watching the whirling time rift, hoping to see the burning Reichstag appear within the mist, as improbable as that seemed.

13

Killing Hitler

Berlin, Germany, February 27, 1933

Paul Joseph Goebbels looked at his reflection in the ornately carved Black Forest mirror that hung above the sideboard. On the apex of the mirror, from within a cluster of splendidly articulated oak leaves, the fierce face of a bear glared down at him, its ears perked, its eyes narrowed, its teeth showing just enough between curled lips to frighten children. Goebbels' gaunt features gave him a nearly delicate aspect, a dangerous supposition to be made by unfamiliar observers who might not live to regret their mistake. Indeed, he had suffered from osteomyelitis and a club foot as a child, a circumstance which exempted him from military service during the Great War. But for what he lacked in manly stature, he was a giant of determination and ire. He was a gifted communicator and wrote and spoke eloquently of German pride—and the world-wide menace of the Jews.

The dinner guests were finishing their custards. Goebbels' daughter, Helga Susanne, now one year old, sat wiggling and giggling on the lap of the newly appointed chancellor, Adolph Hitler. Hitler loved the little girl and would lavish her with attention whenever she was present. Goebbels also loved little Helga and would say openly that she was his favorite. He and his wife, Magda, would eventually have five daughters of their own and one son brought to the marriage by Magda. Only the son would escape the fate of his siblings in the bunker in 1945, during the final fall of the Third Reich. Joseph and Magda, afraid that their children would someday learn that their father was an inhuman monster who had murdered millions, poisoned the girls before committing suicide themselves. Helga would struggle flutily against the placement of the cyanide capsule between her teeth. This would happen as a horrific punctuation to the end of the war…if the two conspirators from the future failed in their mission to assassinate Hitler and Goebbels. If they succeeded…

Hitler had selected Goebbels for his minister of "enlightenment and propaganda." His was now the duty to shore up Hitler's popularity and to regulate the German media. Anti-Semitism was his forte as well as anti-intellectualism and the suppression of anything deemed to be un-German. Goebbels would organize the burning of books as a public spectacle and would end the livelihoods—and later the lives—of artists, actors, and musicians who he saw as decadent, particularly if they were Jewish. The immediate target of the Nazi agenda right now was to rid Germany of the influence of the Communist conspiracy, as Hitler and Goebbels called it. What was needed was an incident to spark outrage, and that was happening tonight over at the Reichstag building.

The Nationalsozialistische Deutsche Arbeiterpartei, or National Socialist German Worker's Party, sprang from the Freikorps paramilitary culture of the 1920s. It fostered a nationalistic and racist agenda to lure workers away from communism. It was also an anti-Semitic movement, and this was the primary attraction it held for Goebbels. Hitler had joined the party in 1921 and soon became its leader, its Führer. When Goebbels met Hitler he was swayed by his dynamic personality. He joined the ranks of the Führer's ardent followers which included Heinrich Himmler and Hermann Göring. The Hitler faction forced out the more moderate members and secretly set as it goal the overthrow of the Weimar Republic and the expulsion of Jews from Germany.

Hitler organized a militant branch of the party which he called the SA, the Storm Troopers, or Brownshirts. Members of opposition parties were sometimes physically attacked by these violent young men. Nazi rallies were held in beer halls and attracted former soldiers, small businessmen, the jobless, and the disenfranchised. The party's popularity grew. But its advance would encounter serious setbacks. In

November of 1923, in Munich, Hitler and his followers attempted a coup d'état. Known as the Beer Hall Putsch, around two thousand Nazis marched to the city center where they were met by police who exchanged fire with the would-be revolutionaries. Sixteen Nazi demonstrators were killed, Hitler himself was wounded, and later arrested and tried for treason.

Hitler was sentenced to 5 years in prison but was released after only 9 months. The Nazi party was banned but continued to operate as the German Worker's Party. While in prison, Hitler, with the help of fellow prisoners, Emil Maurice and Rudolf Hess, wrote the first volume of *Mein Kampf, (My Struggle)*, in which he clarified his anti-Semitic philosophy and his plans to make Germany great again. It would be influential in his rise to power. Those Nazis who had fallen during the Beer Hall Putsch were portrayed by Goebbels as martyrs. By 1930 the Nazi party had won just over 18 percent of the votes in the Reichstag elections. The German President, Paul von Hindenburg, in an effort to appease Hitler, whose growing popularity represented a political threat, offered the Führer the vice-chancellorship, but Hitler turned it down and demanded to be made chancellor. Hindenburg reluctantly agreed, and the rest would be history…or would it?

Magda cleared the dinner dishes and brought two glasses of sherry for her husband and Hitler. She shooed Helga away and she and Harald Quandt, Magda's son from a previous marriage, left the room so that the two Nazi leaders could talk. Briefly they discussed plans to segregate, if not eliminate, Jews, homosexuals, Africans, Jehovah's Witnesses, Poles, Slavs, the physically handicapped and the mentally incompetent, various political enemies, and anyone diluting the Aryan master race through marriage or co-habitation—in short, everyone who was not a good Nazi. Chief among their strategies would be the suppression of civil liberties and an "Enabling Act" to give the cabinet the power of law-making not subject to the consent of the parliament. Hitler would, in effect, become the dictator Führer of Germany. All he needed now was an excuse.

About nine o'clock that evening, as Hitler and Goebbels sipped their sherry, a member of the communist Dutch Counsel named Marinus van der Lubbe along with four other accomplices slipped into the Reichstag assembly building. They had broken a window on the west wall of the building and proceeded through the entry hall to the main Chamber of Deputies. They carried with them incendiary materials such as rags and wood shavings soaked in gasoline. Fires were set in four different areas and soon the building was engulfed in flames. Fire licked upward to ruin the gilded dome and raced across wooden paneling causing extensive damage.

The arsonists hurried from the building but as Lubbes jumped from a window he was apprehended by a local policeman, Sergeant Karl Buwert. He would later be "interviewed" by the Gestapo; this entailed having his naked body fettered with chains that would be tightened until the skin broke. He confessed to having set the fire but maintained he was alone and not affiliated with the Communist party. Lubbe was a 24 year-old homeless person whose drunken father had deserted the family, whose mother had died shortly thereafter, and who was raised by a sister in abject poverty. He had been a bricklayer but was injured on the job and no longer able to work. He would be tried, found guilty, and beheaded by guillotine. The Nazis would have their excuse to outlaw the Communist Party. Some of their opponents, however, would claim that the fire had been set by the orders of Hitler and Goebbels in order to take control of the government. This would never be proven.

The telephone rang in the Goebbels' apartment. Goebbels listened incredibly as his friend, Doctor Hanfstaengl, told him, "The Reichstag is burning!" Goebbels and the doctor often played jokes on one another and Goebbels knew it was Hanfstaengl's turn to hoax him. He laughed and hung up. The phone rang again. "I can see the flames from my window," Hanfstaengl insisted. Something in the tone of his voice convinced Goebbels that this was no hoax. He repeated the message to Hitler. "We must go there," answered Herr Hitler. "Summon my driver."

East Grinstead, West Sussex, England, 1840

Wayland Delaney and Raymond P. Washington, also known as Judo, watched the time rift whirlwind winding and unwinding on the cricket field. The shifting pageant of glimpses into far-gone and far-flung epochs was mesmerizing. They saw Egyptian slaves struggling across the desert, dragging huge blocks of stone toward an unfinished pyramid. They saw a bloody battlefield with men in blue or gray uniforms hacking away at each other while shells exploded among them. They saw a gargantuan ocean liner tipped bow down into an icy sea; saw it break in two; saw people struggling in the water. They saw cities of impossibly tall buildings of shining glass and metal. They could have stepped into the mist and traveled through time and space to any of those scenes. But they waited. They waited for the fire that would flare up within a building in Berlin in 1933.

"Maybe we should go find some weapons while we wait," said Judo. "How do you even know that Berlin will appear in the mist? It's a long shot."

"Notice," answered Wayland, "that most of the scenes that appear in the whirlwind are significant moments in history. Wars, disasters, events that have great emotional trauma connected to them. I believe there is a factor of psychic energy that is part of the mechanism of the anomaly. The alchemist said as much. He was always consulting horoscopes and the like, as if some mystical force was operating the whirlwind. The Reichstag fire *will* appear. We just have to wait. And I don't want to leave here to get weapons and come back to find the whirlwind closed up or gone."

"If you say so. Still, I'd be more comfortable if we was armed."

An hour had elapsed, and the mist was beginning to clear. Judo shivered as the air cooled and the sun started to set behind a stand of oak, casting long shadows across the cricket field. Suddenly, Wayland perked up. "Look!" he said. "A fire." Indeed, a ghostly shimmer of flames could be seen in the mist. It grew closer and brighter. But was it *their* fire? The one that would bring Hitler within their reach?

Wayland pushed at an icon on the tablet device he had brought from the future. He talked to the tablet: "Show me a picture of the Reichstag building in Berlin in 1933." The stately edifice blinked up onto the surface of the tablet. There was the great dome, the neo-classic façade, the twin towers. Wayland looked from the picture to the emerging image within the mist. The building in the mist was engulfed and partly hidden by smoke. But...it was the same!

"That's it!" he exclaimed. "Now we jump into our past...the future of now...into the greatest adventure one could wish for. And we must succeed! I feel it in my bones."

"I hope yo' bones is right," said Judo, and they jumped.

The Reichstag, February 27, 1933

Adolph Hitler and Joseph Goebbels left the official touring car once it arrived at the plaza in front of the burning Reichstag building. The two Nazi flags attached to the car's front fenders which displayed the swastika emblem now drooped—they had fluttered with a furry as the car had raced through the narrow streets of Berlin to reach the fire site. Franz von Papen, Hitler's vice-chancellor, and Nazi leaders Rudolf Diels and Hermann Göering were already on the scene.

Hitler said to von Papen, "This is a God-given signal, Herr Vice-Chancellor! If this fire, as I believe, is the work of the Communists, then we must crush out this murderous pest with an iron fist."

Goebbels interjected a curious pronouncement: "I can assure you it will be found to be the work of the Communists. It is often wise to leave nothing to chance."

Hitler gave Goebbels a knowing look. Then he took up his rant again: "God grant that this is the work of the Communists. You are witnessing the beginning of a great new epoch in German history. This fire is the beginning. You see this flaming building? If this Communist spirit got hold of Europe for but two months it would be all aflame like this building."

Göering then informed Hitler and Goebbels that a communist conspirator named Marinus van der Lubbe had been arrested. "This is the beginning of the Communist Revolt," Göering told them. "They will start their attack now! Not a moment must be lost. There'll be no mercy now."

"I agree," said Hitler. "Extreme measures are now called for."

Göering continued: "Anyone who stands in our way will be cut down. The German people will not tolerate leniency. Every communist official will be shot where he is found."

Wayland and Judo stepped out of the mist. A short distance from them the Reichstag building, a giant torch flickering against the darkened sky, was surrounded by fire wagons and scores of fire-fighters intent on limiting the destruction. The great dome had already been consumed. Directly in the path of the time travers stood a bewildered Storm Trooper. He stared with incredulity at the eerie apparitions who had seemingly materialized from thin air. His hesitation would prove to be his undoing.

Wayland rushed the Storm Trooper, wrapping his hands around the man's throat. Losing balance, the two of them fell to the ground. It is more difficult to strangle a person to death than one might imagine; as his victim struggled, Wayland found his grip loosening. The SA man managed to work his knife from its sheath. But as he began to bring his arm up to plunge the knife, Judo acted. Judo's booted foot slammed down on the outreached arm; the knife fell.

Wayland and the Storm Trooper were now rolling over and over. Neither man had the advantage. Judo picked up the knife. Suddenly the SA man had Wayland pinned under him. He unsnapped the holster holding his pistol and pulled out the weapon. Judo lunged. The knife found its mark squarely in the man's back. It was over.

"Well," said Wayland, after catching his breath, "at least now we have a knife and a pistol."

"And that," said Judo, pointing to a submachine gun that lay near the fallen SA man. "You know how to work one of those things?"

"I'm a quick learner. Now let's go find Hitler."

"Everybody in league with the Communists must be arrested. There will also no longer be leniency for social democrats," Göering was saying. Hitler smiled at the enthusiasm of his supporter. Göering was a former World War I fighter pilot, a decorated "Ace." Hitler would make him an important leader in the Nazi party. Truly now they had an opportunity to sway the masses—even if they had to kill many of them to do it.

A Brownshirt stood next to Hitler's car: the driver and sometimes bodyguard. He watched the group of important Nazis surrounding Hitler, daydreaming, perhaps, of the time he might be elevated up the ranks of the party, not just to guard the Führer, but to advise him. A blow to the back of his head from the pistol wielded by Judo sent him into oblivion. He would awake to a new world.

"There he is," said Wayland, pointing to Hitler. "Jesus, I hate those bastards!"

Wayland hefted the machine gun they had liberated from the SA man. This was a Steyr-made Maschinenpistole 34, loaded with deadly Mauser ammunition and capable of either single-shot or rapid burst shooting modes. It was set for automatic bursts, although Wayland's knowledge of firearms was so limited and the weapon so foreign, that he would have been unable to adjust it. Luckily, automatic firing was exactly what was called for in this situation. The group of Nazis was several yards away. Wayland aimed and pulled the trigger—nothing happened.

"Give me that thing," whispered Judo. He pulled the cocking bolt back until it clicked into place. "I think it's ready now," he said and gave the MP 34 back to Wayland. "Squeeze the trigger...don't jerk it."

Wayland breathed deeply and slowly let the air escape through his open mouth. Again he aimed, and squeezed the trigger gently as Judo had suggested. The gun kicked back at him as a flurry of bullets left the muzzle and sprayed across the five Nazis. One by one they fell like tumbling duck pins, bleeding and torn. Twenty rounds had found their mark in Nazi flesh. Franz von Papen, Rudolf Diels, Hermann Göering, Joseph Goebbels, and Adolph Hitler were dead.

Would the death of Adolph Hitler avert a world war? Paul von Hindenburg, the President of the Weimar Republic, had his own monarchist aspirations and had only tolerated the Nazis in order to rid the government of the Communists. The Nazis, without their charismatic leader, and without Goebbels' propaganda campaign, were now weakened. Who was left who could seize power? Rommel, Himmler, Bormann, Hess—would they be able to enact a military coup, create the Wehrmacht armed forces, the SS, the Gestapo, the concentration camps? Would they invade Poland? Declare war on the United States? Or would the more conservative members of the party prevail and back away from the military extremism of the Hitler faction?

Only time would tell.

14

Saving Lincoln

Wayland and Judo made a run for the time rift. They could hear shouts behind them. Next came a volley of bullets. The time rift whirlwind was dwindling, shrinking in size and intensity. It had stopped revolving and no longer offered options of time and space to the travelers. A Storm Trooper was close on their heels as they jumped into the disappearing mist.

The transition was not instantaneous as it had been before. They hung weightless and blinded by the mist for what seemed like hours—but in a timeless environment, who could really say? Finally there was increased turbulence, as if the whirlwind was regenerating like a brand new hurricane forming at sea—a child of harsh elements. They were deposited—flung unceremoniously—into an alley at some place and time as yet undiscovered.

"Ouch!" said Judo, picking himself up from the trash-strewn alleyway. "Wonder where we are."

Wayland recovered from the jostling in the whirlwind more slowly. He shook his head to clear his thoughts. "One way to find out," he said, and he began running his fingers over the device he had brought from the future. "Where are we?" he said to the tablet.

"Cannot connect," it answered.

"Well, what is the date?"

"Cannot connect," it repeated.

"What do you mean, 'cannot connect?' "

"There are no communication towers in the vicinity. I cannot connect to answer your query."

"One more slight problem," said Judo, tapping Wayland on the shoulder and pointing back down the alley. "We have company."

Slumped in a heap and apparently unconscious was the German Storm Trooper who had followed them into the mist back (or forward) in 1933. Judo rushed to the body of the Nazi and felt for a pulse. "It's alive," he said. "And armed!" Quickly he searched the man and retrieved a luger pistol, a vicious-looking knife, and a small knapsack in which he found some half-eaten rations (which looked terrible), a picture of a young woman (blond hair in braids), and folding money and coins (German currency). Judo confiscated these but left the picture of the woman and the food.

"We'll leave him," said Wayland. "When he comes to, he won't be worrying about us. He'll be disoriented, and he won't know where he is."

"Or when. Can we get out of this alley now?"

Out on the street a crowd was gathering, standing on the wooden sidewalks which lined the dirt roadway. There came the distant sound of music—of a sort—drumming and a discordant trumpet or bugle. Up the street marched a parade. As it drew nearer, Wayland and Judo could see a ragtag collection of soldiers, some in uniforms of faded blue, some in regular clothes. Some shouldering rifles. Some bandaged or walking with crutches. The people on the street cheered as the parade approached.

The color guard at the head of the parade carried an American flag. This encouraged the two time travelers; they were back in their own country! But wait, count the number of stars: 35 stars. "We're in the midst of the Civil War!" blurted out Wayland, oblivious to those spectators nearby.

Someone overheard his exclamation. "The end of the war," the man said. "You haven't heard? Lee has surrendered at Appomattox."

"Oh…well, that's great," Wayland stammered. "By the way, what's the date today?"

"It's the 12th of April. Have you been drinking? And why are you dressed so funny? You part of a circus? You and your Indian?"

Wayland suddenly realized that he was still dressed in the tight-fitting clothing he had gotten when he had visited the future. And Judo, although he had retained his original trousers, worn a fringed deerskin jacket, and must have appeared to the man to be a dark-skinned Indian. He thanked the man and led Judo up a cross street, away from the parade route.

"We need to get some appropriate clothes," he said. "Look for a clothing store." As an afterthought, he pressed an icon on the tablet and asked, "Device, what year did the Civil War end?"

"You may call me Sybil," said the device. "On April 9, 1865, General Lee surrendered to General Grant. There were a few isolated battles after that, but that is the usual date given as the end of the war. President Johnson officially proclaimed the end of the war on August 20."

"Wait a minute…President Johnson? Wasn't Lincoln the president?"

"President Abraham Lincoln was assassinated on April 14," replied Sybil.

"Oh my God! That's in two days!" said Judo who had been listening to the exchange between Wayland and the device. "Say, Wank…do you think…?"

"No, Judo. We can't…"

"But we have already interfered with history. We killed Hitler, remember. If we could stop Lincoln from being assassinated…"

"I wonder if that would really change anything. The war is over."

"But Wank, this is about my people. After Lincoln died Andrew Johnson became president. He was a racist. The Reconstruction era was a disaster for Black people. Remember, that was when the Ku Klux Klan was formed. Lincoln might have prevented that from happening."

"Well, how would we get to Washington in time to stop the assassination?"

"Wank, do you see that big building at the end of the street? The one with the dome with all the scaffolding on it like it's under construction? That is the Capitol dome. We *is* at Washington right now."

They found a mercantile establishment on the next block. After choosing some clothing which would make them less conspicuous, they carried their new things to the front counter where a burly man with bushy mutton chop whiskers stood, ready to take their money and eyeing them suspiciously.

"You ain't deserters, are you?" the man quizzed.

"No Sir. Is there a place we can change into these clothes?"

"Hmm. That will be a dollar and forty cents for the two pairs of trousers and eighty cents for the two shirts. You can use the back room, I suppose."

Judo took the German money from his purloined knapsack. "This is all we have," he told the man.

"What is this? Confederate money?" he said as he thumbed the paper money. "I can't take this."

"We have coins also." Judo poured a handful of coins onto the counter.

"Some of these look to be silver. I'll take these two and this one, and better give me the three copper ones too."

They found a boarding house on E Street, not far from Ford's Theater where the scene of Lincoln's assassination would take place if they were unsuccessful in stopping it. The establishment was run by an old German couple who were happy to take the German money in payment, although they were confused by the design of the bills. The room was on the second floor, with a grimy window that overlooked the street. Wayland immediately took the tablet device from his pocket and thumbed it.

"Sybil," he called, "we need to know more about the Lincoln assassination."

"Low battery warning," answered Sybil. "Recharge in two minutes."

"On April 12, 1865, where was Booth?"

"He roomed at the National Hotel on the corner of Pennsylvania Avenue and 6th Street. He often drank at Tatavull's Star Saloon next to the Ford's Theater. He may have met the other conspirators there on that day. He reportedly went to Mary Surratt's boarding house at 604 H Street to visit George Atzerodt and Lewis Powell. Time unknown. He certainly was in Washington on that day. He…warning…low battery…"

"Sybil, show me a picture of John Wilkes Booth. Sybil? Oh no, I think Sybil just died on us."

"That thing has a battery?" said Judo, thinking of the large, cylindrical "C" cells that went into the flashlight he had used as a child, shining a spot of light across the ceiling of his bedroom to entertain himself.

"I guess we're on our own now. If you really want to do this, we should track down Booth and the other conspirators. We've got two days."

April 14, 1865, Mary Surratt's Boarding House

In a back room of the four-story, gray-brick building on H Street a meeting was taking place that would change history—one way or another. Around a pine dining table sat five men and one woman, a collection of conspirators with loyalties to the now collapsing Confederacy and a common hatred of Abraham Lincoln. The presumptive leader of the conspiracy was a good looking, popular young actor named John Wilkes Booth. He and his cohorts had originally planned to kidnap Lincoln and to hold him hostage in order to secure the release of Confederate prisoners held by the North. They had waited along a lonely country road outside of Washington last March, hoping to stop a carriage transporting Lincoln to the Capitol, but a change in the president's agenda left them unable to fulfill their plan.

"It no longer makes sense to merely kidnap the president," said Booth. "Now that Lee has surrendered, we have to strike a blow for the Confederacy that will cause the South to rise up once again."

"You mean, kill the President?" asked Lewis Powell, a former Confederate soldier who Booth had recruited to his cause.

"Sic semper tyrannis! Thus always to tyrants. Yes, the President and more! The Vice President and the Secretary of State must also die. This will cripple the North."

"It is an admirable idea," offered David Herold, a close friend of the actor and an anti-abolitionist. "But how...and when?"

"You and Lewis will go to Secretary of State William Seward's house tonight. He has taken to his bed to recover from injuries from that accident a couple of days ago. He will be easy to dispatch."

"Let me kill the Vice President," said George Atzerodt. He was a German immigrant who had worked transporting Confederate spies north in his boat. Now he was eager to accomplish more treachery against the Union.

"Yes, do so. I have learned that Lincoln is to attend this evening's performance at Ford's Theater of *Our American Cousin*. I've played at that theater, you know, and it will be simple to gain access through the stage entrance. General Grant is also to attend and be in the President's box. It is delicious to anticipate delivering a bullet to each of their evil heads!"

"What can I do?" asked Samuel Delany, a newcomer from Tennessee.

"We'll need horses to escape and a sanctuary somewhere out of town…maybe a farm. There are many sympathizers who will help you arrange things…but be careful!"

There was a furious knocking at the door. Mary Surratt was startled. "Are you expecting anyone?" she asked Booth.

"No. But you better go see who it is. We don't want to appear suspicious at this late stage."

Mary went to the front door where she found a young white man with a Negro boy standing behind him, holding a cardboard box. She did not know them and was about to slam the door when the white youth said:

"Mizz Surratt, good morning to you. I am a good member of the Sons of Liberty…the Order of the American Knights of the Golden Circle. I am wishing to see Mister John Wilkes Booth who, I am told, is here in your establishment."

"Who are you? What do you want. We don't know you."

"Ah, that is true. I am shortly from Richmond with a package for Mister Booth, to aid him in the Great Cause."

"I don't believe you. Be gone from my door!"

"I know the passwords. Nu Oh Lac. Give me liberty or give me death. Our Supreme Commander is Mister Vallandigham. He sends his regards to Mister Booth and this package which contains materials to construct a deadly weapon which may be of use in the struggle."

"Wait here while I go see if he'll see you."

They waited. Presently, Mary Surratt returned and beckoned them to follow her. "Booth says you know the correct password. He will see you for a few moments. Your boy better wait out here."

"He carries the box which is too heavy for me as I injured my arm in a riding accident. He knows his place."

"Very well."

In the meeting room, Booth quizzed the youth, telling him to take the stance that revealed his level in the Order. Wayland placed his right foot at an angle against his left and folded his arms so that they made an X, with four fingers of the right hand extended. Booth seemed satisfied. "What have you brought for me?" he asked.

Wayland gestured to Judo who opened the cardboard box and drew out two pistols, handing one to Wayland.

"These are pistols of an advanced design, manufactured in Germany. They are capable of rapid fire without reloading. They are called lugers."

"Unglaublich!" exclaimed George Atzerodt. "I am unfamiliar with this weapon, having been away from the homeland for many years. Can I see it, hold it?"

"Oh, we'll give you a demonstration. Ready, Judo?"

During the next few minutes the room reverberated with the cracking of lugers spattering shells into the bleeding, jerking bodies of the five men. When it was over, some were slumped across the pine boards of the table, their life fluids soaking into the wood. Others lay in tangled heaps on the floor. Mary Surratt had fled. Lincoln would be able to enjoy the play tonight.

Two days later in Baltimore, Maryland

Wayland and Judo not only were mass-murders, albeit in the best interests of the nation, but robbers: they had taken the time to fleece the pockets of the dead conspirators for any cash currency or loose change they could grab. Some of the bills they discarded, being too blood-soaked to use, but they had sufficient funds now for a decent hotel room at Baltimore's Barnum City Hotel on the southwest corner of Fayette and Calvert Streets. The hotel had been a favorite of such notables as the former President John Quincy Adams, Davy Crocket, and Charles Dickens. Ironically, it was also the location of one of the first meetings the year before of the conspirators gathered together by John Wilkes Booth.

Wayland was relaxing in an easy chair next to a window overlooking Battle Monument Square, where the marble statue of a woman in the Greek Revival style stood, laurel wreath in hand, atop a

Romanesque column set upon an Egyptian Revival cenotaph. She was known locally as "Lady Baltimore." She was attended by a fluttering of sea gulls.

Wayland perused the Baltimore Sun for news of the day. Scanning the headlines, he noted that although the South had surrendered to the North at Appomattox over one week ago, Wilson's Raiders, under Brigadier General James H. Wilson, had marched into Georgia to do battle with hold-out Confederate troops. It was Easter Sunday, and President Lincoln was entertaining his family and selected members of the congress at the White House. Wayland's eye stopped at a small news item on the inside of the front page:

TRAGIC SHOOTING AT D.C. BOARDING HOUSE

Owner of a boarding house on H Street, Mary Surratt, reported that on last Friday, the 14th, members of a local social club, including the actor, John Wilkes Booth, who were playing a friendly game of cards, were brutally accosted by a ruffian and his Negro assistant. The gunmen entered the boarding house and drew pistols, killing five men. The culprits escaped and are now being sought by police. The dead, besides Booth, include Lewis Powell, a former Confederate soldier, George Atzerodt, a German immigrant lately from New York City, David Herold who like Booth, had lived in Baltimore, and Samuel Delaney, from Tennessee.

The newspaper slipped from Wayland's hands. "Samuel Delany from Tennessee?" he moaned. "Oh my God! I think I've killed my own grandfather!"

"What do you mean?" asked Judo. "How could that be possible?"

"There was a story that my grandfather…I hardly knew him, had once been a Confederate sympathizer. But he didn't marry my grandmother until much later than this. So if the man described in the newspaper article was *my* Samuel Delany…"

"That would mean you were never born. You don't exist…but Wank, you do exist. Again I ask, how is that possible?"

"The professor always said, time is relative to the observer. Maybe I don't exist anymore only in my own time frame. But because I am here, now, I am the person that I am. It just means that I can't ever go back to my own time."

"Well, so what? There are some advantages to this time-travel thing. We could play the stock market. Maybe go back and do some more adjusting of history. Say…we could repeat the assassination of the conspirators, but not kill this Delany guy."

"I don't know, Judo. I think I may be trapped right here in 1865."

"Wank, how did you know all that Sons of Liberty stuff? The password and so forth?"

"Just a good-old Tennessee boy, Judo. Just a good-old Tennessee boy"

Byron Grush

15

The Alchemist's Solution

East Grinstead, West Sussex, England, 1840

It seemed like a nice little town, set against a rugged forest to the south and a band of chalk hills to the north. It had its share of historical edifices: a long row of 14th century houses framed in old-growth timber, 12th century churches (Church of England mostly), the Sackville College with its sandstone almshouses. A decade or so from now, the newly established Prime Meridian would run right through the town. By the Twentieth Century, nearby Gatwick Airport and other developments would bring little East Grinstead a rush of suburbanites who would commute by rail to London, only twenty-seven miles distant.

Now it was quaint, quiet, and colloquial. It might have stepped out of a story by Dickens. The rag man strolled the main streets. The fish monger called out to advertise his offerings. Carriages ambled, pulled by lazy horses; no one was in a hurry here. Two men, one from the future and one from the past, wandered up High Street, absorbing the ambiance. They considered their plight. They had found a farm house near the cricket field where a clothes lines was stretched between wooden posts. Thus they obtained period clothing for themselves and also took two outfits for Wayland and Judo, who had failed to follow them, stubbornly standing by the whirling time rift, waiting for…what?

When the alchemist and McGinley returned to the cricket field the whirlwind had disappeared, and with it, Wayland and Judo. McGinley could not help but worry about where Wayland had gone and what he might be planning. Without the whirlwind they had no hope of following, even if they knew what era to enter. Although McGinley suspected he did know, the point was moot.

For Lorcan Mac Conmara, East Grinstead was a very modern city filled with wonders: the cluster of houses three and four stories high, the tall chimneys spewing woodsmoke, the tower and spires of St. Swithun's Church which sat on a hilltop above the town and dominated the skyline. For Dr. Madison McGinley it was a grubby relic of the past with little to offer them in their quest for a resolution to the errant and uncontrollable time rift.

A stand on the corner sold books, magazines, and current newspapers. Here, without seeming obtuse, they were able to learn the name of the town, its location, and the exact date: February 9, 1840. The headline jumped out at them. It read, "Queen to Marry Prince Albert of Saxe-Coburg and Gotha in the Royal Chapel at St James's Palace, Westminster, tomorrow."

"Oh no," said Mac Conmara, "is England forever to be plagued with female monarchs?"

"Yes it is," answered McGinley. "Elizabeth the First in your time, Elizabeth the Second in mine, and Victoria in this time. Say, would you like to go to a royal wedding?"

"This queen, is she accessible? Might she offer us resources if we explained…"

"Explain that we traveled through time and now we need to build a machine to stop the temporal whirlwind that threatens to cause unspeakable damage to the word as we know it? If I remember my history, Victoria is still a very young woman and those around her do not trust her to reign without guidance. Her finance is a German, which confounds her situation. However…"

It rained the next day, the morning of the wedding. Nonetheless, the streets were crowded with people anxious to see the young queen and her prince as they made their way from Buckingham Palace to St.

James' Palace where the wedding would take place in the Chapel Royal. The Bride wore a long white dress of satin and silk, trimmed with Honiton lace, a lace veil, diamond necklace and earrings, and a sapphire brooch which Albert had given her. The groom wore the uniform of a British field marshal, fiery red. As the carriage passed by the crowds cheered.

There were comments favorable to the Queen's attire, in simple white instead of the traditional colors worn by brides. The bridesmaids, also all in white, were said, however, to look quite common. The Prince garnered no compliments. One woman who had been standing next to Mac Conmara and McGinley said Prince Albert looked as if he had needed to borrow some clothes in which to be married. McGinley couldn't help overhearing this and when he turned to look at the woman he felt there was something about her slim and attractive appearance, her plain but neat clothing, and her confident stature that made her seem familiar, iconic even. It was as if she had stepped from a portrait of some historical person or off a postage stamp. He suddenly realized he was staring at her, and she was staring back at him.

"I am truly sorry for being so rude, madam," he said. "I didn't mean to stare. It is just that I feel I know you, or that I have seen you somewhere before. But that couldn't be true, could it?"

"I would think not," said the woman. "Would the gentleman wish to introduce himself so that we may continue to stare at each other properly?"

"Oh, of course. My name is Dr. Madison McGinley. I am visiting from…from the United States. This is my companion, Lorcan Mac Conmara. He is Irish."

"Ah! A doctor. My name is Florence Nightingale, from Embley Park in Hampshire. I am very interested in entering the nursing field although my family is set against it. What do you think of my idea?"

McGinley quickly reviewed his meager knowledge of history. The Crimean war…had that happened yet? No, it would take place a dozen years from now. This was the young Florence Nightingale. Not yet Longfellow's "Lady with the Lamp," the ministering angel of the war, the reformer of nursing practices, the figurehead for women's independence.

"I am not that kind of a doctor, I'm afraid. I am a professor of physics. We are both scientists. But I would strongly encourage you to follow the calling you have felt."

"It is a calling from God, I believe."

"Miss Nightingale, I predict a life of valuable service to mankind for you. It has been a pleasure meeting you, and take my advice, don't listen to your parents…follow your heart."

"Wait a moment," said Mac Conmara. "May I ask a somewhat pertinent question? Are your family well off?"

"Lorcan! That's very rude," complained McGinley.

"No, it is all right. I do come from wealth. I was born in Florence, Italy, hence my given name. My father inherited the estate here at Lea Hurst. He is very interested in science, by the way…although that does not, unfortunately, allow him to condone his daughter's desire to forgo the trap of marriage and to enter a scientific profession like medicine. He is a member of the Royal Society for the Encouragement of Arts, Manufactures and Commerce. That is Britain's answer to the French and their unending exhibitions…their Exposition des produits de l'industrie française which seems to pop up nearly every year. Father's committee would like to organize such an exhibition here in England. He is looking for inventions and scientific achievements to put on display."

"Is that so?" said McGinley. "Well, Miss Nightingale, I think we are about to begin a wonderful new relationship, we two, yourself, and your father."

Crystal Palace, Hyde Park, London, May, 1851

> *As though 'twere by a wizard's rod*
> *As blazing arch of lucid glass*
> *Leaps like a fountain from the grass*
> *To meet the sun.*
> ——William Makepeace Thackeray

Queen Victoria stood on a raised platform in the center of the great hall. Two of her five children were by her side and flanking the Royals were her mother on her right, and Prince Albert on her left. She was about to open the Great Exhibition of the Works of Industry of All Nations, the Great Exhibition of 1851. Above them hung a large tapestry resembling a decorative umbrella from India (the jewel of Britain's crown) and above that, rising four stories in height, was a domed ceiling of glass and steel, delicate and intricate, the dazzling brainchild of architect Joseph Paxton. The building was called "the Great Shalimar," the Crystal Palace.

The building, constructed expressly for the exhibition, was 1,848 feet long and 454 feet wide. It resembled a gigantic glass house. Its grids of iron framing held panes of clear glass, allowing sunlight to illuminate each and every corner. A fountain of pink glass 27 feet high occupied a central location. Just behind the ceremonial group surrounding the Queen rose one of Hyde Park's stately ancient oaks.

Standing behind the Queen's family on the dais were dignitaries including members of the Royal Society for the Encouragement of Arts, Manufactures and Commerce. Principle organizer of the Prince's Royal Commission for the Exhibition, Henry Cole, and his fellows, Francis Henry, George Wallis, Charles Dilke, and William Edward Nightingale, stood shoulder to shoulder as the Queen announced to the world that here and now, the works of industry of Britain, its colonies and dependencies, and forty-four foreign states of Europe and the Americas, would show the world that technology (most importantly, although she did not thus specify—the technology of Great Britain) was the key to a better future.

And what an exhibition! Charlotte Bronte, in a letter to a friend, described the "bazaar or fair as Eastern genii might have created" with its "great compartments filled with railway engines and boilers, with mill machinery in full work, with splendid carriages of all kinds, with harness of every description,…the glass-covered and velvet-spread stands loaded with the most gorgeous work of the goldsmith and silversmith, and the carefully guarded caskets full of real diamonds and pearls worth hundreds of thousands of pounds….a blaze and contrast of colours and marvelous power of effect."

Besides the Koh-i-Noor, the world's largest diamond, there were modern kitchen appliances, Cyrus McCormack's reaping machine, an envelope-making machine, an automatic voting machine, Frederick Bakewell's facsimile machine, Mathew Brady's daguerreotypes, Samuel Colt's revolvers, a telescope with an 11 inch lens, George Jennings' pay toilets that cost a penny to use, a giant hydraulic press, a large steam-hammer, a high-speed printing press, early versions of the bicycle, and a very curious machine that displayed moving images—brought to the exhibition by William Edward Nightingale, who was at a loss to explain its workings.

Nightingale had obtained the device from two men his daughter Florence had brought to dinner one day over ten years ago. He had been hopeful that Florence's interest in the men indicated a more general interest, one which might lead to matrimony—although the American was obviously too old for her and the Irishman—well, he was an Irishman. Florence had been courted unsuccessfully by the poet, Richard Monckton Milnes, but she seemed to prefer the company of other women, principally Mary Clarke, whom she called "Clarkey." William Nightingale, in desperation, had sent his daughter on a world tour and she was now in Germany. There, she had visited the Kaiserswerth Institute where she had become inspired by the work that religious community was doing with the sick. Her experiences would influence the noble deeds that would bring her fame during the Crimean War, three years from now.

Ten years before at dinner, the two men, McGinley and Mac Conmara, had impressed William Nightingale with their discourse on scientific research as they supped and later sat, sampling a fine sherry. Nightingale's interest in the subject was more than that of an amateur, as he had, for more years than he could count, amassed a collection of dried insects, butterflies, small stuffed rodents, some exotic bird drawings bound into volumes, and other curiosities. Although a naturalist by nature, he was fascinated by McGinley's talk of galvanism and the relationship of electrical forces to the life force present in humans and animals.

Nightingale had read Mary Shelly's revised edition of *Frankenstein* in which the author had indicated that galvanic shock was used to resurrect the monster. Although a work of fiction, the suggestion intrigued Nightingale. When McGinley revealed that he hoped someday to build a large machine to create electrical magnetism and other effects, Nightingale offered to support him in his research. Eventually, the two scientists from the past and the future found a sponsor in William Nightingale. They were afforded a carriage house on the property and it was all they could do to prevent Nightingale from camping on the doorstep, so infatuated was he at witnessing the process of invention.

The curious device that Nightingale had brought to the Great Exhibition was a prototype for the new time machine they were building. With it, they could select an epoch to view and to derive from it coordinates useful in locating said space-time. A larger, transportable machine took several years to build. When it was finished and tested, they found they could travel into a time in the future or the past and, without mishap, return. The machine did not use the time rift whirlwind they had accidently created—therefore they were convinced they could counteract that anomaly without themselves being stranded in some time frame or another. Their plan was to travel back to the future to prevent themselves from initiating the whirlwind. But how?

"Suppose we do go to the future and stop ourselves from creating the whirlwind," Mac Conmara had said. "That would mean our future selves would be unable to travel to this time to create this time machine. Therefore we would be unable to travel to the future to stop the whirlwind..."

"That is called a paradox," replied McGinley. "However, it seems to me that although changing the past will certainly have an effect upon the future, it is possible that changing the future will not affect the past. We would still exist in this past even though we had no way of reaching it."

"That makes no sense. I think it is too risky. But what if (here the alchemist presented his solution) we go to the future just before we build the rift machine and kidnap ourselves, bringing us back to this time?"

"Or even dropping each of our other selves off in their own times. That might work. There is another consideration, however...Wayland is there in the future too. And somewhere else in time as well. Do we leave Wayland in the future, in which case he might not be able to leave it? Or do we bring him back, thereby creating duplicates of him as well as of ourselves?"

"Can we even be twice in the same time? And if so, how do we sort that paradox out? Maybe we'd better just let well enough alone."

"No, I like your solution. But is there a way we can kidnap ourselves without encountering them? I just have a sense that meeting yourself in another time presents, not just a paradox but potentially a dangerous situation. Perhaps it might cause another rift...one of some other kind."

New York, 2152

The time machine materialized nicely on the lowest floor of the Empire State Building that still remained above the water line. The machine itself was an innocuous-looking black box, about the size of a small automobile. The travelers stepped from the box into a musty room occupied only by rats and roaches—survivors of man's destructive tenure of the earth. The plan was to locate the other scientists, Leith Carlyle and Albert Breckinridge, and enlist them in spiriting away their other selves, without revealing that there were two McGinleys and two Mac Conmaras.

The wolfhound, Teige, bolted through the doorway and lunged at Mac Conmara, thrusting his paws against the alchemist's chest and licking his face with enough force to nearly remove the man's features. "He's happy to see you," said McGinley.

"That is so. Down, Teige. Down boy!"

"Too bad we can't send him upstairs to bring our other selves down. He isn't exactly Lassie, now is he?"

"Lassie? No, he's a boy dog, McGinley."

"No, I mean…Lassie the movie dog…oh, never mind. Let's get this little merriment over with. Up the stairs we go!"

They entered the break room and found Wayland sitting alone at a table. There was nothing to do but to tell the youth the truth. Wayland was incredulous although he noted they wore clothing from a past era. He agreed to go with them to the lower level where they showed him the time machine and explained about the disastrous time rift that would occur unless they could send their duplicate selves back to the past. Their explanation left out the fact that in the unaltered past, using the whirlwind, Wayland would venture off on his own, most likely with a devious plan to kill Hitler.

"Okay," Wayland said, "I'll humor you. Weirder things have happened. I'll go get…you two and bring you down here. Then can we go home?"

"Absolutely. We'll file this time travel business away until we can approach it without changing history."

If the reader has ever experienced meeting someone who strongly resembled them, they would know perhaps a fraction of the astonishment the four men felt when they finally met. Even the McGinley and the Mac Conmara who had arrived in the time machine, who had expected the meeting, were dumfounded. But the world didn't end, and time didn't grind to a halt. At least not yet.

The five humans and the dog stuffed themselves into the time machine—it was cramped quarters. The McGinley who knew the operations of the device, set coordinates for 1572 Ireland. He would return the two Mac Conmaras and the dog to their own time, then he and the other McGinley and Wayland would travel to 1953 Oakridge, Tennessee. The world would be free of the threat of the whirlwind plummeting its way through time and creating chaos. Or so he thought.

Byron Grush

Part Two

Tangled up in Time

Byron Grush

Preface to Part Two:

Tangled up in Time

The time is…well, that's relative, isn't it? As we continue our story, our characters are fairly well scattered throughout the time-space continuum. Dr. Madison James McGinley, lately from 1851 London and his duplicate, Dr. Madison James McGinley lately from 2153 New York (both originally from 1953 Oakridge, Tennessee), and their apprentice, Wayland Delaney, also from 2153 New York, are in a time machine of McGinley's design. Also in the machine are the alchemist, Lorcan Mac Conmara, and his duplicate, each lately from 1851 London or 2153 New York, and both originally from 1572 County Cork, Ireland. Oh yes, and a dog named Teige, lately from 2153 New York, also travels with them in the time machine. The machine has been set to return to 1572—but that is not likely to happen.

Another Wayland Delaney, a duplicate of the aforementioned Wayland Delaney, was last seen in Baltimore, Maryland in 1863, along with his companion, Raymond P. Washington, also known as Judo. They are both from 1953 Tennessee. It is possible they are now stranded in their current time frame, but then, all things are possible.

And alas, our poor lass, Melanie Langford (from 1953 Tennessee) stepped into the time rift whirlwind in Virginia in 1571 and hasn't managed to extricate herself from those buffeting winds of temporal chaos. We do hope she will escape into a space-time that is less hostile than the one she has (just?) left.

Then there are Enrico Fermi and Leona Libby, famous nuclear

scientists from 1952 Chicago, who had found themselves in 1905 Zürich, Switzerland, along with Riordan Ó Ciardha, the alchemist's apprentice from 1572 Ireland, and a duplicate of the dog, Teige. In their time frame the whirlwind still exists and they could use it to travel to some other time and space (except that McGinley and Mac Conmara have, or will have, stopped the creation of that whirlwind in 2153).

And now if the reader is not too confused (preferably less confused than the writer), We can pick up the story where we left it. And that would be…

16

The Girl in the Whirlwind

Melanie Langford was floating in a strange space disconnected from temporal reality—a timeless, mist-filled void where sensations of up and down existed sporadically if at all. Things floated beside her or zoomed passed in an endless Alice in Wonderland caucus race of material objects: furniture, debris that might have come from smashed houses, wheels spinning on invisible axles, plucked from locomotives or the machinery that drives huge turbines, bits and pieces of clothing, great iron pots, and tiny things that might have been toys. No other humans or animals were present in the whirlwind.

Melanie was alone in a fantastic dream world that moved, or maybe didn't move, where sounds eluded her, where smells were impossible to identify, and where time—time was a mystery she only vaguely remembered. It had something to do with alarm clocks that were about to clang and clatter, about being late for school, about being scolded for returning from a date after midnight. But there were no clocks here.

"Have I been here like this for a day, a week, a year? Has it only been minutes?" She realized she had been speaking out loud, to the broken picture frame that hovered next to her. Crazy! The mist—the mist was something she recognized from the time rift she and Judo had stepped through, transferring them to pre-colonial Virginia where they had lived for a time in a Native American village. Then…then this thing, whatever it was, swallowed her up and spun her around. Where was Judo? Then a horrible thought presented itself: she had died, and this was…it wasn't Heaven, or Hell…perhaps it was Purgatory.

Another timeless period passed and these thoughts that had frightened her were gone. She wished…she wished she could go home…click her ruby slippers together and go home. Then, suddenly, if there were such a thing as sudden in a world that was timeless, the mist disappeared and she felt herself dropping. She landed on a soft carpet of flowers. All around her the landscape was blanketed with blooms: bright purple, hazel-tinted, delicate pink, shocking orange, deep scarlet, many-colored blooms. The tiny blossoms were held inches above the ground of coarse black dirt on slender stalks the color of golden corn.

She rose and began to walk. It seemed the flowers turned their heads to watch her progress across the field. She thought she heard buzzing—not of bees for there were none—but the faint murmur of many small voices, lowered as if a hushed conversation in a library ensued. The landscape, covered with the strange flowers, stretched to the horizon in all directions. Here and there a hillock erupted to break the monotony of the flat land. Well, she thought, I've finally reached heaven. But where are the angels strumming on their harps?

She walked without purpose, for no destination occurred to her—how could it? But she must keep walking. Walking showed her that she was alive. Perhaps over the next hill….

It rose up before her on four spindly legs. It resembled an insect, a praying mantis. Except it was the size of a horse. Its arms were held in front of it, angled and swaying, the (hands?) drooped downward, just like the insect named for this gesture. The face was less like that of an insect, almost human-like. The eyes were not multi-faceted; instead two orbs bulged forward from within leathery lids. They were like great elephant eyes on the small head. Gaping slits served as a nose. Antennae wiggled and twitched from its forehead and a long tongue darted out from a small circular opening that must have been a mouth, no doubt testing the air to get her scent.

The mantis-being and Melanie were startled; which one was more shocked and stunned cannot be stated. But neither turned and ran, nor did one or the other attack. Perhaps fascination overcame fear. It was certain that neither being had ever encountered such a thing as that which now stood before it.

Melanie realized she hadn't taken a breath in minutes. She forced herself to breathe. Then she thought she heard a soft giggling like the tinkling of tiny bells. The sound resolved into a chorus of singing soprano voices. Melanie heard, or thought she heard:

"Our two visitors are surprised by each other, yet they cannot look away. How droll and how quizzical it is to witness such amazement at the unexpected!"

Melanie was astounded for the second time today. "Who said that?" she said.

"No one *said* that. We communicate nonverbally." A ripple ran through the bed of flowers surrounding her.

"You...you are the flowers? You can read my mind?"

"Not read. We listen. We hear. We have no need of language or the use of air pushed out to touch off vibrations in feeble organs. And, just so you know, we are not the many that you see. We are one together—the many in the one, the one of the many. We are called the Pyroon."

Melanie suddenly remembered the monstrous bug-thing standing in front of her. "This...big insect. Do you talk to it too?" she asked.

"We can communicate with it, yes. It is curious about you. What are you, it wants to know?"

"I'm...I'm a human girl. From Tennessee. I'm Melanie. Is this...this isn't earth, is it?"

"This is not the planet from which you come. No. Some come here—by what means we do not know. The big insect, as you call him, is from another planet as well. We assume it is not your planet that sent him."

"Sent him?"

"How else? He is called a rhillw. His given name is Veetit. Although we refer to him as a he, he has no actual sex. He reproduces by fission, not involving the union of gametes."

"Is he communicating with you now?"

"Yes. He thinks you are quite bizarre-looking and a bit frightening. You aren't hostile, are you? No...we can sense that you are not. We will reassure him of your friendship if that is what you wish."

"Yes, please. Tell him that I think he has beautiful eyes."

"We do not think he has the concept of beauty in the way in which you have it, but we will communicate your compliment."

The mantis-being named Veetit twitched his antennae and thrust his long tongue at Melanie. Was it a gesture of friendship? She hoped so. Veetit began stomping his feet in place.

"He would like you to follow him," said the Pyroon. "He wants to show you something. He says it is all right if you would like to ride on his back."

"Oh my God…no! I'll just walk."

"He travels very fast. We suggest you mount him and ride. It is some distance."

Melanie's thighs ached from wrapping them around the mantis-being and holding on tightly so she wouldn't fall off. Her posterior was also sore and her pride hurt because, although she had ridden horses and was a fair equestrian, her skill at posting on a rhillw left much to be desired. They had reached their destination, at least the destination that Veetit had in mind. They stopped at the foot of a large hill, perhaps a foothill of the mountain range she could see in the distance. There was a shallow valley in its shade and the never-ending carpet of sentient flowers extended to its edge but went no further. Melanie dismounted but lingered near the flowers, unwilling to leave the vicinity of their ability to communicate.

"Well? What is it you wanted to show me?" Melanie asked Veetit, hoping the Pyroon would translate for the rhillw. The mantis-being pointed with his claw-like hands at the hill where, once Melanie was able to penetrate the deep shadows which fell across it, she could just make out the outline of a cave opening. "What? You want me to go in there?" she said—it was more of a statement than a question.

"He has no intention of harming you," said the Pyroon. "We cannot live in that environment, but you should have no trouble. Trust the rhillw."

Melanie had, up to now, no sense of the temperature of the air of this strange planet. Not hot, not cold, but even—a restorative balm for one who had been buffeted relentlessly in a temporal cyclone. Entering the cave, which she did reluctantly, a cold, dank, and vaporous ambience numbed and depressed her. The darkness deepened as she followed the rhillw along a low-ceilinged corridor where tendrils of cobweb touched her head and shoulders and unseen things crunched beneath her feet.

Just as she was about to turn and bolt from the claustrophobic cave the walls took on a soft iridescence, a glow that gave hope of deliverance from the oppressive blackness. It brightened just enough that she could see that the walls were not etched from primordial stone but tiled with brick or hand-shaped limestone—the obvious work of some intelligent being with (unlike the rhillw) hands with opposable thumbs. Curious.

Soon they emerged into a circular chamber, perhaps thirty feet in diameter, twenty feet in height, open to the sky, and walled with the same stone-work that Melanie had noticed in the tunnel. There were two openings into the chamber other than the one from which they had come. The rhillw hesitated here, as if waiting for someone or something. Melanie looked at the sky above them and noticed that it was taking on a hue resembling green pea soup. Shadows falling from the walls seemed to lengthen as if the sun was setting rapidly. The pea soup sky darkened and she saw a small moon rising. As she watched the silver orb move slowly above the rim of the chamber, a second moon followed close behind it. Curiouser.

As the twilight descended upon the chamber the walls began to glow, just as they had within the tunnel. Soon the two moons and the walls were the only source of illumination. Still the rhillw waited. Melanie wished for the bed of flowers so that she could talk to her strange companion. Even as this thought entered her mind so too came a voice…or the sensation of a voice…which responded to her: "I will talk with you. Do not despair."

Something was coming from one of the openings on the wall. Something large and fur-covered. Something that might have been a rodent—a large rat?—but it was even too large for a rat. Of course, Melanie thought to herself, why should anything on this planet be of normal size?

"I *am* of normal size," said the thing. As it drew closer she saw that it looked a bit like a rotund teddy bear, but nearly six feet tall with a long snout and an ugly, naked, rat-like tail. Its fur was striped like a tiger's, reddish-brown and white, and it had a mane of golden fur that would have made any earth-based lion jealous. A pair of wicked-looking incisors overlapped its lower lips. Curiouser still!

"Oh, Christ! Does everything on this planet read minds?"

Melanie said.

"Not all of us," it answered. "The rhillw for example. Of course, people's minds are cluttered up with all sorts of nonsense. Yours, for example."

"Who are you? What are you? What is this place?"

"One thing at a time. First I must thank the rhillw for bringing you to me." He (it?) paused for a moment, then continued to place thoughts into Melanie's mind: "I am called Shylan. My race is known as the hokablz. I am in charge of meeting new arrivals. I am something of a constable, with special privileges. That is due to my superior size and strength."

"I don't follow…what is this place?"

"This is a prison planet…a penal colony for the worse offenders of the galaxy. You would not be sent here without having committed some dire crime. What was your crime, by the way? Your mind is a bit hazy where that is concerned."

"Crime? I…I am not a criminal. And I wasn't sent here, I fell out of the time rift."

"Nothing you can think of? Oh come now."

"Well, we did kill a man back in Nashville and hid his body in the trunk of his car. But the man was trying to rape me and it was Roy who actually killed him…stabbed him with a knife. He deserved it."

"So you were an accomplice. Hmm…what am I to do with you? That will be for the committee to decide. Perhaps you would make good breeding stock."

The two moons had traversed the sky rapidly and were about to set beneath the rim of the chamber. The sky began to brighten. It had only been a matter of minutes since day became night, and now the sequence was reversed. Short nights around here, thought Melanie. The hokablz called Shylan made no comment.

"What was Veetit's crime? He seems so mild mannered."

"It is hard to say. He doesn't have the concept of criminality. Nor of much else. His kind are not the most intelligent beings in the universe. Maybe he is a political prisoner."

"And you?"

"My kind have been scavengers, living off the misfortunes of others. But I took it one step further. Well, I was hungry, wasn't I? And now my little human girl, it is time for me to take you to the committee."

"And if I refuse?"

"Then I would have to eat you."

"Well, I'll be going now," said Melanie and she ran for the entrance of the tunnel. Maybe if I could get back to where the whirlwind dropped me, she thought. Maybe it would reappear and I could leave this awful place. The flowers...the flowers will help me!

But as she flew through the tunnel she heard laughter—demonic, horrible laughter from the hokablz which seemed to increase in volume the more she ran. It was then that she realized she had entered, not the tunnel from which she and the rhillw had come, nor the one from which the hokablz had come, but the third tunnel. It was wider and darker and it twisted and turned, disorienting her. There were cross tunnels and dead ends like a maze. She was hopelessly lost. She sat down and did something she hadn't done in years: she cried.

What had begun as uncontrollable sobbing and heaving of her breast eventually subsided and now only a few tears rolled down her cheeks. Something poked at her shoulder. She looked up to see Veetit standing next to her shaking his head as if to beckon. He squatted and Melanie climbed upon his back. Swiftly the rhillw galloped down the tunnel, taking a turn here and another there until finally they reached the end of it, where it opened unto a broad valley bordered by spartan hills. There were no flowers, no Pyroon carpeting the ground, but trees (or something that looked like trees) dotted the valley floor. Odd-looking fruit colored purple or chartreuse hung from drooping limbs and yellow vines twisted up the trunks and along the branches.

Veetit took Melanie into a stand of the trees which sheltered a small clearing. There, in the open space within the strange forest, a congregation of many rhillws stood or lay with curled legs or climbed the trees to pick the fruit. Melanie dismounted and Veetit went to one of the rhillws. The two mantis-creatures joined antennae and seemed to be talking. Melanie's mind raced through several possible explanations for the isolated grouping of oversized insects. If this were, indeed, a penal colony, then perhaps segregation was practiced; there were no other creatures—thankfully no hokablzs or other bizarre entities. Or, this group were renegades, hiding out from the hokablz. If they were, in fact, political prisoners, the later theory would make sense. Too bad they weren't mind-readers.

One of the rhillws offered Melanie a purple fruit. It was pulpy and dripped juice. She sniffed it and experimentally ran her tongue across the skin of the fruit. The rhillw grabbed it away from her with its claw-like hands and tore the fruit apart, handing one of the two pieces back to her. It extended its long tongue and began to slurp the tender meat of the half he held. Melanie thought, if it kills me, I won't be too much worse off, and so she raised the fruit to her mouth and took a bite. It wasn't delicious, but it had some flavor born of a slight acidity tinged with sweetness. It was probably the only food she would encounter on this surreal planet. And it hadn't killed her.

Days went by, punctuated by the swift fall of nights with dual moons and an equally swift rising morning sun. Although the nights were short—a matter of ten or fifteen minutes, the days lingered on well past what Melanie had been used to on earth. The explanation for this escaped her: her knowledge of astronomical physics was nil. Maybe the planet wobbled or rotated sporadically or circled its sun in an odd, oval-shaped orbit. Curious. It meant sleeping during the day.

The rhillws had adopted her and treated her, she thought, as if she were their pet. They brought her food and entertained her with a sort of dance during which two or more of the creatures swayed and rubbed antennae and bumped abdomens. She later found out this was a mating ritual although the big bugs were asexual and reproduced by fission. She was privileged to witness one such fission-birth which took place during one of the short nights; the rhillw's body glistened in the double moonlight as it split into two new beings.

Although they pampered her, the rhillw would not allow Melanie to leave the shelter of the woods. One day she found out why. She had edged her way to where the woods gave way to the rest of the valley and had looked out across the plain to where, in the distance, she could see another dense stand of trees. To her dismay, many large brown shapes were emerging from that tree line—hokablzs! They were marching in a line toward her own sheltered sanctum. Was it an attack? She remembered that they were meat-eaters. In horror, she fled back to the clearing and tried to communicate what she had seen. The rhillws sensed her fear and one went to the edge of the woods to observe the approaching horde. When he returned there was much intertwining of antennae and a general chaos. These were relatively helpless creatures when it came to battle. They were all, Melanie thought, probably doomed to become dinner for the hokablzs!

Suddenly, just above the clearing, in a sky not yet turned to the pea soup green of evening, a thick mist was forming. Its appearance caused even more anxiety and turmoil for the rhillw. But Melanie's outlook brightened: the time rift! Only it was too high for her to reach. Too bad these bugs did not have wings. Just as her mood dropped, two shapes fell from the mist cloud and landed right in front of her. The mist then disappeared. Her emotions now were a mix of thrill and dread for the shapes were human bodies and familiar ones at that.

This was hope, but impossible hope. For the two humans that had dropped from the rift were Wayland and Judo, lately come from post-Civil War Baltimore. Yes, they could help fight the hokablzs. But they might die along with the rest of them on this God-forsaken prison planet.

Byron Grush

17

The Hokablzs Attack

Wayland and Judo hit the ground hard, the wind knocked out of them. There was a pair of sandaled feet standing next to them right at eye level. Looking up, Judo was surprised to see Melanie looking down, anguish distorting her face. He and Wayland picked themselves up thinking to embrace the girl they had been missing, but stopped short once the rhillws came into view. Their first sight of a dozen giant praying mantises naturally gave them pause. Bewilderment gave way to incredulity, then a sort of anger at the helplessness the situation had imposed. Traveling through time was bizarre enough, but this…

"What the fuck?" said Judo.

"No time to explain fully," said Melanie. "We are on another planet. Those big bugs are called the rhillw. They are the good guys. We are about to be attacked by the bad guys…giant rats called the hokablz. It's fight or flight, so decide quickly."

"Giant rats?" Wayland began to laugh. "We'll see about that." His hand went to his pocket and withdrew the German luger he had been carrying with him since the assault on Hitler. Judo also found his pistol in the knapsack slung over his shoulder.

"How many bullets have we left?" Judo asked.

"Not enough, but we'll make a stand."

One of the rhillws approached. Melanie recognized it as Veetit as it had a peculiar mark on its back: a sore from when she had ridden on it. Veetit knelt down and beckoned her to mount. He was preparing to run. Melanie shook her head and pointed to Wayland and Judo. "These are my friends," she said, knowing that the rhillw wouldn't understand her words but hoping he would decipher her actions.

Veetit sprinted across the clearing. Soon he was twitching antennae with two other mantis-beings. Presently, the three rhillws returned to where the humans stood and then knelt. "They want us to ride on their backs," Melanie told the others. "They can travel very fast."

"Too late," said Wayland. "Look!"

Emerging from the line of trees were the first few hokablzs. Their large faces, framed by great golden manes, were filled with hatred for the rhillws. Saliva dripped from gleaming incisors. Six of the monster rat-beings advanced, cautiously at first, then hesitated when they saw the three humans. Wayland didn't hesitate: he fired rapidly. Three shots found their marks. Three hokablzs fell forward, bleeding and writhing in pain. The other three turned and ran into the woods.

"Well, that's that," said Wayland.

"I think not," said Judo. "Here they come again!"

This time there were a dozen or more. They charged, leaping on the nearest rhillws and sinking sharp teeth into their necks. Wayland and Judo opened fire with the lugers, taking down a few of the monsters, but soon they were out of ammunition. The line of hokablzs advanced; the rhillws, although they fought bravely, were being ripped to shreds by claw and tooth. One of the hokablzs approached the humans but did not attack them. Instead:

"Hello, human called Melanie. It is I, Shylan. I mean you no harm."

"That is hard to believe. Why are you killing those poor rhillws?"

"Well, we are hungry, aren't we? You will come with me now, you and your mates. You must procreate for us. You will be most beneficial in providing us with food in the days to come."

Melanie turned to Judo. "Can you hear what he is saying? He communicates by telepathy." Judo shook his head. "He wants us to mate so they can eat our children!"

Shocked and repulsed, Judo had a flash of memory—of course from some old movie he had seen as a child. Here was Johnny Weissmuller as Tarzan of the apes, fighting the golden lion with only a knife (where did he buy a knife in the jungle?). Judo had a knife, liberated from a Nazi Brown Shirt. His hand found the weapon and with a yell, not quite a Tarzan yodel but adequate, he rushed the hokablz.

Surprise was on his side as his momentum knocked the rat-thing off balance. Judo was on top of the beast, thrusting his knife into its flesh, over and over. Blood flew into his eyes, momentarily blinding him. Shylan rolled over on top of Judo. His great weight pinned Judo down. His jaws opened red and dripping, and fastened on Judo's shoulder, tearing open the skin—but luckily for Judo, just missing the artery. With an effort supplied by adrenaline, fright, and anger, Judo swung the knife up one final time, severing the hokablz's juggler.

Wayland and Melanie struggled to roll the dead rat-thing off Judo. This accomplished, they examined Judo's wound. Melanie tore some cloth from her blouse and tied it around Judo's shoulder: a makeshift bandage, but it would stop the bleeding—she hoped. Other hokablzs now noticed the humans and began charging toward them.

"Time to make like an atom and split," yelled Wayland. Melanie climbed onto Veetit's back and Wayland and Judo mounted the other two rhillws. Wayland had to restrain himself from shouting, "Giddyap!"

The big bugs raced away from the clearing, away from the slaughter that was ensuing, away from their own kind whom they could not help. They could help the humans, and so they did. They could outrun the aggressors, but they would be followed. Instinctively, the rhillws ran for the tunnels in the base of the hills. It was some distance but it was the only hope of evading the hokablzs.

The shining cliffs they had seen in the distance now loomed before them. They were abnormally smooth and shaped into large cubes like a stack of children' alphabet blocks. There was no doubt

161

this was the work of intelligent beings, but no sign of life was apparent. A chasm in the rock face offered an avenue through the cliff face and into this trotted the rhillws carrying their human cargo. The passageway was narrow, with walls like flat brushed copper. The sky could be seen as a small slit of light many hundreds of feet above them.

Judo was delirious and teetered on the threshold of unconsciousness. The ride on the rhillw's back had been perilous. Several times he nearly slipped off. His wound was bleeding again. The pain that raced through his body was not limited to the bite on his shoulder; the jostling was bruising him and his good arm ached from the tension of holding onto the rhillw's neck.

They came to the end of the passage and entered a large cavern which had been created in the shape of a bowl with an arched ceiling. The sense of it was that they were inside a huge egg. The walls and ceiling of the egg emitted a soft glow. At the other end of the chamber was a round object, as tall as a man. Melanie and Wayland dropped to the floor from their mounts and went to examine the round object.

"I think it's a door," said Wayland. "But how do we open it?"

There were no apparent hinges nor knobs nor keyholes. Wayland pushed and pulled at the edges of the thing but nothing happened. "Maybe you have to say, 'Open Sesame' or something," he said. Melanie studied the door for a moment, then pushed it sideways; it rolled away, revealing another passage. "Elementary," she said. They continued their journey into the depths of the mountain, walking along with the rhillws with Judo still slumped across his mount.

Another dreary tunnel, low ceiling, uneven floor, faint glow from the walls hardly adequate to prevent them from stumbling. And on and on it went. Was it a mistake to come here? Judo needed attention. They were hungry, thirsty, weary. Then a sharp turn to the left…and an opening!

They exited the tunnel into an expansive box canyon, open to the sky but enclosed by steep walls hundreds of feet high. Here were trees, gardens, a bubbling stream. And a pool of glass-clear water that beckoned. Here they lay Judo down on a soft mound of moss while the rhillws drank deeply from the pool. Judo motioned toward the knapsack he still carried; it contained the Nazi soldier's mess kit. Food gone but there was a cup. Melanie brought water from the pool in the cup and managed to get some of the liquid past Judo's parched lips. They rested.

The days passed without incident. The Rhillws had gone to the other end of the canyon. When they returned there were six of them; the mating rituals had been carried out in private this time. Melanie couldn't get the idea of Eden out of her mind—this place was heavenly. It provided food in abundance and the water of the pool seemed to have restorative properties. Indeed, Judo was improving. Cleansing his wounds with water from the pool had hastened the healing. But she was irritated by Wayland's relentless references to Adam and Eve. His advances had been subtle...so far. It was Judo she felt herself drawn to if there ever were a need for them to perpetuate the human race, as the rhillws had perpetuated theirs. Not yet, she assured herself...not yet.

They explored their Eden. Some of the walls had been decorated with carvings and paintings by former residents now long gone. It looked to Wayland like hieroglyphics, as the Egyptians and the Mayans once used. There were also scenes of everyday life. The depictions of the long-gone inhabitants were startling: so very human-looking with long slender fingers and elongated craniums. Wayland said:

"Did you ever read about the theory that the pyramids were actually built by aliens from another planet? The Egyptians would not have had the technology to accomplish it. The Mayan pyramids too."

"That's a lot of nonsense," said Melanie. Flying saucers and ancient astronauts! Poppycock!"

"No, it is a theory given some weight by scientists," said Judo. "And look over here." He pointed to an image that had partially eroded. Faint outlines showed a man wearing a helmet who was seated in some sort of capsule. "A space man. Just like Buck Rogers or Flash Gordon."

"You get all your knowledge from comic books, Judo."

"No, Mel, I read newspapers. I ain't ignorant."

The first time it rained they realized they needed to build a shelter. Running into the tunnel was not a solution as the place was dreadfully sparse and depressing. Melanie and Judo had lived in the Chiskiack village along Chesapeake Bay where the Native Americans constructed yehakin huts from bent saplings. The only tools they had were Judo's knife and the two lugers, but they made do. Soon a domed structure rose near the bank of the pool. Big enough for the three of them.

One day, as Judo had left the camp to explore the box canyon, Wayland and Melanie sat along the bank of the pool watching falling leaves landing one by one on its crystalline surface. Too bad there were no small fish or frogs to entertain them...or to be caught and eaten.

"Do you think we'll be here forever?" Wayland asked.

"There are worse places to be stuck at," she answered. "It's kind of a paradise, isn't it?"

"But lonely. What if we ventured outside? Do you think we could find the whirlwind again?"

"I think we would be eaten by giant rats, is what I think. Aren't you happy here, Wayland?"

"I'd be happier if we could start a little family, Mel. You know how I feel about you."

"Wayland, I love you like a brother, you know that. I'm just not into incest. I don't feel sexual about you. And besides, there's Judo to consider…"

"Judo? What's he got to do with it?"

"Don't you think he'd become an outsider? How would he feel if we…"

"I suppose you *are* attracted to *him*. Is that what this is about?"

"Well, there *is* a sort of animal attraction to him. He has avoided me in the past, in that way. I think he is sensitive about our race difference or some stupid thing. But he's a sweet boy."

"Who's a sweet boy?" Judo had just returned but only heard the very end of the conversation.

"You are, my dear," answered Melanie. "Did you bring me anything?"

"Right. A donut maybe, or a coke? But look, I've been studying those hieroglyphs. I can't read them, of course, but they are a kind of picture writing, aren't they? Certain pictures are repeated, almost as if they were letters of an alphabet. And, you know, there are ones that look like birds or snakes. No birds or snakes here abouts. How did they know what they look like?"

"Maybe they did go to our Earth in their flying saucers and came back. The writing is a diary," offered Wayland.

"Like a photo album. What I did on my summer vacation."

"So, were they the ones who built this place? Lined the tunnels with iridescent stone? Or were they originally from Earth? Came here...and died?" Wayland cut his thought off short. No sense worrying the others about their future.

"From Earth's past, or its future...our future, I mean. If they were time travelers..."

"Lots of questions," said Melanie, "few answers. I'm just going to enjoy our little Garden of Eden. You boys can rack your brains about its mysteries."

A few days later, Melanie and Judo were walking through the gardens past the pool. The sudden fall of night overtook them and they looked up at the twin moons moving across the night sky. The moonlight obscured the stars, but as the orbs passed beyond the canyon's rim, a myriad dancing diamonds appeared.

"Isn't it romantic?" Melanie asked, not expecting an answer—at least, not the answer she would have preferred to hear.

Judo said nothing. He did not pull away, however, when Melanie put her arms around his neck and pulled him toward her. The kiss was deep and long. All of the instances when Judo had been transported through time were as nothing to this entrance into the world of passion. If he had been reluctant to admit his attraction to Melanie because of the difference in their races, that little obstacle no longer existed. It was that, and sex, and a fond regard that was blossoming into love. It was a whirlwind he rode into ecstasy. Time, this time, had indeed stopped.

"What are we going to do about this?" Melanie asked. She had not forgotten about her recent conversation with Wayland. Now they were potentially a vicious triangle. Tensions would rise. Things would be said that were veiled recriminations. "Perhaps we should forget about this. Pretend it didn't happen," she said. "Not take it any further."

"But it did happen. And I'm glad. Why should we hide our feelings now? It will be too hard."

"It's Wayland I'm thinking about. He'll be hurt."

"Ya, well, he's a sweet boy, ain't he?"

They made love there in the garden under the stars, surrounded by exotic blooms and tendrils, their discarded clothing scattered about. It was a good thing these flowers couldn't talk, thought Melanie. After it was over, she said, "Please, don't tell Wayland."

It was one week later when they found the round stone door hidden behind bushes near the other end of the box canyon. They had been visiting the rhillws, whose numbers continued to increase. Judo thought he saw some hieroglyphs on the canyon wall. He forced his way through the brambles to get a better look, and there it was.

They rolled the stone aside expecting a long passageway, but the opening led to a large roofed chamber filled with tables and strange pieces of equipment. It was a laboratory, certainly. Wayland was familiar with many kinds of scientific apparatus from his days at Oakridge, but here he recognized nothing. There were things that looked vaguely electrical, but there were no wires. There were vials and retorts, but no liquids filled them. There were tools, but to what use they had been put he could not say. All in all, it was a mysterious place that suggested either advanced science or occult experimentation.

Judo, for his part, had expected to see a flying saucer or some kind of time machine, but nothing was apparent that would prove his theory that these aliens had built the pyramids. And so they explored and examined and touched. The place was long ago deserted. Just another inexplicable mystery. They were about to return to their own camp when Judo said, "Hold on a moment. There's something behind that bookcase. Wayland? Help me move it?"

There was a floor-to-ceiling bookcase, sans books of course, but piled with paraphernalia and accumulated dust, up against a back wall of the chamber. Peeking from the edge of the case was a bit of molding that indicated a possible doorway. Wayland and Judo put their shoulders to the task and soon had the case away from what was, indeed, a door. Not a round one this time, but a narrow rectangle, taller than the average human and just wide enough for the passage of a single entity, be they human or otherwise. This door did not roll away, nor did it swing sideways: it was hinged from the top like the flap on a dog door—for very tall dogs. Beyond they could see the outside world; it was a scene of endless sand under a dull sun.

"Incredible!" said Wayland. "I did not think we were so close to the other side of the mountain."

"Is that a camel?" exclaimed Melanie, pointing to a hump-backed creature in the distance.

"What are we waiting for?" asked Judo. With that, he was

through the doorway, beckoning for the others to follow. But as he had turned back toward the doorway, he froze in amazement.

"What is it?" Melanie said, and she left the chamber to stand on the sand next to Judo. She turned around. Her expression matched his: utter astonishment. The was nothing left for Wayland to do but to join them and he too turned back toward the doorway and saw...

They had just come through a doorway that was not in the side of a mountain or a hill. It was the obscure entrance to a large stone building shaped incredibly like...

"A Sphinx! Body of a lion, face of a woman, a fucking Egyptian Sphinx," said Wayland.

"Look," said Judo, "the nose has not yet been broken off. I read that Napoleon's army used the Sphinx for artillery practice and shot the nose off. So we are here at some time before that happened."

"That's not all," said Wayland. "Look beyond the Sphinx. What do you see?"

"Nothing. So what?"

"We should be able to see the Great Pyramid. There is nothing there. It hasn't been built yet!"

Byron Grush

18

Einstein, Newton, and the Gravity of the Situation

Zürich, Switzerland, 1905

In Lindenhof Square a giant whirlwind of mist was spitting out objects of antiquity and things from future years and the occasional live specimen of epochs so distant that the clutter on the lawn was like a Surrealist's bad dream. A prehistoric fish lay flapping next to a smooth sphere the size of a basketball on whose surface three-dimensional images danced. A woman, coiffured with a mountain of perfumed hair sat down hard, her voluminous skirts in disarray, a stream of caustic French issuing from her ruby painted lips. A ball used in a Mesoamerican ballgame in long-ago Mayan Belize rolled out of the mist—it was a human head. Something that might have been a pterosaur, a flying reptile from the Triassic period, winged away from the turmoil on delicate membranous wings. And a large Irish wolfhound named Teige appeared and leaped onto Riordan, the alchemist's apprentice, and licked his face in the happy reunion of boy and dog.

Leona Libby and Enrico Fermi watched the boy and the dog. They knew that this whirlwind was the time rift and that it was their chance to return to their own time. "We had better jump into this thing," said Fermi, "before it peters out."

"Enrico," said Libby, "what if we took Einstein back with us?"

"What? Why, then he wouldn't publish his theories. That could drastically alter scientific development. We'd never make the bomb and end the war. At least, I think that is what would happen."

"Perhaps. But he could publish in our time. We could help him."

"Co-author it, you mean. That's a bit presumptuous and certainly unethical."

"But in our time there are so many advances to the theory. If Albert put that wonderful mind of his in congress with our own contemporary thinkers..."

"If he knew that time travel was possible..."

"If we all went into the future beyond our own time..."

"Excuse me, Sir and Madam," said Riordan, "but I think the mist is, as you say, petering out."

The whirlwind had slowed and was diminishing in size and density. In a few moments it would disappear altogether and the chance to return to 1953 would be gone with it. It was time to jump into another era. As they neared the whirling mist a man came running toward them. His unruly head of hair and threadbare suit identified him even from a distance. He was waving his hands and shouting something they could not quite hear.

"Oh my God," said Libby, "it's Einstein!"

"Hello, my colleagues," Einstein said when he reached them. "I wanted to tell you..."

Libby grabbed the famous scientist by the arm and dragged him into the whirlwind. Fermi, Riordan and Teige followed—what else could they do? Enrico Fermi was not about to let Albert Einstein out of his sight, especially since he did not trust Libby's ability to think clearly about the consequences. Riordan simply followed with Teige at his heels. The two scientists from 1953 assumed, without any foundation for the theory, that the mist would return them to their own time. They were wrong.

London, England, 1704

Isaac Newton was still in disguise when he returned to the Tower of London from the Green Sparrow Pub where he had been gathering evidence against Thomas Carlisle, a prisoner currently held in Newgate Prison for the alleged crime of counterfeiting. Carlisle had been observed by Maggie Brighton, bar maid at the Green Sparrow, whom he had enticed by offer of money to visit him at his lodgings in Convent Garden. She testified to having seen Carlisle engaged in the casting of a mold through the use of a white clay earth the consistency she said, of pudding, into which he pressed a sovereign. He then baked the clay to a hardness and poured melted shillings mixed with large amounts of impure pewter into the mold to cast counterfeit coins.

The technique, he had confessed to her, was learned from the now infamous William Chaloner. A man Newton had trapped and brought to justice. Newton had left Cambridge in 1696 to accept the appointment of Warden of the Mint at the Tower of London, a post which helped to cure his financial problems and to give relief after two major mental breakdowns which had threatened his academic career. During his early tenure at the mint he encountered Chaloner who pretended to offer an improved technique to the coiners but really wished to learn more about casting in order to produce superior counterfeits. Newton's investigation of the man had brought him up on trial and by 1699, Chaloner was found guilty, hung, drawn, and quartered. That same year, the Master of the Mint fell ill and died, and Newton was offered the post.

He had continued to track down and persecute counterfeiters and often frequented pubs and boarding houses in disguise for evidence. The state of the mint before Newton's management had been one of chaos. He had set his keen mind to the problems, requiring old coins to be returned and recast and improving the quality and integrity of Britain's money. He would be knighted later next year by Queen Anne (assuming he was still present in this time frame).

The beefeater guard at the gate of the outer ward of the Tower recognized Newton, in spite of his false beard and slouch hat.

Newton devested himself of the beard, hat, and a grubby coat as he entered the complex next to the Lion Tower and crossed by the Royal Menagerie where the snarls of the caged great cats exactly echoed his own mood.

The mint was in a building next to the Salt Tower. From the top of that tower, located on the south-east corner of the wall separating the inner wad from the outer ward, Newton could look at the original fortification built by William the Conqueror in 1078 which was called The White Tower. The square-within a square design of the current complex reminded Newton of one of his fascinations in his study of religion and the occult: The Temple of Solomon. The Temple of Solomon, for Newton, was an example of Sacred Geometry, a sort of map or time-line of the chronology of Hebrew history. Such things greatly interested Newton the alchemist.

In his spare time, when he wasn't acting as a detective or developing better recipes for coinage, Newton experimented with what he called "The Chymistry." It was possible that some of these experiments which involved the tasting of various metals such as lead, gold, mercury, and arsenic, may have led to his mental breakdowns. Although he wrote extensively on alchemical theories, Newton, in Einstein's time, would be best remembered for his Laws of Motion, his theories on Universal Gravitation, his confirmation of Kepler's theories of planetary motion and his theory of color. In fact, he was just about to publish his book, Opticks, in which he would postulate, and demonstrate though the use of prisms, that white light was a composition of the colors of the (visible) spectrum—colors which he conceived being of immutable "corpuscles" which traveled in waves. And of course, he would be credited with co-authoring the Calculus.

Thus it should not have been surprising that Newton would immerse himself in metallurgy for the good of the country. What might have been surprising to some was his expertise in administration. He was not considered the most pleasant of men, but he clearly understood diplomacy. And he brought the chaos at the mint to a controlled situation.

In his own time, Einstein idealized him (although his own theories would supersede Newton's) and kept a picture of him on the wall of his study. So it was the second great surprise of Einstein's life (the first being that he had been abducted into a time warp—

although he was not yet aware of the reality of this) that as he and Libby and Fermi and Riordan (and the dog), rose from where they had landed and dusted themselves off, that he, Einstein, saw the incomprehensible and impossible figure of Isaac Newton lumbering toward them.

"Gott im Himmel," shouted Einstein, "es ist Newton! Ist es möglich?"

"Do I know you, Sir?" asked Newton.

Libby translated for Einstein. "He is astounded to see you, Sir Newton. He knows of your great achievements in science and mathematics. He is also a scientist...Albert Einstein. Lately from Switzerland."

"I am not knighted...not yet, although there is talk of it. A scientist, you say? And you?"

"I am Leona Libby and this is Enrico Fermi, from the United States...you know it as America. We are both scientists. The boy is called Riordan Ó Ciardha, from Ireland. He is...was...an apprentice to the alchemist, Lorcan Mac Conmara."

"I know not of this Mac Conmara, and I have read many a treatise on the Chymistry. But I should very much like to have a dialogue with you all. I have a small workshop here next to the Mint. Please come be my guests. And you may bring your dog. Is he too a scientist?"

Throughout the discourse, Einstein remained befuddled. He was only able to catch a word or two of the English spoken but he reasoned that something very unique was happening...something that foretold of a great revelation that might add to his knowledge of the workings of the universe. As they walked to the workshop, Fermi said to Libby that it might be propitious to enlighten Einstein as to who, and from when, they were, and how they had gotten here. Einstein already had his suspicions.

While Newton demonstrated his light experiments, sending a beam of sunlight through a prism to be splashed as a rainbow of colors against the wall (to the delight and fascination of Riordan), Libby took Einstein aside and began to tell him their story in German.

"You will not believe me, but we all, you included now, are travelers through time. Enrico and I embarked from the U.S. in 1953 and found ourselves in Zürich in 1905. Of course we had to look you up…meet you as you are quite famous in our time for your theories. I'm sorry I more or less kidnapped you and brought you to the 17th century. You must admit though, meeting Isaac Newton is worth the inconvenience."

"This is a trick, or a I am dreaming. You cannot travel through time…certainly not into the past!"

"We would have agreed with you then, but we met Riordan, the lad who claimed to be an alchemist's apprentice from the 16th century. The more we talked and listened to him, the more he seemed credible. Then a colleague of ours, another scientist named Dr. Madison James McGinley, disappeared. He had been experimenting with time and had succeeded in bringing back objects from the past with a device of his own design. We began our own experiments, Enrico and I, and…here we are! We couldn't tell you this before because we didn't want to influence the past and possibly change the future. We don't want to tell Newton about this for the same reason."

But Isaac Newton now stood next to them, a crooked smile on his face. "You didn't know I read and speak the German language to aid in my studies of the Chymistry?" he said. Then to Einstein, in perfect 17th century German, he said, "Herr Einstein, what shall we do with these charlatans? Send them to the torture chamber beneath the White Tower until they start to tell the truth? Or are you part of this conspiracy? Are you all counterfeiters? That is punishable by death!"

"Oh this is a farce," exclaimed Einstein. "You, who purport to be a man who has been dead for 250 years, disbelieve in me? Did an apple really fall on your head?"

"Something much larger seems to have fallen on yours. At least…at least we agree on one thing: we can't both be right."

"If you are really Isaac Newton, then answer me this: what is your theory of gravity…and don't tell me about apples."

"Ah, an inquisition. The mass of an object…you understand the term, mass?…exerts a force which attracts other objects. The greater the mass, the stronger the force. The distance between the objects is a factor which I describe as influencing gravity by the inverse square of its proportions. This coincides with Kepler's Law of Harmonies."

"And you require mass to exist whenever there is gravity?"

"Well, that would follow, wouldn't it?"

"How then, how does gravity bend light, when light has no mass? You have followed the only way that a man of the highest degree of intelligence in your age might use to conclude what the laws governing the workings of the universe might be. But you have fallen somewhat short of the answer. Your explanations work locally, but not universally. You believe that time and space are constants. I say that they are not. I say that matter can affect space and that space can affect matter. I say time is not a constant."

"Gravity," complained Newton, "is an instantaneous force which acts at a distance. It is a vector traveling through 3-dimensional space at a constant rate relative to the amount of mass which generates it."

"Space," answered Einsein, "is curved and warped by gravity which depends not on the presence of mass. Time is a fourth dimension we may add to the equation."

"Space is absolute. Absolute space, without regard to anything external, always remains similar and immovable. If you talk about relative space, then this is some movable dimension or measure of the actual absolute space."

"You are talking about what we might call the 'aether.' The aether is not absolute with no physical properties. It is geodesic and within it, the presence of matter determines the structure of spacetime."

"This is not within our experience. This cannot be proven by the calculus as can my view of the universe. I do not know who you are or whence you came, but your ideas will never supersede mine. Now as to this claim of time travel…"

"Here, said Einstein, "we certainly agree. If I am Einstein, then you cannot be Newton. Conversely, if you are Newton, then I cannot be Einstein. If we are both who we say we are, then at least one of us has traveled in time and space. It is an intriguing thought."

"I have enjoyed our intellectual sparring, I must say. Your ideas, although obviously flawed, will be on my mind for the near future. Curved space…gravity regardless of mass…well, there may be something there. Or not."

"And you, Newton, have given us the basis for every new idea that has and will come along. You are a man for all seasons."

"I have only but stood on the shoulders of giants."

Libby had been translating as best she could for Fermi's benefit. Now that the discourse between Einstein and Newton had turned to mutual congratulations, Libby and Fermi focused their own thoughts on the dilemma into which they had fallen. Would Newton really consider Einstein's "wild" theories? How would that change the evolution of scientific thought? If Einstein never returned to his own time, would others envision general relativity? Would there be an atomic bomb? In this day and age, could another time machine be constructed? Where would the enormous energy required to set it in motion come from?

Meanwhile, Riordan Ó Ciardha was perusing Newton's substantial library that occupied one whole wall of the workshop. Of interest to him were various works on alchemy and the occult. Here he found a copy of Robert Fludd's *Apologia Commendiaria Fraternitatem de Rosea Cruce*, an "appology" for the Brethren of the Rosy Cross in support of their doctrines, and his *Tractatus Theologo-Philosophicus*, which was his mystical account of life, death, and resurrection. There were manuscripts such as Roger Bacon's *Tract on the Tincture and Oil of Antimony*, *The Art of Distillation* by John French, Francis Bacon's *Experiments touching Sulphur and Mercury*, and his *The Making of Gold*, Edward Kelly's *Theatre of Terrestrial Astronomy*, and his *The Stone of the Philosophers*.

He was unfamiliar with many of these titles but concerning their subject matter, Riordan was a proficient student, having poured through many a treatise in the workshop of the alchemist, Lorcan Mac Conmara. Thus, once there was a lull in the conversation, Riordan boldly asked Isaac Newton, "Have you found the Philosopher's Stone?"

This prompted Newton to question Leona Libby with the following: "You say you are from the future. By your time, has the Philosopher's Stone been found? Has the transmutation of metals been achieved? Have you made gold from lead?"

"As to the Philosopher's Stone," answered Libby, "it depends on what you mean by that term. If you mean by it that it is a process which can modify elements, purifying them, such as turning vulgar lead into angelic gold, and that this same process may be used to purify the soul, then…no. You see, I know a little of your alchemy too. The human soul is far from pure in our own age. As to the metals, certain compounds may, of course, be made, but changing one base metal into another is patently impractical. Making gold would cost more than its eventual worth after production. Sorry."

"I might add," said Fermi, abandoning his taboo of not revealing the future, "that some elements may be changed through natural processes. We have achieved the release of energy through bombarding unstable elements with the parts of atoms of which your time has not yet dreamed. This," he said, turning to Einstein, "was built upon your theories of General Relativity that you will refine in the coming years."

"I don't think I understand," said Einstein, after Libby translated for him.

"Sir, we split the atom and in a chain reaction, released energy of the greatest magnitude. It may have been a boon…or the beginning of the end for us all. You see, with the technology that science created, the politicians built a bomb that could destroy an entire city. It was used to end a war. But it has ironically perverted the opportunity for peace."

"And this is my fault?"

"Enrico is exaggerating," said Libby. "If it was anyone's fault it was all of us together. How do you harness the power of the Sun without burning your fingers?"

Riordan had just found a copy of a translation of the *Corpus Hermeticum* of Hermes Trismegistus and was carefully pulling it from the bookshelf when something white and wispy began to flow under the door. A tendril of mist had wound its way through the courtyards and over the battlements of the Tower of London, as if searching for something…or someone.

Isaac Newton noticed the tendril as it pushed into the room. It looked to him like so much bloody ectoplasm unraveling from the spirits of the dead—Anne Boleyn or Catherine Howard or Lady Jane Grey, all of whom were executed in the Tower during the reign of Henry VIII. Or perhaps it was the ghosts of the two children of Edward IV whose skeletons would one day be found buried beneath what was called The Bloodier Tower. Or the ghost of Arbella Stuart, Elizabeth I's cousin, who starved to death during her arrest in the Tower; she had married without having permission from the Queen. Yes, there were plenty of ghosts at the Tower of London.

The tendril rose from the floor like a translucent dancing snake. A ghostly hand formed at the end of it as it wound around the hapless scientists, the boy, and the dog. They were wrapped in mist and pulled into an even denser miasmas where they vanished from the century of Isaac Newton. Their destination would surprise even Riordan Ó Ciardha, who was not easy to surprise.

19

How Times Have Changed

St. Charles Avenue, New Orleans, 1869

It was crowded in the time machine. Dr. Madison James McGinley, lately from 1851 London and his duplicate, Dr. Madison James McGinley lately from 2153 New York, Lorcan Mac Conmara, and his duplicate, one lately from 1851 London and the other from 2153 New York, Wayland Delaney, and a dog named Teige also from 2153 New York, were shoulder to shoulder and elbow to elbow as the machine settled down in an alley off St. Charles Avenue, just behind the Saint Nicholas concert saloon.

Kathy O'Neal had just emerged from the side entrance of the saloon carrying a basket of empty bottles to deposit in the trash bin as the time machine materialized in front of her. She dropped the basket. Bottles rolled along the cobblestone pavement. A door opened in the large black box and out of it came two men who must be twins (she thought) followed by two more men (also twins—a rare occurrence in these parts to see even one set of twins much less two), a young man and a dog. "Golly!" she said.

McGinley from 1851 London, realizing that the girl had witnessed their arrival, quickly tried to divert her attention. "Excuse me, Miss, I see that you have been sun-struck by this awfully intense daylight we have today, and that you'd dropped your bottles. May we help you retrieve them?'

"Golly," repeated Kathy O'Neal. "Who are y'all, and how…how did you get this carriage into the alley without no horses? And no wheels, neither!"

"Um, it's just a large packing crate that has fallen off from a wagon. We were…just checking the contents to see if there was any damage. Luckily, there is not."

But McGinley was not so sure about possible damage to the time machine. He had accurately, he thought, entered the proper coordinates for County Cork in the sixteenth century. This was clearly not Ireland. It was…

"Where are you from? Are you Yankees? Y'all ain't from N'awlins, now are ya?"

McGinley introduced himself and his traveling companions as Wayland scampered to collect the scattered bottles. Teige took the opportunity to stroll over to the trash bin, lift his leg, and pee for many long minutes. After all, his bladder had been inactive for 284 years. Kathy O'Neal explained that she worked in the St. Nicholas as a bar maid.

"It's 'bar jerker' that they calls us, but us girls prefer waitress."

Now Wayland perked up, always thinking of the pleasures of life such as food and drink. "Would you have something to eat inside? I'm mighty hungry…and thirsty."

"Again I ask, you aren't Yankees, are ya? My boss, Mr. Clements, he was in the war, on the Confederate side, of course. He hates Yankees."

"Miss, we are from Tennessee. And the Mac Conmara's are from Ireland."

"Tennessee? Well, that's kind of north, but I guess y'all fought on the side of the Secession. Ireland? Hmmf. Come in and I'll fix you up with something to wet your thirst. Early, it is. The entertainment doesn't start until six o'clock. But it's oh, so splendidly decorated inside. There's a big ol' mural and a picture of Don Coyote to see."

Once they were seated at a large round table under the painting that even Wayland identified as Don Quixote and Sancho Panza, McGinley determined to pin down the exact date.

"With the war over," he said to the girl when she returned with a tray of mugs filled with frothy beer, "are there still troubles...you know, with the Negroes?"

"What with that President Lincoln winning his third term, there's been a heap of trouble. He just barely sneaked by that Andrew Johnson and won by only a few votes, they say. And Johnson...he was the vice president, that's true, but he were a Democrat. He would of kept the darkies in their place, oh yes. Imagine. Lincoln, he no longer calls his party the Union, it now the Republics. And Reconstruction that he went and made us do...that's caused a whole lot of trouble. Yes sir! A whole lot of trouble."

"Lincoln...he wasn't assassinated?" blurted Wayland.

"Assassinated? Don't be talkin' aloud about that. There's people might be thinkin' along those lines, of course...but...the walls have ears, ya know."

McGinley from 1851 leaned over to McGinley from 2153 and said, in a low voice, "Somethings is clearly wrong with the space-time continuum."

The other McGinley answered, "Someone may have altered history. Or, someone will alter history. Obviously, the time machine isn't functioning correctly."

"You weren't there in England when Wayland...the other Wayland...disappeared, but I was, and I worried then that he might be meddling with time."

"This is serious." He looked up at the painting of Don Quixote. "Ironic, but apropos. We seem to be chasing windmills!"

Wayland had his own ideas—amorous ones. He whispered to Kathy O'Neal, "Would you like to see inside of the...packing crate? That's not what it is, you know."

"I thought not. Yes, I do."

"Come outside in a few minutes." Then to the others: "I'm going outside to check on Teige. Be right back."

Perhaps he was just showing off. Perhaps it was the low cut of her blouse. Perhaps he was just lonely. Perhaps, as usual, he hadn't thought things through. And Kathy? Well, he might be just a boy, but he was cute. And she really did wonder what was inside of the big boxy thing in the alley. Wayland held the time machine's door open and she went inside. He followed and Teige followed him.

Kathy stared at the assortment of dials and switches and blinking lights. It was like nothing that she had ever seen before. "What is it?" she asked.

"It's a time machine," said Wayland. "See, I can set the coordinates for any time and place I want and…zoom, we're there."

"No you can't. That's not possible." This was not the thing to say to a love-starved youth who was desperate to impress a lady.

"I can and I will. Here, I'll set the time machine to take us to my own time, 1953 in Oakridge, Tennessee. We'll go, take a look, then come right back before the others miss us."

And so he manipulated the dials and switches as he had seen the scientists do and threw the main lever. There was a hum which became a sort of grinding sound, some buzzing, flashing lights, a jolt…and the machine settled down again. But not in Oakridge, Tennessee in 1953.

Inside the St. Nicholas, the four scientists were getting restless:

"Wayland has been gone a long time," said one of the McGinleys.

"If he's wandered off, then he's on his own," said the other McGinley.

"We should be off ourselves," said one of the Mac Conmaras.

"Anyone have any money?" asked the other Mac Conmara.

"I've got a fiver," said one of the McGinleys.

"Twentieth century money," said the other McGinley, "and with a picture of Lincoln on it!"

They threw down the bill, although useless to the proprietor, and made for the exit. Outside in the alley, they were astounded to find that the time machine was gone, and probably Wayland with it.

Inside the saloon, John Clements, the proprietor, saw the men leave, saw that his bar jerker girl was nowhere to be seen, saw the bill on the table with its picture of Lincoln, and he also made for the exit. He was just in time to see a white sphere of translucent mist forming at the end of the alley, rolling swiftly toward the four men, enveloping them, and then rolling away as it slowly faded out of existence. John Clements reentered his saloon and poured himself a large glass of whiskey.

San Francisco Bay, 1949

Wayland eased open the door of the time machine and took a look. A great expanse of waterfront was all he saw. That and the gray hulk of a battleship bobbing impatiently at the end of a long pier, a swarm of sea gulls lifting up and gliding with the updrafts, a myriad of men in uniforms hustling back and forth, a tall crane swinging a rope net filled with boxes out and over the edge of the ship, and a sun like the blurry red eye of a drunken sailor inching its way into the morning sky.

"I think we missed our mark," Wayland told the girl. "There ain't no ocean in Tennessee."

"This ain't the bayou neither," said Kathy. "That's a hell of a big boat, that is."

"I see a bar up the boardwalk. Let's go see if we can find out where and when we are."

"I *am* a bit thirsty."

The Plucky Pelican occupied a prime spot near the dock side of the Naval pier. Ocean spray had eroded most of the paint on the wooden slats that served as an outside wall and the windows were so dusty and dirty it was hard to tell if the establishment was open or not. But, of course, a bar like the Plucky Pelican never closed. Wayland and Kathy entered the bar to the disapproval of the bartender, who looked askance at the girl.

"This may not be an appropriate venue for the missy," he told Wayland. "It be a rough place here."

"I've handled rougher than you can bring on," answered Kathy, "back at the St. Nick. I'll have a whisky, neat, and hurry it up!"

"Rum and coke for me," said Wayland.

They sat in a wooden booth that needed more paint than the outside of the bar itself. Patrons had carved their initials in the wood and attempted crude drawings of nude women. As they waited for their drinks, Wayland looked around. On one wall was a poster with block lettering that said, "Loose lips sink ships," and which showed two men talking while the racist caricature of an Asian man with an oversized ear hovered over them. Across the room on another wall hung a calendar featuring a realistic painting of a naked girl reclining against a blue velvet backdrop. Wayland couldn't quite make out the date, but the month appeared to be February. He was about to amble over to check it out when the bartender arrived with their drinks.

"That'll be a dollar, fifty-five," he said. "You ain't in uniform. You a deserter, or did you score a furlow?"

"I'm…I'm not a soldier. 4F. What's the big hullabaloo going on out on the pier?"

The bartender glanced at the poster. Loose lips. "Dunno. Think maybe they saw another Jap sub out in the bay yesterday."

"War's still on," said Wayland, absentmindedly voicing what should have obvious. "That calendar correct? It doesn't feel like February."

"Ha! That's an old one. Can't make myself take it down and part with the lovely thing. You probably noticed it says 1947. Two years it's hung there, waiting for the next issue, but what with the war…"

"It's 1949? We're still fighting Japan? I though we ended the war by dropping the atom bomb on them."

"The what? What's an atom bomb? If we had one, you can be sure we'd a dropped it on 'em. Say…what's with you? Been in a coma since Pearl Harbor?"

"Um…I've been out of the country. South America."

"They don't have newspapers in South America?"

"And Hitler. Are we still fighting Hitler?"

"Who, may I be so bold to ask, is Hitler?"

"You know, Nazis…Germany. Heil Hitler and all that."

"Why would we be fighting Germany, you idiot? We sent troops to fight along side of them when Russia attacked them. Fucking Stalin has eaten up most of Europe now…Germany, Czechoslovakia, Hungary, Austria, and now he's entering France. We're spread so thin in the Pacific we can't help them anymore. You must have escaped from a loony bin. I'm calling the MPs."

"That's all right…we're leaving. Thanks for the info."

"Wayland, honey," said Kathy, "I'm still nursin' this whisky. This really *bad* whiskey."

"Out!" said the bartender. "You get out now before I get really angry."

Back in the time machine, Kathy asked Wayland, "What dat all that about? You gave that bar jerker quite a conniption."

"In my time, history was that we fought the Japanese, and the

Germans, and the Italians in what is called World War Two. We won that war. But it would seem that history has been changed, at least according to the bartender."

"Maybe he be drinking his own liquor."

"I'm going to bump us forward in time just a bit. I have to see for myself."

Wayland flipped the control lever quickly up, then down. Opening the door slowly, he peered out to see...

"Japanese soldiers marching up the street! There are signs on the buildings written in Japanese characters! The Plucky Pelican is a Japanese bar now. Oh, Kathy, I don't think we're in Kansas anymore."

"Kansas?"

"Never mind. We've got to go back to your time and find the professors. First Lincoln and now this. Something is wrong with time."

"I still don't believe you been takin' us to the future. It's a trick! Some sort of magic lantern show. But even if true...so what? So what if the Japanese are marching through town? It's all the same to me."

"No, it means we lost the big war. It means there was no atom bomb to make the Japs surrender. And no Hitler? There was a time when I fantasized about going back in time and killing Hitler. That would have saved the lives of six million Jewish people! Something has prevented his rise to power in this time frame. I wonder...oh God! What if I...my other self...what if I did go back? Have I changed history? And not for the good? Oh, Kathy, what am I going to do?"

"You are going to take me back to N'awlins and we'll have a good stiff drink and forget all about this."

"But the time machine...it isn't hitting space-time right. I set the coordinates, but it misses the mark."

"My daddy said, if you're trying to shoot a running wild turkey, you need to aim a little ahead of it."

"Ahead or behind? And how much? All I can do is set the coordinates for New Orleans...what was the year?"

"1869. April 21st."

"Jesus! Okay, here goes nothing."

Dials dialed, switches switched, levers flipped, and the time machine hummed obediently, jerked a little, shook a little, and settled with a gentle jostle. Wayland gingerly eased open the door. "Oh shit!" he said.

Sand. Endless tracks of sand. A dull sun hanging in the haze of a distant sand storm. No people. No towns. No trees. Not even a lizard or a snake. But…

"Is that a camel?" asked Kathy.

"Well this sure as hell isn't New Orleans. I guess we better try again…this time leading the turkey at little."

But when Wayland threw the lever to start the machine…

"Oh-oh. I think we're out of gas."

Nothing he did could persuade the machine to spring to life. It didn't run on gasoline, of course, and Wayland had no idea where to look for the gauge or whatever, that might lend a clue as to the machine's demise. In frustration, he exited the time machine and thrust his hands down into the sand, scooping up a quantity to fling into the air without purpose except to feed his anger. He had expected the sand to be hot, or at least warm, but it was cool. The sun at the horizon was not setting, it was rising, and it had yet to warm the dessert terrain.

Behind him came a low mewing sound such as a camel might make to get attention. He turned to see the creature standing next to him. Only it wasn't exactly a camel. It was the creature Kathy had seen off in the distance that looked like a camel. But up close the differences were dramatic: thick stocky legs like a shortened elephant, a wispy long tail like that of a Clydesdale horse (and flapping rapidly), short spotted hair much like a dalmatian's, if such a dog had yellow skin and purple spots, the face and bulbous lips of a camel, to be sure, but with a pair of hairy antennae that wiggled and jiggled like the wind-blown branches of a willow.

"Kathy," Wayland called, "come out and see what just came to visit."

Once Kathy had emerged from the time machine and registered her amazement, the two humans thought they heard the camel-like thing speaking—a voice intruded into their minds. The voice told them not to be alarmed. It told them their machine was useless now. They would have to trust him.

"Did you hear that too?" asked Kathy, hoping that Wayland would answer in the negative—this just couldn't be happening.

"Unless we've fallen asleep while reading a Doctor Seuss book and we're both dreaming the same dream, I think we've just met an alien being," said Wayland.

"Doctor who?" asked Kathy.

"Correction," said the camel-like thing, "it is you who are the aliens here."

A second voice rang out behind them: "Wayland! What are you doing over here? Come back and help Judo and me find the door." It was Melanie, who had wandered over from the Sphinx to investigate the strange appearance of the black box that was the time machine. Then: "Oh! Another human! Who is this, Wayland? What does it all mean?"

"Judo is here?" asked Wayland. "You are here? Where *is* here? and...a talking camel? I'm losing my mind!"

Too many questions, not enough answers. The camel-like thing was no help, but it suggested moving on before the sun rose to its zenith and made the world insufferably hot. Melanie led them back to where the Sphinx stood, just over a large dune. Wayland came face to face with Wayland, his double, created when their time-frames had overlapped. Or was it he who was the double?

Explanations flew back and forth as the time travelers looked in vain for the door into the Sphinx which had disappeared. They pushed and pulled and poked, but to no avail. The sun was climbing higher and the air was becoming warmer and warmer. The camel-like thing strolled off; perhaps it knew where there was some shade—but it wasn't talking.

"I don't understand," Melanie said to Wayland, "how there can be two of you."

"I have to ditto that," said Kathy. "Talking camels and so-called time traveling has been enough for one day. Now there are two Waylands."

"What is worse," said the Wayland who had just arrived in the time machine, "is that you (talking to the other Wayland), have totally screwed up time by killing Hitler."

"You would have done the same thing," the other Wayland answered. "After all, you *are* me!"

"If we don't find this door," said Judo, "we'll all be in big trouble. We have no water, no shade, and it's getting hotter and hotter."

They had worked their way around to the front of the Sphinx.

There were indentations in the stone that seemed promising, but so far, nothing budged.

"Do you remember what the riddle of the Sphinx was?" asked Judo. "It was some Greek guy that answered the riddle and the Sphinx died."

"Judo," said Melanie, "that is just a myth. You may as well say something like, 'open sesame' and it will help as much."

It was just then that a brief cloud of mist appeared and from it stepped the two alchemists, the two professors, and the dog, Teige.

"Oh my God" said Kathy, "the twins again!"

20

The Riddle of the Sphinx

The present issues from the past, and the future from the present. Everything is made one by this continuity. Time is like a circle, where all the points are so linked that one cannot say where it begins or ends, for all points precede and follow one another for ever.

—— Hermes Trismegistus, *Corpus Hermeticum*

They had worked their way around to the front of the Sphinx, walking between the long outstretched arms of the lion-figure. They had still not found the door. Judo was musing about the riddle of the Sphinx. It was just then that a brief cloud of mist appeared and from it stepped the two Lorcan Mac Conmaras, the two Dr. Madison James McGinleys, and the dog, Teige.

"Oh my God" said Kathy, "the twins again!"

Lorcan Mac Conmara, the one lately from 1851 London, looked

189

up at the face of the Sphinx before him. Undaunted by this encounter with the other time travelers or even by the strange location where they now they found themselves, he was fascinated with the ancient structure. The other Mac Conmara stood next to him, nodding.

"Do you think?" said the one to the other.

"Perhaps," was the answer. This Mac Conmara turned to Judo and said, "You were asking about the riddle of the Sphinx just as we came out of the mist. Do you know what that was?"

Judo said, "It was something like, what walks on four legs in the morning, two legs at noon, and three legs in the evening? The answer is…man. A baby crawls on all fours, the adult walks on two, and the old man uses a cane."

"Very good. But there was another. There are two sisters: one gives birth to the other and she, in turn, gives birth to the first. Who are the two sisters?"

"Oh, that's a good one. I don't know. What's the answer?"

"They are night and day. The Greek's name was Oedipus, and answering the riddle caused the Sphinx to cast herself down from the high rock where she stood guarding the entrance to Thebes."

"But isn't it all just a myth?" asked Melanie, getting a little frustrated with the discussion which was keeping them from finding the door. It was just then that another brief cloud of mist appeared and from it stepped Leona Libby, Enrico Fermi, Albert Einstein, Isaac Newton, Riordan Ó Ciardha, and another Irish wolfhound named Teige, who was, in fact, the first dog's double (or was it the other way around?)

"I think I'm going to be sick," said Kathy O'Neal. "There are just too many people here to deal with for my poor little brain."

The two Teiges were sniffing each other's hind quarters. They seemed nonplused by the fact of their doubling. Enrico Fermi embraced Dr. McGinley. "I'm so happy to see you," he said, "we thought you had been lost in the fire." Then he noticed the other Dr. McGinley. Riordan looked from one alchemist to the other, threw up his hands and said, "Masters! We are united again." Einstein simply sat down on the sand, exhausted from the events he was witnessing which were clearly impossible, and therefore would require the utmost thinking in order to bring them into a theoretical but logical rationality.

Newton, like the alchemists next to him, stared up at the face of the Sphinx. "Yes, of course," he mumbled. The two alchemists heard him and said to him, "Sir, we were just talking about the riddle of the Sphinx. Perhaps you are familiar with the story."

"There was a book of emblems by Michael Maier called *Atlanta Fugiens*, which came out in 1617, I believe," said Newton. "I have it in my library. He talks about the riddle in it. He thinks that the answer about the three ages of man is misleading. It is the Quadrangle of the Four Elements which is most important. The Stone, he maintains, is only the Triangle in essence …that is, the Body, the Soul, and the Spirit. It is most importantly the Quadrangle in its quality. I remember having read this just recently."

"Sir," said one or the other of the Mac Conmaras, "you are an alchemist? I do not know of this Maier, but the Triangle of Sol, Luna, and Mercury is very familiar. The Quadrangle of Earth, Fire, Air, and Water is, as you say, the most important to consider."

Riordan still clutched the copy of the *Corpus Hermeticum* of Hermes Trismegistus, which he had taken from Newton's bookshelf. Newton saw this and said to the boy, "Yes, the Hermes Trismegistus. Here in what may be ancient Egypt, that book may have meaning for us."

Riordan began to thumb through the book; its pages were creased and soiled from much use.

"There is the Asclepius dialogue in it," continued Newton, "in which Hermes describes how to imprison the souls of angels and demons within statues so as to make them speak and prophesize the future. Perhaps this Sphinx has been visited by magicians of yore."

Riordan had found a certain page which interested him and so he began to read:

> *Aye, I saw the great path opened*
> *and looked for the instant into the beyond.*
>
> *Knew I then that all that has being*
> *is growing to meet yet another being*
> *in a far-off grouping of space and of time.*
>
> *Knew I then that in Words are power*
> *to open the planes that are hidden from man.*

*Aye, that even in Words lies hidden the key
that will open above and below.*

*Hark ye, now man, this word I leave with thee.
Use it and ye shall find power in its sound.*

*Say ye the word:
"ZIN-URU"
and power ye shall find.*

Perhaps it was a coincidence. Perhaps it was fate. Or perhaps it was the power of the sound of the Word. The ground shook and the front of the great Sphinx began to tremble. Gradually an opening appeared where before there had been only the weathered bedrock of the statue's construction. They had found the door.

Entering, Melanie had expected to find the Eden-like garden from which they had come when exiting through another door had placed them outside of the Sphinx. Instead, she now looked into a cavernous chamber with a high vaulted ceiling. The walls and the ceiling were covered with paintings and niches along the walls held statues of men wearing headdresses and tunics, just like pictures she had seen of Egyptian carvings. At the very end of the chamber stood a large statue that gleamed in sunlight that entered the chamber through the open door; it was covered with gold. Once the group had all entered the chamber of the Sphinx, the door closed and threw the chamber into darkness.

"I saw a torch hanging on that wall," said Newton. "How can we light it?"

"I've a match here somewhere," said one of the McGinleys, searching through his vest pocket where he kept his pipe, a tin of Virginia flake, and a box of safety matches. Stumbling toward what he vaguely remembered to be the location of the torch, McGinley began feeling across the wall. His hand touched the wooden handle and a few seconds later, he had struck a match and held it to the wad of linen that was the torch. The linen burst into flame so suddenly and intensely that McGinley fell backwards. But being ancient, like everything in the surrounding chamber, the fire lasted only momentarily.

"Drat it!" said Newton.

As they stood in darkness, unsure of their next move, they began to see a subtle luminescence emanating from the walls. The glow increased gradually until a rosy brightness like that of early dawn filled the large space. Now they saw, centered in the chamber, a long table of blackest obsidian. On the table sat a row of goblets of pounded copper filled with some pinkish liquid. Next to these were plates made of purest amber, and on the plates were whole fish, recently cooked to perfection and staring up at them with smoky eyes.

Seated at the far end of the table was a man, good looking, with coal black hair tied with a black ribbon in back, dressed in the clothing of an 18th century country gentleman—all in black and white, ruffles and buttons. His hands, which betrayed an extreme age not noticeable in face or figure, were bejeweled with rings of platinum and precious stones. His shoes sported buckles studded with gems and pearls. He smiled at the startled group before him and gestured. "Please sit and partake of food and drink," he told them. "Do not be surprised at my presence. We will talk, and soon, all will become clear to you."

There was a natural hesitation by all except the two Waylands. Both sat immediately and lifted goblets to their lips. "Delicious," said one. "Agreed," said the other. Meanwhile, the two Teiges were exploring the chamber. One lifted his leg at the golden statue and peed upon it. The man in black saw this and laughed. Finally, the rest did sit and sample the fare before them.

"My name," began the man, "is le Comte de Saint Germain. I have been known by other titles—le Marquis de Montferrat, le Comte Bellamarre, and Prinz Rakoczi, to name a few. I will be 500 years old next Thursday. Voltaire called me 'der Wundermann, a man who knows everything and never dies.' Giacomo Casanova referred to me as a celebrated and learned impostor, but I assure you, I am no fake.

"I speak all the languages of Europe and the Middle East, compose and play music, and I can transmute other metals into gold. Ah! This interests you? I also know how to melt diamonds and can combine several small ones together to form large and very valuable gems. I invented Masonry and taught Alessandro Count di Cagliostro about the Elixir of Life and the Kabbalah.

"I studied with Gian Gastone, the last of the Medici. I have met and am known by the crown heads of France, Germany, and England. I helped Catherine the Great in her quest to become Queen of Russia. I held seances for King Louis XV. I was the favorite of Madame de Pompadour. I warned Marie Antoinette that there were dire changes to come. I have traveled to the Hague, Saint Petersburg, London, Berlin, Venice, Nierenberg, Amsterdam, and of course, Paris. And now I am here to entertain and possibly enlighten you."

One of the McGinleys looked askance at the Count. He had a vague recollection of reading about this man: a legend and a brilliant con man! But no matter what he claimed, he was now a source of information which they desperately needed. He asked: "Count, exactly where *is* here? Are we in Giza, Egypt, at the site where the pyramids will someday rise?"

"It is difficult to say. You must wait until She arrives to answer all questions and determine your fate."

"She? Who is this She you speak of?"

"Ah, I see the young man there has a tome purporting to be a collection from her many writings… the *Corpus Hermeticum*. That is who She is."

Riordan still clutched the book by Hermes Trismegistus. "But Sir," he said, "Hermes is a woman?"

"Sometimes, when it suits her. She is the last of the Old Ones. It was She who brought you all here to answer for your indiscretions. You have meddled with Time, have you not? Tsk, tsk. Naughty, naughty. She is not pleased."

Libby leaned over to Fermi and whispered, "Who is this fruitcake?" Fermi shrugged.

Newton now confronted the Count: "If indeed you know the way to make gold, you must tell me. What is the Philosopher's Stone? What is the secret to eternal life?"

"Ah, my friend, but that would be telling," the Count answered.

"I don't believe you could know Hermes Trismegistus. He dates to the time of Moses. Cagliostro, maybe. But you profess too much nonsense…melting diamonds, indeed!"

Now both of the Mac Conmaras chimed in at the same time. Then: "You go first," said the one. No, you go first," said the other. Finally: "Count Saint Germain, you know that at least four of our group are students of the alchemy. We, and particularly, young Riordan here, would enjoy hearing of your experiences in pursuing the Philosopher's Stone. Will you not enlighten us?"

"Ah...you may know that I published, in France, my book which I called, *La Tres Sainte Trinosophie*? It has a subtitle of 'The Holy Magic revealed to Moses, discovered within an Egyptian monument and preciously preserved in Asia under the emblem of the Winged Dragon.' You should look to that tome if you wish to peruse my philosophic enterprises."

"I have heard of that book," said Newton, "although I have been unable to obtain a copy for my library. I thought, however, that it was Cagliostro who penned it. And anyway, it is purportedly in cypher. A triangular shaped book with writings missing vowels, sometimes upside down, littered with obscure symbols and drawings. Incomprehensible."

"Incomprehensible?" said the Count. "Shall I tell you a story? Shall I allow you to enter into that sanctuary of the sublime sciences wherein the Eternal has secured its secrets? Shall I lift for you the impenetrable veil which prevents the eyes of common man from seeing this mystical spectacle? Shall I tell you of my own journey through the Hall of Thrones into the Palace of Wisdom where I performed certain rites to become master of the elemental spirits who opened for me the doors of immortality? Yes?

"Then listen, but beware of thoughts to follow exactly in the path I took...names of certain things I will withhold for your safety. At Pozzuoli near Naples is the crater of the Solfatara. Upon its crags the vapors of sulfur can be seen even by moonlight. That night, however, clouds obscured the moon. My head was covered with a linen veil. In my hands was the golden bough...these things I brought as it was told to me to do by wise men I knew. I stepped over the burning sand until I found an altar of rocks of lava, and there I placed the bough and spoke the required words...no I won't say them to you here. The earth trembled, the golden bough burst into flames, I thought I heard a chorus of voices of angels, and a thick mist enveloped me. I seemed to descend into an abyss!

"I was in a cavern, alone, far away from the upper world. Nearby me lay a long, white linen robe. On a granite boulder sat a copper lamp engraved with Greek words describing the way I was to follow. I took the lamp, put on the robe, and entered a narrow passage with walls of black marble. It was three miles long. At last I found a door that opened onto a flight of steps. I descended.

"I came to a square chamber. In the middle of this chamber was a square black table; on its center was the image of a crystal star. On a wall was a painting representing a woman. She was naked to the waist. In her hand was a crystal rod which she placed against the forehead of a man facing her across a table. A flame rose from the ground and seemed to envelop the man.

"Then, as if the painting had been a prophesy, a lake of fire presented itself. I smelled burning Sulphur and bitumen. I shuttered at the sight. Then I heard a voice commanding me to pass through the flames. I obeyed, and the flames harmed me not. I walked through the conflagration for a long time.

"I found myself suddenly in a great hall: The Hall of Thrones. Many ornate thrones lined the walls. In the center of this place stood an altar in the form of a dragon. A greenish gold embellished its scales. Its eyes looked like rubies. A golden plaque with an inscription was placed near it and a rich sword had been driven into the ground near the dragon. On its head rested a golden cup. I heard the choir of the celestial spirits again and a voice said to me: 'The end of thy labors draws near. Take the sword and smite the dragon.'

"I did so: I drew the sword from its sheath and approaching the altar, I took the cup with one hand and with the other I swung the sword against the neck of the dragon. The sword bounced back and the sound of it re-echoed as if I had struck a brass bell. No sooner had I obeyed the voice than the altar disappeared. I swooned. I know not how long I remained in this condition. When I awoke I was lying on a green velvet couch; in the air was the fragrance of jasmine. A blue robe spangled with golden stars had replaced my linen garment. A yellow altar stood opposite me; a flame rose from it.

"Letters in black were engraved at the base of the altar. A lighted torch stood beside it, shining like the sun; hovering above it was a bird with black feet, a silvery body, a red head, black wings and a golden neck. It was motionless, not using its wings. It was if it could only fly when in the midst of the flames. In its beak was a green branch. Altar, bird and torch are the symbol of all things. Nothing can be done without them. They themselves are all that is good and great!

"I left the Hall of Thrones by a narrow door and entered a circular apartment paneled in ash and sandal wood. At the further end of the apartment was a pedestal upon which lay a mass of white and shining salt. Above was a picture showing a crowned white lion and a cluster of grapes; both rested on a salver suspended in the air by the smoke of a lighted brazier.

"I approached the altar and took some of the white and shining salt and rubbed my entire body with it. I exited through a door and found myself on the banks of a lake. At some distance from the shore I saw the sumptuous Palace of Wisdom with its alabaster columns. The stately edifice was of a light and airy architecture having porticos of flaming color. As I approached the portals, I saw that the front was decorated with the figure of a butterfly. No sooner had I entered the palace when I saw fluttering in front of me a bird similar to the one I had seen within the flames in the great hall. A voice echoing within the palace commanded me to seize and to affix it. I darted forth after it. I seized the bird, and driving steel nails through its wings, I affixed it to the floor. It did not move but its eyes began to shine like topaz.

"I now went through another doorway into a large, perfectly round chamber; it resembled the interior of a globe composed of a hard and transparent material like crystal, so that light entered from all sides. Its lower part rested upon a vast basin filled with red sand. A gentle warmth reached me in this circular enclosure and calmed me. From the floor of the hall ascended a gentle mist, moist and saffron yellow. It enveloped me, raised me gently and bore me to the upper part of the crystal globe. Thereafter the vapor thinned; little by little I descended and finally found myself again on the floor. My robe had changed its color. It had been blue when I entered the hall, but now had changed to a brilliant red.

"Another phenomenon then occurred: I noticed with astonishment that I had somehow re-entered the Hall of Thrones. The triangular altar was still in the center of this hall but the bird, the altar and the torch were joined and formed a single body. Near them was a golden sun. A sword lay a few paces distant on the cushion of one of the thrones; I took up the sword and struck the sun, reducing it to dust. I then touched it and each particle of it flew up and became a golden sun like the one I had broken. At that instant a loud and melodious voice exclaimed, 'The work is perfect!'. Hearing this, the children of light hastened to join me, the doors of immortality were opened to me, and the cloud which covers the eyes of all mortals was dissipated. I SAW and the spirits which preside over the elements knew me for their master."

There was a silence born of awe, or perhaps, of incredulity. No one around the table stirred. Even the dogs were immobile. Yet suddenly both dogs issued a low growl. Their ears perked and their noses twitched. Melanie looked in their direction and thought she saw a small dark shape dart across the floor. It seemed a cat had entered the chamber, indifferent to the presence of the dogs. It ran behind the golden statue. Gradually, in front of the statue, a swirling mist appeared. A voice, rhapsodic and melodious came from the mist. They heard:

"Man is only that which he believeth in…a brother of darkness or a child of light. Come ye now into the light, my children. Walk in the pathway that leads to the sun."

The mist dissipated. The figure of a woman appeared. Count Saint Germain announced, "Behold, Hermes, The Thrice Great…SHE!"

21

SHE

Einstein was pouting. Leona Libby had been attempting to translate the Count's soliloquy as he voiced it, but missed much of it and muddled the rest. It didn't much matter, however, as the great mathematician was irritated by what he characterized, once Libby asked him what he thought of the Count, as an audition for the side show of a bad traveling circus. "What kind of fools does he take us for?" he asked Libby. It was a rhetorical question.

Mist formed in front of the golden statue and She stepped out of it. Her words added nothing but further mystery to the time travelers' perplexing situation: "Come ye now into the light, my children. Walk in the pathway that leads to the sun." While that sounded like a capital idea, it was vague and theatrical and, given the twilight glow of the chamber, somewhat comical.

The woman identified by the Count as Hermes Trismegistus, who was called "She," stood in front of the golden statue. She seemed to exhibit an inner glow that dimmed the statue by comparison. Her attire was ancient Egyptian in style; a long, diaphanous, pleated linen sheath supported by two beaded strands which fell from her shoulders across her bare breasts; a necklace of turquoise and gold radiating around her slender neck like the rays of a jeweled sun; a headdress shaped like eagle wings, gilded and studded with more turquoise; leopard skin sandals from which painted toe nails shone like rubies. With one hand she grasped a staff that ended on top with the craved head of a spitting cobra; with the other she held a golden ankh, the ancient Egyptian symbol of life.

To Einstein she seemed yet another part of the menagerie of the silly one-ring costume charade to which they were being subjected. More theatrics. More subterfuge, more sophistry, more sleight-of-hand. More misdirection. He would confront both the Count and this apparition as soon as the opportunity presented itself.

The two Waylands were too busy ogling the lady to consider the significance of her abrupt intrusion into this gathering—this mad tea party hosted by a crazy count. She was delightfully semi-naked and on a par with any given Hollywood starlet that came to mind. None did for the lads. None would suffice to break the spell. She was Helen, launching their mutual ship of fools. She was Venus, balancing seductively on a cockle shell. She was Diana the huntress, Delilah the clipper of locks, Cleopatra the enchantress, Salome the seductress, Jezebel the painted woman, Brünhild the warrior, Phryne the courtesan, Guinevere of Camelot, the Lady of the Lake, Nefertiti, Lady Godiva, Joan of Arc—all rolled into one delectable desirable dish. She was…She.

The Mac Conmaras saw something else. Here, potentially, was proof that the occult did exist! They had been introduced and indoctrinated into the scientific philosophy of the twentieth century by the McGinleys. Always however, the alchemists had thought that the modern empirical belief in the scientific process, in the notion that nothing could exist which could not be explained, was flawed. Yes, the alchemical explanations fell short, the quest for eternal life and easy access to wealth was self-indulgent and often misleading. But parallel theories did sometimes point toward the same reality. Astrology, the Tarot, Spiritualism, and yes, even and especially, religion, were no less valid than Plank's constant or Schrödinger's quantum theory.

Newton would not have agreed. Newton was still skeptical and suspected the Count and She were simply charlatans. Many false alchemists existed in his own time. Many were sent to the gallows. Riordan, the alchemist's apprentice, did believe. Riordan was enthralled. He was like a small boy whose fairy tale book has just come alive and he was watching fantasy characters dancing across his bedspread. Enrico Fermi, like Einstein, was bored with the entire tableau. This just wasn't worth the time it was wasting. He put his mind to working out just how they were to escape from the Sphinx and return to their own time. He wasn't far along toward a solution.

Leona Libby was torn. She wanted to believe yet couldn't reconcile these characters who seemed to have stepped from the pages of a comic book with general relativity theory and the invention of time travel. Unless...wasn't there a "many worlds theory" that sprang up along with other wild ideas after Einstein? The McGinleys were already contemplating a similar notion. They had traveled through time, or so they thought, to other eras...yet...what if they had not traveled through time but merely stepped across the rift into alternate universes?

Melanie Langford saw She as a rival for Judo's affections. True, he wasn't drooling over her the way the Waylands were, but the tall shapely woman, the gown, the jewels, the bare breasts! How could she compete with that? Kathy O'Neal wasn't similarly intimidated by the ethereal beauty that stood before them—she was amused. Like Einstein, the circus quality of the tableau had occurred to her. A circus! They have taken me to a circus, she thought. Where are the elephants? And Judo? Judo was taken back in memory to those endless Sundays at Oakridge in the Baptist Church where his parents took him to listen to the old preacher with his singsong sermons. Only this preacher was a woman, was naked from the waist up, and she was white! It was that line about coming into the light that made the connection for Judo. Come ye now into the light, my children.

Then She said, "Close your eyes and let your minds expand. Let no fear of death or darkness arrest its course. Allow your minds to merge with The Mind. Let it flow out upon the great curve of consciousness. Let it soar on the wings of the great bird of duration, up to the very Circle of Eternity."

Kathy O'Neal began to laugh. This was getting to be more and more preposterous, but, she had to admit, it was very entertaining. She/Hermes heard the girl laugh and a terrible fire flared behind her eyes. She slowly raised the ankh she held and pointed it at Kathy.

"So, you do not believe? Never turn your thoughts to the darkness! You shut up your soul in your body and abase yourself. Hark to me now as I give you the evidence your unthinking mind thirsts for!"

The ankh was pointed directly at Kathy O'Neal. It began to glow with the redness of a heated ember. Wayland saw this and understood the ankh to be a weapon. He leaped in front of Kathy. But just at that moment, the cat that had so bothered the two dogs jumped from behind the golden statue. The woman called "She" swung the ankh around and aimed it at the cat. A silvery ray of light leaped from the tip of the ankh and struck the cat in mid jump. The cat vanished and all that remained was a puff of orange smoke. She spoke:

"Listen ye and hear a mystery stranger than all that lies beneath the Sun. Know ye that all space is filled by worlds within worlds; aye, one within the other yet separate by Law. Know ye that even though in this time ye are separate, yet in all times existent ye still are ONE."

Sometimes, thought McGinley, we are TWO.

"She just described the Many Worlds Theory," said Libby to Fermi. "All possibilities as set forth by quantum theory occur simultaneously in independent parallel universes…the 'multiverse,' as Everett calls it. Are we really traveling in time, or is all this nonsense just the result of our observations of alternate realities?"

"Realities," aid Fermi, "which we experience according to our own concepts of our preferred world. We feel the same weight, see the same brightness, measure existence with a bias instilled in us by language, habit, and a certain laziness to remain in our comfort zones."

"We will have to run this by Einstein. He worked with Everett on extensions to general relativity, didn't he?"

"Not yet he hasn't. Remember, he is living in 1905, no matter what space-time dimension we may have entered."

"I wonder, Enrico, does time really have direction? It is relative to space, I know, but when you consider that entropy increases as the universe ages…"

"Are there more than four space-time dimensions, then? And these 'worlds within worlds' that She mentions…are there separate laws that govern the physics of those worlds?"

Kathy O'Neal, who had just barely escaped the fate of the vanished feline, uttered a gasp. And, "Yikes! That could have been me! You...you didn't have to kill that poor puss, you...monster!"

The woman named She shook her head. "He has only been sent to a new reality," She said. "Change into another state is not death...it is only the ending of an individual awareness that began with birth. And now I must deal with you all. Some among you are innocents brought abroad by circumstances not of your own doing. You I will return to your beginnings and without malice. You will retain an essence of what grace I may bestow upon you so that at the crucial time, your behavior will satisfy the gods of destiny."

She waved the ankh in an arc across the company of time travelers. The very air solidified and they found themselves immobilized, unable to resist. One by one the ankh selected Kathy O'Neal, Albert Einstein, and Isaac Newton, and a fountain of silvery mist issued forth to strike them. One by one they disappeared.

Kathy O'Neal carried a basket of empty bottles out the side door of the Saint Nicholas concert saloon to deposit in the trash bin. It was 1869 again. The time machine materialized in front of her. She dropped the basket. Bottles rolled along the cobblestone pavement. She ran back into the saloon, terrorized. When she regained composure, prompted by her voracious curiosity, she ventured back out into the alley. Nothing was there but a score of shattered glass bottles.

Albert Einstein was working on an equation in his cubby hole at the Polytechnikum physics building in 1905 when Mileva Marić intruded, bringing a man, a woman, and a boy with her. "Some visitors to see you, Albert," she said. "Tell them to go away," said the scientist. "I am too busy to see anyone." Fermi and Libby were disappointed, but at least they had gotten a glimpse of the great man at work. Einstein finished his equation just as the others left the room. He wrote, "$E=mc^2$" on the chalk board.

Isaac Newton was still in disguise when he returned to the Tower of London from the Green Sparrow Pub in 1704. He was about to enter his small workshop next to the Mint when he was accosted by Fermi, Libby, Riordan and the dog. (In this reality, Einstein was no longer part of the time travelers' entourage.) "Guard!" he yelled. "Take these interlopers away. I have work to do." The beefeater sprang from his post at the gate and led the time travelers away.

All was well with (some of) the worlds.

She released the others from their temporary paralysis. She spoke with a timbre of voice that bedeviled the time travelers; her tone was like the terrible ringing of a bell or trumpet calls from frigid mountain heights—startling, compelling, frightening. "I can send you back, but the wrongs you have done to time must be repaired. And there is the problem of the doppelgangers. This is beyond my skill. I must take you to the Realm of the Old Ones. I must talk with the Dweller. Come ye now as I lead you…or else stay and suffer slow painful death by dehydration in this tomb-like place!"

No one argued. No one hesitated. A door appeared on one wall as the statue that stood in a niche there swung away. They followed behind She as she led them outside the Sphinx to a waiting vehicle. Vehicle? It was, to the surprise of all, a long, yellow bus with black stripes and lettering which read, "Long Island School District 204." A school bus in the desert, in ancient Egypt, next to the Sphinx, waiting to load the sorry time travelers for their journey to the Realm of the Old Ones!

Wayland and Wayland hunkered down in one of the forward seats. Yes, it was just like the school buses they had ridden years before (or should that be, *will* ride in years to come?) The same ripped plastic seats, polished nearly bare by children's' butts. The same strange steel seat backs with that funny embossed diamond pattern, and kick marks from mud-soiled shoes. The same smells of discarded sack lunches, kid sweat, and kid vomit. The same gobs of dried gum stuck under, and sometimes on the seats. Windows you couldn't open. Windows that showed nothing of the desert—only a thick greenish mist that swirled around the bus and took it like a leaf in a stream.

It moved, but it didn't move. A few seats back sat Melanie and Judo. Melanie buried her face in Judo's shoulder and sobbed. It was the first time she had been able to let go, and it was a blessing. Behind them Riordan occupied the seat with the two Teiges. The dogs licked his face from both sides. Oh, I hope She lets both of you stay with me, he thought. I couldn't stand to part with either of you.

There was no driver; there was no steering wheel and nothing to see out the front window. She stood at the head of the bus with the Count standing dutifully behind her. The two Mac Conmaras were anxious to question her and approached guardedly. She acknowledged the alchemists with a nod. Those seeking knowledge were always welcome in her presence.

"What think you of all of this?" She asked, then answered for them: "It is possible to think a thing apart from your senses, as those who fancy sights in dreams. But unto me it seems that both of these activities occur in dream-sight, and therefore sense doth pass out of the sleeping to the waking state. For man is separated into soul and body, and only when the two sides of his sense agree together, does utterance of its thought conceived by mind take place."

"And what of science, alchemy, astrology? Are these too the stuff of dreams?" asked one of the Mac Conmaras.

"All science is incorporeal, the instrument it uses being the mind, just as the mind employs the body. Both then come into bodies, I mean, both things that are cognizable by mind alone are things material. For all things must consist out of antithesis and contrariety; and this can otherwise not be so."

"And the Cosmos? Is it real? What is man's place in it?"

"Man hath the same ensouling power in him as all the rest of living things; yet is he not only not good, but even evil, and for that he is subject unto death. Now Genesis and Time, in Heaven and upon the Earth, are of two natures. In Heaven they are unchangeable and indestructible, but on the Earth they are subject unto change and to destruction. The people call change death, because the body is dissolved, and life, when it's dissolved, withdraws to the unmanifest. I say the Cosmos also suffers change, for that a part of it each day is made to be in the unmanifest. Yet it is never dissolved. These are the passions of the Cosmos—revolvings and concealments; revolving is conversion and concealment renovation."

The Mac Conmaras nodded, seeming to understand, because the allegorical was part and parcel of their own studies. They asked, "What then of death?"

"He who hath learned to know himself, hath reached that Good which doth transcend abundance; but he who through a love that leads astray, expends his love upon his body, he stays in Darkness wandering through his sense of things of Death. Why do they merit death who are in Death? It is because the gloomy Darkness is the root and base of the material frame; from it came the Moist Nature; from this the body in the sense-world was composed; and from this body Death doth the Water drain.

"When the material body is to be dissolved, first thou surrender the body unto the work of change, and thus the form thou had doth vanish, and thou surrender thy way of life, void of its energy, unto the Demon. The body's senses next pass back into their sources, becoming separate, and resurrect as energies; and passion and desire withdraw unto that nature which is void of reason."

"And then forgotten?"

"There shall be memorials mighty of these handiworks upon the earth, leaving dim trace behind when cycles are renewed. For every birth of flesh ensouled, and of the fruit of seed, and every handiwork, though it decay, shall of necessity renew itself, both by the renovation of the Gods and by the turning-round of Nature's rhythmic wheel."

The two McGinleys were also listening to She's soliloquy (a spiel Riordan could have told them was right out of the *Corpus Hermeticum*—She had repeated her "sermon" so many times that she knew it now by heart and repeated it at will by rote). Einstein, they remembered, had postulated a single possible past, the Block Universe of his field theory. All physical variables were locally determined. But the new theories being put forth in the McGinelys' time suggested the existence of multiple worlds where the multiple possible worlds of the future derived from multiple parallel worlds of the past—something akin to She's "worlds within worlds." Did a translation through space-time have an effect on the physical laws of an independent universe? Or, as She had said, was the Law the same for all possible worlds? It was the old question of Fate verses Free Will. Determinism verses indeterminism. The arrow of time might not be flying straight…or it might be unwaveringly right on target. Analysis was up to the observer, and the observer could not see into other worlds. Or could he?

Libby looked at Fermi. "If we could figure out how this thing works," she said, meaning the school bus, "maybe we could steal it and take it back to our future."

"But look," answered Fermi, "there is no driver and there are no controls."

The sense of motion they experienced escalated rapidly and the bus began to shake as if it were traveling over a bumpy, rut-worn road. Then with a jerk, the motion stopped.

"This is as far as we go by this form of transportation," said She. "The rest of the way will be by more traditional means. Please exit at the rear of the bus and watch your step!"

They stood once again before the great Sphinx. However, its time worn surface was no longer pitted and scarred. Instead, it gleamed with a covering of burnished gold. The desert was gone. All around them lush vegetation flourished. The lacey fronds of palm trees danced in a warm and mild breeze. Birds of Paradise flitted and spider monkeys called one another with chattering voices.

"This is as far back in time as I dare go," said She. "There," She pointed to a distant snow-capped mountain, "is our final destination. There we will summon the Dweller and the judgement will take place."

Across the verdant plain were a score of golden Sphinx monuments. The way to the mountain wound among them and along rushing rivers and deep canyons and forests of twisted vine. "How can we…?" asked Libby, and no sooner had she voiced her concern, She/Hermes waved again that terrible ankh she carried. Yellow tendrils of mist encircled them. Then:

They all stood on a ragged cliff where scattered clumps of snow were melting under a blazing sun. Much of the apex of the mountain rose above them. The valley below fell away to depths that dizzied them to look down into. Against the wall of rock before them a thick mist hung, impenetrable to vision or entry.

She approached the mist saying, "I am Hermes Trismegistus, the Thrice Great, known in Egypt as Thoth, known in Greece as Asclepius, the grandson of Adam, the vanquisher of the dragon Typhon, son of the Nile, master of alchemy, astrology, and theurgy. I beseech you, oh Dweller, for an audience. For I have brought these poor mortals to you for judgement. They have sinned against Time itself."

The company of time travelers felt, not heard, the booming acknowledgement of the Dweller. Now She/Hermes turned to them and spoke:

"All men are subject to Fate, and to Genesis, and Change, for these things are the beginning and the end of Fate. Although all men do suffer fated things, those led by reason, whom the Mind doth guide, do not suffer as the rest as they have freed themselves from viciousness and pride. Approach now with humility and behold…the Dweller!"

22

The Dweller in the Mist

The sense of the sound was that of the roaring of a waterfall and the flapping of monstrous wings mixed with a tinkling of tiny bells and the distant howl of hungry wolves. All this combined to form word-ideas in the minds of the time travelers as they stood before the wall of mist wherein the Dweller was. Recriminations and admonishments were implied, and also understood. The sense of the sound created shame along with doubt and a smattering of fear. But none could turn away. Then the Dweller addressed each one separately.

"Hermes Trismegistus," said the voice, "You I will treat first. Typhon and Argus Panoptes you slew. Abraham you counseled. King, priest and philosopher you have been called. The Emerald Tablet you have written. The Great pyramids you have caused to be built. But you have meddled with demons and spirits and played with the workings of the Genesis and the Fate and for this you shall be banished back to the time of your prescribed birth and death. You will have papyrus to inscribe with your philosophy. Many will revere you in the far future. But no longer will you twist through the eons like a snake.

"Long ago I said to you that in the beginning, there was eternal thought. For thought to be eternal, time must exist. Into the all-pervading thought grew the Law of Time. And so Time became the force that holds events separate. To protect Time I will forbid you the Serpent Drum, the purple robe and silver crown, and the circle of invocation. Go you and speak not to Zoroaster nor to Enoch nor to Imhotep ever again. I am the door-keeper and I close now your avenue to the Seven Rulers of the Cosmos. Begone!"

A wispy tendril issued forth from the wall of mist and twisted around and around the form of Hermes Trismegistus who was called She. In an instant, She was gone from the icy cliff upon which the company of time travelers stood.

She reverted to Hermes' original sex during the transfer, and so She became He. He emerged in Karnak, Egypt, in the year 1346 BC. It was the year that the Pharaoh, Amenhotep IV, changed his name to Akhenaten. Hermes went to the temple where the Royal Wife, Nefertiti, was holding court. Nefertiti agreed to an audience with Hermes once he had announced himself as the son of the god, Thoth, calling himself Thutmose. Eagerly, the woman consulted with Thutmose on a most pressing problem that had occupied her husband and kept him away from their bedchamber. A leader of the Hebrew slaves named Osarsiph had been petitioning Akhenaten to let him lead his people out of Egypt. Osarsiph had begun to influence the Pharaoh in his religious beliefs; Akhenaten primarily worshiped Ra, the Sun God, and slowly was becoming monotheistic—a situation which would cause his successors to destroy all the images and mention of him in the future. Akhenaten wavered concerning Osariph's passionate plea for the freedom for his people. "What should I do?" asked the Royal Wife. Hermes/Thumose answered, "Tell the Pharaoh to let those people go." Osarsiph would later change his name. To Moses.

The time travelers felt threatened by the wrath with which the Dweller had addressed She. They had no chance to escape; behind them was a steep drop to the valley, hundreds of feet below, and before them was the wall of mist. They waited and listened.

"Next I speak to le Comte de Saint Germain," said the voice from the mist. "You have been a false prophet and a grifter in your time. You have learned the mysteries that are prohibited from common men and used this knowledge for aggrandizement and ennoblement. You have called yourself an Ascended Master and peddled an elixir barely capable relieving a headache much less of bestowing eternal life upon your victims. None of these are crimes against the Cosmos, but against mankind. This is not within my purview. However, your presence here at this Holy site is annoying. I can see no solution but to send you back to your own time and to forbid you translation to other worlds. Sell your fake diamonds if you will, but conjure not the mystical elements...or you will suffer grave consequences."

The mist picked up the Count rather roughly and deposited him in the year 1779 at the Louisenlund Castle at Güby in the Duchy of Schleswiq, near what is present day Hamburg, Germany. The Duchy was then under Danish rule and Prince Charles of Hesse-Kassel, a Danish field marshal, had been appointed governor of the Duchy by his wife's brother, the Danish King Christian VII. The castle had been built on an estate which the king had gifted to his sister, Louise, and was named after her. It so happened, luckily for Count Germain, that Prince Charles was a devotee of mysticism. The Count lost no time in impressing the Prince with his expertise in the arts of alchemy and gem making and soon found himself installed in a private laboratory constructed within an abandoned factory where he and the Prince set to making imitation diamonds and other gems. The Philosopher's Stone and the Elixir of Life were put on the back burner, so to speak, as the Count did not want to come under scrutiny again by the Dweller. Of course, it would just be a matter of time...

The ledge upon which they stood seemed to shrink with each departure. Perhaps, though, the Dweller would send them back, one by one, without the dire consequences they imagined awaited them after the meddling they had done with time. Or perhaps, as the cliff diminished, their next journey would be down into oblivion, down to dissolve and pass without ceremony to the source of their senses, their passions and desires, to their deserved fates. Who would be next?

"Enrico Fermi and Leona Libby, you who call yourselves nuclear physicists, you have much work still to accomplish. You I would return to your time, but alas, I cannot erase from you the memory of your achievement...the invention of time travel which you stumbled unto so aptly. Your era is not yet ready for this knowledge. You think of Time as a rushing river and you struggle against it like salmon swimming upstream. But learn: Time is expanding in all directions, just as the universe, which began as a single particle, multiplied and hurled its many possible forms out into the void."

Libby and Fermi looked at each other, voicing, simultaneously, "The Big Bang!"

"Yes, an explosion of sorts. You understand this. If I send you back you must concentrate not on the enormity of the Cosmos and the evolution of Fate, but upon the simplest and tiniest particles. For know you that within these miniscule things is Time contained, just as within your blood the pattern of your ultimate form and future lies."

"What if we promise…"

"Promises are made to be broken. I cannot trust you not to discover Truth, nor would I wish you not to follow your intellect. I can only alter the event which set you on your path: your meeting with the youth named Riordan Éamon Ó Ciardha. Him I will keep with me for the present, at least until you move past that event."

Hearing this, Riordan gasped. Not returning me to my own time? Riordan watched as the mist grabbed the two scientists and seemed to devour them. He would truly miss Leona Libby, with whom he had lived and studied and learned. That would not happen now. And the icy mountain ledge narrowed again.

At the Bernard Albert Eckhart Hall on the campus of the University of Chicago in 1952, a group of atomic scientists who had been involved in the world's first controlled chain reaction ten years before had just finished posing for a portrait documenting their reunion. Eugene Wigner, Leona Libby, James Franck, Leo Szilard, and Enrico Fermi, tired from standing for so long as the photographer had fiddled with his camera, focusing cloth, and film holders, ambled up University Avenue on their way to the Quadrangle Club where they could finally relax. A rusty red pickup came roaring up the street. Driving it was a red-haired young woman and seated next to her was a young Black man. The pickup did not stop.

"And now to the problem of the doppelgangers," said the Dweller. "It should not be possible that your one self and your other self should in the same plane exist…but somehow, it is true! The Seven Rulers of the Cosmos are offended by this infraction of the Law. However, if I eliminate one of your selves, the other will also be sacrificed. Then Death would know you doubled, and this also cannot be. So what do we do?'

"Begging your pardon, Mister Dweller," said one of the Waylands, "if it's all the same to you, we would be happy to coexist. In our time there are twins and triplets and even quadruplets."

"Don't forget the Dionne quintuplets," said the other Wayland.

"Yes," continued the first Wayland, "so no one would think anything of seeing us together."

"Except maybe our mother," added the second Wayland.

"The boy's got a point," said one of the McGinleys. "We all seem to be harmonious and no damage is done by our duplications."

"No damage?" returned an angry retort from the Dweller. "You have fractured Time by crossing what should have been independent paths. Elements of Eternity have stuck to your beings like sticky honey on a bee's wings. Damage will continue to occur unless I separate you. All I can do is split you up and send you into -space-time each as far away from the other as possible. One of each pair will go 'home' to you own time, but the other of you will remain here with me until I decide what to do with you."

"This ledge is going to be awfully crowed," said Wayland number one.

"You, alchemist," said the Dweller, "return now to your humble laboratory and think not to pierce the veil of Time again. Seek ye the Philosopher's Stone if you will, but do not meddle with Time!"

In a puff of mist, one of the Mac Conmaras disappeared. The Dweller spoke again:

"Professor McGinley and Wayland Delaney, I will send half of your number back to your own time. It shall happen after the fire that burned your apparatus. You are admonished not to rebuild the machine! Look to some other enterprise. Hear me and obey!"

"We would never get funding again anyway," grumbled McGinley.

Tendrils of mist, a crackling sound, and one of the McGinleys and one of the Waylands were gone. The ledge again became smaller. Now, huddled together on an icy overhang, were Lorcan Mac Conmara the alchemist, Riordan Éamon Ó Ciardha the alchemist's apprentice, Dr. Madison James McGinley, Wayland Delany, Raymond P. Washington aka Judo, Melanie Langford, and two Irish Wolfhounds named Teige.

The other Dr. McGinley and the other Wayland Delany had been transported by the Dweller to the Oak Ridge laboratory where the

Space-Time Accelerating Reciprocator, or time machine, as Wayland called it, was a smoldering ruin. Dr. Frederick Duban, McGinly's long-time friend and fellow scientist, was already there surveying the damages and ready to "tsk tsk" McGinley when he walked in.

"See," said Duban, "I told you so. Now you'll never get funding to replicate the project. Just as well, I say."

"Do they know what happened?" asked McGinley.

"Overheated. Curious though, the machine shouldn't have been running at the time. Somebody turned it on."

"Or perhaps someone left it on. I must have done. My own mistake. Freddie, I may be let go for this."

"I'll certainly support you. Accidents happen. The powers that be will actually be pleased to be rid of this albatross."

Later, as McGinley walked home to check on Scheherazade, his time-traveled cat, Wayland said, "We should go to Chicago and talk to Fermi and that lady scientist. There are still things we can do with time travel, in spite of that mist monster. He can't hurt us here."

"Don't you ever learn, Wayland? We're out of it and we are going to stay out of it. I took the blame for ruining the STAR so you are off the hook. Please don't give me any cause for concern."

"Oh crap. I guess you're right," said Wayland, but his mind was churning with bad ideas.

The alchemist, Lorcan Mac Conmara, materialized in his laboratory. Items there were in disarray; flasks and retorts were toppled, their contents dribbled out and evaporated, books were strewn about. The cat was nowhere to be seen, nor was there any longer a dog to act as sentry. Had Teige been at his usual station, he would have been barking furiously at the approaching townspeople who were crunching their way through the forest toward Mac Conmara's castle. Some held ugly-looking truncheons and some carried torches, as yet unlit. There came a banging at the main door.

Some minutes later, back on the cliff where the mist still hung thick and impenetrable, the other Mac Conmara suddenly clutched his chest. A shock had run through him and he staggered momentarily.

"What is the matter, Master?" asked Riordan.

"It is nothing," the alchemist answered, "For a minute I felt…diminished. I am better now. Give it no thought." But he knew something was very wrong, something irreversible.

"Dweller," shouted Judo, "this young lady and I were not doubled. Why do you keep us here?"

"Have I overlooked you? I cannot send you to your own time for I cannot erase your memory of where and when you have been. Although you have not the means to traverse the temporal vastness, you still are a danger. However, after consideration, I have decided to send you into a future just far enough ahead of your life spans where you will be insignificant. You will have no knowledge of that future until you live it for yourselves. I think perhaps seventy years will do it. So...be gone!"

When the mist cleared for Judo and Melanie, they found they were on a street corner in a large city. "2022," said Melanie, "if my arithmetic isn't faulty." One of the dogs named Teige was by their side and he was growling fiercely. Just up the broad avenue was a familiar looking edifice, a grand white mansion surrounded by a black wrought iron fence. Crowds of people milled around the entrance to the building's grounds carrying signs and chanting. Judo and Melanie could not make out what they were saying but they could read some of the signs.

"What do you suppose '45 must go' means?" asked Judo.

Suddenly a platoon of men in black battle dress charged through a gate in the fence with drawn weapons. Someone in the crowd of protestors pointed an assault rifle at the police. Shots were fired. People dropped. Tear gas started to drift down the street toward Judo and Melanie.

"Let's get out of here before we get hit by a stray bullet!" shouted Judo. They ran.

Back on the cliff the mist was pulsing slightly, as if a light breeze were rippling across its surface. This caused Riordan, ever curious and now determined to understand the supernatural phenomenon that had trapped them there, to stare deeply into the thickness of it. The thickness abated to the extent that Riordan saw, or thought he saw, the figure of a small stooped man at work at the console of a strange machine. He blinked and the vision disappeared. An illusion? He nudged Wayland and told him what he had seen.

Wayland answered, "I saw a movie once called *The Wizard of Oz*. The wizard in this film turned out to be an incompetent man hidden behind a curtain with a machine that made loud noises and smoke and stuff. I wonder..."

Not content to wonder, Riordan pushed his way into the mist at the point at which he had seen the man. With a little effort he was through and had entered a chamber filled with scientific-looking apparatus: wires and tubes and flashing screens. And yes, there was a small stooped man bent over a control panel of some sort. The man saw Riordan and started, bumping a lever with his elbow. Suddenly, the wall of mist disappeared and the entire company of time travelers, those who were left on the cliff, witnessed what Riordan had discovered.

The man had leathery skin, splotched with liver marks and creased with the inevitable seminal scribblings of age. His clothing was simple, a mere cloak with no ornament, although brilliant red ribbons tied back wisps of hair on either side of his head. His name, he told the company, was Grisha Viktorov. He was from Tatarstan, in Russia, from an age far flung from any they had frequented in their travels. He did not apologize for the subterfuge and theatrics which he had caused, nor did he offer any explanation except to point out that he was only one to their many; his worry was to be cast out and his facilities stolen. This was not a pleasant place to become marooned, he said.

"But you would have left us here with no regrets?" said McGinley. "How far into the future was your home?"

"I can only answer you with a story you must trust is the truth. In my time, many hundreds of years beyond yours, there is turmoil. Yes, we have technology that pales your own. But those in power heed not the dangers inherent in a science that pierces the fabric of the universe. They seek only more power, more wealth, more suppression of the masses.

"In your own time there was a similar situation, was there not? The planet was devastated by environmental catastrophes brought on by ignorant denial and greed. Hundreds of years passed before any semblance of Earth's former magnificence and splendor returned. And then it began again. Only this time the science was not ignored. It was exploited. I was a scientist. I worked to develop this system of temporal manipulation for which I was handsomely paid. When I discovered how it was to be used, I did the only moral thing I could…I stole it. I moved to this time-distant place where the others would not be able to find me. I observed the passage ot events from this vantage point, ever wary.

"I found out that some individuals throughout history were on the verge of discovering the secrets I had pledged to protect. One by one I brought you here, to the near beginnings of time itself, to stop you. And I have stopped you. Now that you have heard my story, what will you do? If Time can be controlled by those who have no regard for humankind and seek only to profit…I am afraid that it will spell the death of Time!"

Part Three

The Death of Time

Byron Grush

Preface to Part Three
The Death of Time

As I write this, in 2019, our planet is facing a crisis. Years of ignoring the inevitable effects of global warming have resulted in a dangerously short shelf life; we may be past the time when we can reverse the damage we have done to our environment. Many nations have stepped up to the challenge. Unfortunately, with the election of our current president and the balance of political power too often in conservative hands—hands bought and paid for by vested interests—we the people, like Sisyphus, seem to be pushing an enormous rock uphill only to watch it roll back again. Not every politician may be deemed evil, but.... We are a house divided and, as Lincoln once said, that cannot stand.

What may we say of the future, if we and the planet survive? Will we go out into space, mine the moon and the other planets for the resources we have squandered here and in doing so, set these celestial places on their own paths for destruction? Will we tilt the universe on its axis and let loose chaos? From Big Bang to Big Black Hole, will we cause the Death of Time? It may be the ultimate pessimism to say so, but we are only hampered by a lack of the required technology to cause such a catastrophe. We have the necessary greed, intolerance, jealousy, ignorance, sophistry, zealousness, bigotry, faux supremacy, fearfulness, and hatred to do the deed.

On the positive side, some of us are intelligent, nonconforming risk-takers who, as we approach an understanding of the unknown, fight for human dignity and reason. The Wizard of Oz, in the movie of 1939, was portrayed as a bumbling charlatan who didn't even know how his hot air balloon worked. The wizard in our story, the Russian, Grisha Viktorov, is the antithesis of Professor Marvel. He has considered all the answers to the great mysteries of the Cosmos and he *knows*. Unfortunately, he has chosen to run and hide instead of to stand and fight. Perhaps our own time-traveling crew can persuade him to attack the problem of the Death of Time.

One can imagine Lorcan Mac Conmara quizzing Viktorov on certain metaphysical subjects. For instance, he might ask, "What is God?" Viktorov might tell the old alchemist that society had abandoned religion and other superstitions long ago (in the future, that is). And yet, as a scientist, he might add:

"There is the notion that the universe had a beginning and may someday have an end, and that the question then arises: does the universe have free will...a purpose...or is there only random chaos? There is your God...in that. You may answer that question in your own way as others have done since...since the beginning of time, so to speak."

"And other worlds? Alien intelligence such as some of our group have seen?"

"When anything is possible, and you have eternity before you, it is inevitable that strange things will manifest. You are only limited by your powers of observation. Seek illusive shapes in shadows and in starlight. You may find wonderous things therein."

And again, as the time travelers confront the Dweller, he asks them the most important question of their lives: "Now that you have heard my story, what will you do?"

23

May Day Comes Early this Year

Washington, D. C., Spring, 2022

Crowds of people milled around the entrance to the White House grounds carrying signs and chanting. Judo and Melanie could not make out what they were saying but they could read the signs.

"What do you suppose '45 must go' means?" asked Judo.

A platoon of men in black battle dress charged through a gate in the fence with drawn weapons. Jeers and taunts came from the protestors. Helmets with plastic face visors hid the features of the soldiers; any fear they might have shown was obscured. People in the crowd gestured with raised and clenched fists. One or two held rocks, ready to hurl at the oppressors.

Then, someone in the crowd of protestors pointed an assault rifle at the police. Firearms were easy to obtain now that gun control laws had been abolished by the administration. The ugliness of the AR-15 was silhouetted against the cardboard signs with their variety of slogans. One of the White House soldiers saw the rifle and fired a shot over the heads of the crowd. With an uproar, the protestors moved backwards—all but two who began throwing rocks at the soldiers. A tear gas grenade was tossed into the crowd. Another report from the weapon of a soldier, a returning shot from the protestor who held the AR-15, and pandemonium descended upon the scene.

More shots were fired. People dropped. Tear gas started to drift down the street toward Judo and Melanie.

"Let's get out of here before we get hit by a stray bullet!" shouted Judo.

They ran down E Street to Pennsylvania Avenue with the dog, Teige, on their heels. Turning up 10th Street they found themselves in front of Ford's Theater. A plaque stated that here in 1865, President Abraham Lincoln had been assassinated by John Wilkes Booth. Except Judo had the distinct memory of killing Booth and his fellow conspirators on that day in April before they could kill Lincoln.

"I don't like this future much," he said.

They walked south then, past the Capitol, zigging and zagging through Capitol Hill, and crossing over the Anacostia River on the 11th Street bridge, dodging over-loaded trucks and a barrage of motorcycles whose riders had sewn Confederate flags to the backs of their leather jackets. It seemed like a nice residential neighborhood, away from the government buildings and museums and monuments. It seemed…

They followed signs directing them to the Frederick Douglass National Historic site as Judo was eager to see where the great African-American leader had lived. What they found, however, was a smoldering ruins—the mansion had been recently torched and the steps leading up the hill to the house had been covered with slogans of white supremacy such as "Blood and Soil," and crudely drawn images such as the Valknot, or knot of the slain, an old Norse symbol appropriated by white supremacists. The cindered remnants of what had been a burning cross lay on the blackened lawn.

They wandered through neighborhoods that had not fared much better. There was evidence of violence to property and persons in equal measure. From the rear of a house with blistered paint and broken windows came a pack of feral dogs. They ran at Teige, barking and drooling and ready to attack. Teige took off running; the pack gave chase. Judo and Melanie yelled at the dogs but the only result was that a large bull terrier stopped and turned toward them, growling viciously. As the dog inched toward them, a man appeared at a window of the house. He held a rifle which he aimed at the growling dog and he fired three shots. One. Two, three—little tornadoes of dust erupted next to the bull terrier. This was enough to cause the dog to turn tail and run.

"Damn!" said the man. "Missed the little bastard. Y'all better git inside off the street. It's dangerous around here."

The house, like many on this street, reflected a 19th century Italianate style with its overhanging eaves, porticoed porch and tall windows. It had once been repainted in a bright blue, but the wooden exterior was now dingy, and the paint was blistered and peeling. Inside, the floors were covered with cheap and worn carpeting, hiding what once must have been beautiful hard oak boards. The heavy molding, devoid of ornament, was painted, and this showed the chips and scratches of years of wear. An older davenport, occupying the center of the front room, was draped with a patchwork quilt. For all its age and apparent neglect, the interior was neat and orderly, clean, and smelling sweetly of the baking of an apple pie.

"Love it when that woman cooks," said the man. He gestured for Judo and Melanie to sit on the davenport while he pulled up a wooden chair for himself. "I can git her to rustle up some coffee if you like," he added.

"No thanks," answered Melanie. "We're fine. Thank you for scaring that rabid dog away. Our dog…Teige…will he be okay?"

"He'll either join the pack or be eaten by it. Just like us humans these days."

He was an African-American man nearing thirty and his clothing, like the house, was neat but oddly dated. His name was Bernard Montgomery he told them, Bernie for short. He had to leave for his shift within the hour but he would try to entertain them, at least until his wife, Effy, was ready to serve the pie. Bernie and Effy had moved to the Anacostia neighborhood after Bernie had graduated from a trade school in Virginia. He was initially disappointed in the employment opportunities in Richmond and had heard from a cousin living in D.C. about a wholesale meat vending company there that needed a technician. Bernie applied and soon worked an afternoon shift monitoring thermometers in walk-in refrigerators, checking the freeze dates on packaged frankfurters, replacing light bulbs, and other tasks for which he was over-qualified. It was a job, the pay was good, the hours were reasonable, and the company had just added paid employee health insurance. And there wasn't much else he could get.

"Y'all not from around here," Bernie said.

Judo started to say, "We're from…" but Melanie interrupted with, "Tennessee."

"Well, if you're here for the cherry blossoms, you're on the wrong side of the river."

"We were just up by the White House. There was a disturbance…a protest of some kind, and the police fired on the crowd," said Melanie. "You said it was dangerous around here, I hope this sort of thing isn't usual."

Bernie laughed. "Bunch of white kids, I bet. They haven't learned yet that carrying signs isn't gonna work. Oh, and those weren't the cops. They was the president's private police force."

"Oh, you mean like the Secret Service?"

"No, no. They all left or were fired by President Orange. He recruits from the worst of the worst. They don't tell this on the news no more…there's no more news that ain't controlled by 45. But you must know all this."

"We've been out of the country," said Melanie. "Please tell us about this 45 person. Is he a good president?"

"Man, have you been in outer space or somthin'? Ever where in the world he is known for the stupid asshole that he is. Oh, sorry for the language, but I get perturbed on talking about him."

"We're from 1952," said Judo. "Our president is Dwight Eisenhower. He was a war hero."

"Ha! That's a good one. I like your sense of humor, son. 45 was a draft dodger. He is a criminal, a bigot, a racist, and a traitor to our country. But don't get me started."

"How is he a traitor?" asked Melanie.

Bernie shifted uncomfortably on the wooden chair. Just then Effy entered the front room with a slice of apple pie, still warm from the oven. "What was that shooting I heard?" she asked.

"Just those same dogs again. Missed again, of course. Oh, Effy, these folks is visiting D.C. from Tennessee. Justin and Marie."

"Judo and Melanie," corrected Melanie.

"Could you get them each a slice of your delicious pie? Thanks, sweet thing."

As Effy returned to the kitchen, Melanie said, "You were saying? About the President being a traitor?"

"It was more or less proven he was a pawn of the Russians. They helped elect him, poisoning the minds of voters who were ready to be poisoned anyway. He did everything he could do to undermine our democracy. He lied, he cheated, he obstructed justice, he brought incompetence and vested interests into government. He called the free press 'the enemy of the people' and sowed seeds of hatred and intolerance to keep the support of the slime that would keep him in power."

"Why didn't they impeach him, put him in jail?"

"Oh, they tried. But he filled the courts with racist and bigoted judges, and he had most of the Republicans in congress protecting him. Then the worst of it began."

"He was reelected, after all that?"

"He declared presidential elections to be unconstitutional. That was his biggest lie, but it took. Free elections, he argued, allowed Muslims, and illegal Mexican drug runners, and homosexuals to vote. And women. He basically made himself king of America."

"It's too bad," commented Judo, "that my buddy, Wayland isn't here now. We'd take care of him. We killed Hitler, once upon a time."

Bernie looked at Judo with a frown that indicated that he was getting tired of the joke.

"You said something about joining the pack or being eaten by it when we came in," said Melanie.

"Yes, but there is a third alternative. Now don't say anything to Effy when she comes back, but there are meetings...the Panthers are reforming."

Effy chose that moment to enter with two generous slices of warm pie which she gave to Judo and Melanie.

"Panthers? What are the Panthers?"

"You know, the Black Panthers. Before any of our times, of course, but they were the militant arm of the Civil Rights Movement during the Vietnam War."

Vietman War? Civil Rights Movement? We missed a lot of history, Melanie thought to herself.

"Don't you be hangin' with those Panthers," said Effy. "You get yourself killed."

"Any coffee left, honey bunch?" replied Bernie. "I could use a cup to wash down this delicious pie. Either of you? No?"

Effy wiped her hands on her faded house dress, as if to rid herself of the anger that rose from her husband's treatment of her.

Begrudgingly, she did return to the kitchen for the coffee pot.

Bernie said to Judo, in a low voice, "You come back here about eleven o'clock if you're interested in meeting some people that want to do more than just carry around signs and get beat up by 45's storm troopers. Don't think your white lady be too welcome, though. Sorry to say so, Ma'am."

Metropolitan Police Sargent Jimmy Dale Peskowitz didn't think of himself as a white supremacist, nor did he affiliate himself with the Neo-Nazis or the Ku Klux Klan, but when his president called for him to serve and protect, he was Jimmy-on-the-spot. He didn't much like immigrants and was happy that Muslims and Mexicans had been kicked out of the country by his president. The Blacks…well, that was another problem. They hadn't exactly been immigrants, so what to do?

So he led his squad of six tried-and-true to raid an abandoned warehouse near the railyard in the D.C. neighborhood called Brentwood. An informant had told the police about a meeting there tonight: The New Black Panthers. Meetings, especially those held in secret, were illegal but hard to detect. Tonight, Jimmy Dale Peskowitz might earn a citation for arresting the leaders of the militant group. He might even get to meet the president!

Inside the warehouse, as the police were sneaking up through the darkness and grit of the railyard, Judo sat next to Bernard Montgomery on makeshift seats that formerly had been shipping crates. People were still trickling in as the main speaker waited patiently to begin what he hoped would be a powerful speech—one to inspire and possibly to launch a full-fledged revolution.

"How did all these people know about this?" asked Judo. "Telephone tree?"

"Cell phones are monitored. Facebook and Twitter are censored and controlled by the government. Can't even put an ad in a newspaper…all of them are right-wing now. TV won't cover us. So, we use word of mouth. Runners. Code words…that sort of thing. Didn't start that way, though. You familiar with the song, 'Follow the Drinkin' Gourd?' "

"An old folk song, isn't it?"

"The drinkin' gourd referred to the Big Dipper, which was a constellation that pointed to the north star. It was during the years of slavery when our people fled to the northern free states. The song was code for the directions they'd follow: 'The riva's bank am a very good road, the dead trees show the way. Lef' foot, peg foot goin' on, foller the drinkin' gou'd'...and so on.

"Well, in these modern times the people listen to Rap music. Could get a crowd together for a concert and weave messages into the lyrics...whitey can't understand them lyrics anyhow. But the government caught on and now we can't form groups over six or seven without gettin' our asses tossed in jail. So it be the word of mouth that spreads the word."

Cell phones? Facebook? Rap music? What a world, thought Judo...what a world! "So what will the Panthers do?" he asked.

"First off, we kidnap that son of a bitch that was the senate majority leader, before President Outrage disbanded Congress. You know the one, some Irish or Scotch name...McMuffin or somethin'. We'll give him a fair trial before we hang him. He kept the congress from opposing President Mushroom-dick. Goes way back to when he obstructed everything our God-given Black president tried to do."

"We had a Black president?"

"Oh boy, Jules, your joke has gone on long enough!"

"Judo. And it's no joke. How did we get from having a Black president to this evil number 45 guy?"

"Hush, the meeting is starting!"

The crowd, Judo noticed, was mostly teenagers and young men with but a few women and older citizens. A low murmur, like the purring of an angry cat—a panther—subsided as the speaker banged with his fist on the abandoned packing crate that was his makeshift podium. For the second time in his career as a time-traveler Judo was brought back in memory to that little Baptist church in Oakridge. But this venue, the disused warehouse, darkened due to missing bulbs in the hanging lamps, with cobwebs coating some kind of pulley system hanging limp and useless, with high windows so dingy with the dust of time that it was impossible to see outside save for broken panes— this was an unlikely place for a religious gathering. And yet...

The speaker, so preacher-like to Judo, was a large man with a demeaner which commanded respect and attention. He was dressed all in black. On his lapel was a pin-back button with the image of a charging black panther. His voice reverberated even in that voluminous space.

"We had a dream," he began, "a dream from which we have been rudely awakened. Remember the 'I have a dream' speech? You and I, all of us in this room today, are those little Black boys and Black girls that Martin Luther King Jr. dreamed would one day join hands with little white boys and white girls as sisters and brothers. It was not a bad dream. But it has not come true!

"Since the abolishment of slavery in this country we have suffered the indignation of being separate and unequal. We have suffered the continuation of Jim Crow and every effort on the part of white supremacists to hold us back, keep us ignorant, keep us from voting, keep us from living where we like. We have been jailed, beaten, lynched. The dream…the dream urged us to resist, to march, to protest. The dream cautioned us to be non-violent. We were met with fire hoses, dogs, and even bullets. Still we dreamed on.

"We made great strides, eliminated the legality of segregation, although not the de facto face of it. Then the glorious day came when we had our own president, a man of color, a man of integrity, honor, intelligence, and humanity…the opposite of what we have now. So how did it happen that the tide turned so brutally back against us and against every right thinking, socially conscious, tolerant and fore-thinking person in or out of government?

"Whitey got scared. Whitey saw that our dream might just come true. Whitey's vision of his own supremacy was being chipped away. He reached deep into his playbook of nastiness and hate. He rallied his troops and took over. He changed laws that got in his way. He began to strangle democracy with the help of the wealthy and powerful. And those who just stood and watched.

"And Martin, were he alive today, might caution against violence. And I say to you, brothers and sister, let us not panic. Let us not riot…for that can only hurt our own communities. Let us not throw away our lives in useless struggles against overwhelming odds. Yet, let us not be afraid to fight and to fight intelligently. Small groups placed strategically can illuminate key figures. One by one we can weaken them. Remember that in the days of another Republican president the Vietcong were facing the power of the American Army: an overwhelming force. They faced napalm and flame-throwers and the rape and murder of innocents in the villages where they hid. But they won. As we will win if we organize intelligently and without undue passion."

As the speaker paused a man ran up to him and whispered something. The speaker smiled, then turned back to the crowd. "It seems we have visitors," he told them. "There are some white folks at the door wishing to come. Shall we let them?" The crowd roared their consensus.

The door was opened and there stood Metropolitan Police Sargent Jimmy Dale Peskowitz and his entourage, armed and dangerous. They hesitated upon seeing the large crowd of Black faces all staring at them.

"Come in and join our celebration," said the speaker. "We were just talking about you and your handlers."

The police inched forward. Peskowitz raised his rifle, pointed it at the speaker. "I am here to arrest you for illegal assembly and conspiracy to attack the government of the United States," he said. "Will you come quietly, or do we have to use force?" There was laughter.

All at once the audience moved to surround the police. It happened so quickly that none of the officers had a chance to resist the crush, nor to fire a shot, nor to lift a baton. There was a constriction, like a huge hand closing around some soft, rotten fruit to squeeze out the rancid juice. The police were overwhelmed by the sheer numbers of the opposition. Soon they were battered and lay bleeding on the dirty warehouse floor.

"We shall overcome," said the speaker, we shall overcome."

Byron Grush

24

Strange Fruit Hanging from the Cherry Trees

Washington D.C., Spring, 2024

Killing them once had not been sufficient to quench the anger and undo the horrors of the regime. Bodies, still bleeding from bullet holes, were dragged along the walkway next to the National Mall Tidal Basin. Water flooding the banks of the basin covered much of the walk so the angry crowd tugged the bodies up across the grass and laid them under the cherry trees where kicks were applied at random to the swelling cadavers. Someone emptied a handgun into the very dead victims. Someone else brought a coil of rope, and soon there swung by the feet from the stoutest of the tree limbs, the former would-be dictator, his daughter, one of his sons, and a son-in-law. The scene was reminiscent of the last public appearance of Benito Mussolini and his mistress, hanging in the Piazzale Loreto in Milan in 1945.

It had taken two years for the revolution to mature to the point where at last it seemed an end was in sight. What had started as a covert operation by the militant New Black Panthers had soon spread to other groups and non-groups across the country, especially within poor and disenfranchised communities. Members of the Armed Forces and the Police had come over to the cause, usually undercover, as this war—and it was a full-fledged war—was not being fought in the open yet. Now there was talk of reform—a reformation along the lines of the old constitution, with added safeguards to assure that something like this could never happen again. Never?

Dangers existed that foreign interests might intercede and influence the process, just as Russia had done years ago when elections were still being held and computerized voting machines could be hacked. It would be a long, slow, and painful journey to "make America great again"—a slogan whose perverted meaning would now be redefined.

It was just the beginning of a new struggle. Four Southern states, Alabama, Georgia, South Carolina, and Florida, seceded from the Union for the second time in nearly two-hundred years. There were many in the North who said, "good riddance." There were still many politicians and judges in place who were appointees of the would-be dictator. A purge began. More blood. Even a Supreme Court judge met the fate of the First (or was it the Last?) Family.

Those with a modicum of wealth stepped up to be leaders for the birthing of the new democracy. They made sure that their own interests were placed in the forefront. Others, not so fortunate financially, who struggled day to day, fell back into the old gang mentality which fostered separatism and channeled anxiety into violence. The divide which had always existed deepened; there was no common enemy to unify the down-trodden. And the rich saw a path toward becoming richer—an exclusive path.

It was too late to reverse the damage done to the environment. Already the signs of an approaching doomsday were evident: sea levels were rising, the weather was intense and often devastating—bringing droughts that brought firestorms and winds that brought hurricanes and tornadoes, floods and mudslides. A new dust bowl developed in the west. Some said it was God's punishment for (fill in the blanks with whatever or whomever you most despise). Some said, with the utmost irony, we should have acted sooner.

Melanie and Judo had been active in the struggle since those first days when they had materialized in D.C. and met Effy and Bernard Montgomery. Bernie was skeptical about Melanie's ability to fit in with the New Black Panthers but soon gained respect for her once she started planning burglaries for the group to obtain weapons and other supplies. Her experience as a fugitive, when she and Judo had robbed service stations, gave her an insight into the use of subterfuge and misdirection during an act as simple as shoplifting or as complex as a midnight "crash and grab" at a Walmart or a Fleet Farm. Judo became an expert at disabling burglar alarms and surveillance cameras.

Now that the first phase of the revolution was over, the pair of weary time travelers was ready for a road trip to a less volatile realm. Both desired to return to Tennessee to their original home town of Oak Ridge. It had been over 70 chronological years since they had left although the actual elapsed time they had experienced only totaled three or four years. Their parents and friends would no longer be alive. Yet their need for closure was strong so they prepared themselves mentally for the changes they would find—and the losses.

They liberated a 1972 Volkswagen Beetle from a parking lot and switched its license plates with a late model Buick they found on a side street. In the back seat they found an old Rand McNally which they consulted for the best route between D. C. and Oak Ridge. They decided on Interstates 66 and 81, a journey of over 500 miles through rural Virginia to Knoxville, where I40 would take them into Oak Ridge.

80 miles out of D.C. they pulled off the interstate at Strasburg for fuel; the VW only held about 10 gallons of gasoline. There was an Exxon station next to a McDonalds and it seemed like a good idea to get some take-out they could eat on the road. The door opened easily but the place was deserted. Even the smell of grease and salt and spilled catsup was gone.

At least the gas pumps still worked and the stolen credit card they used hadn't been canceled yet. Melanie had just finished topping off the tank when a gang of angry young white men came around the corner of the station and headed straight for them.

"What has this world become?" she said as they jumped into the Beetle. Melanie nearly flooded the old car as she stomped on the gas pedal. The gang chased the car but luckily, the Beetle outdistanced them. Back on the interstate, Melanie said, "Now I have to wonder what Oak Ridge will be like!"

"I agree," said Judo, "but the farther from Washington we get, the better. Why did the Dweller send us to this time? It really sucks."

"Maybe to punish us."

"If only we had the time machine again. We could go back and…"

"And create an even bigger mess than this is!"

"It would be worth a try."

A few years ago, in the distant past

Grisha Viktorov, known to the time-travelers as The Dweller in the Mist, had just asked, "Now that you have heard my story, what will you do?" The people of the Dweller's own time had no regard for humankind, he had said. They would misuse the technology of time travel for their own gain, he had said. It would spell the death of Time, he had said. I am opposed to altering Time, he had said.

"You have at your disposal an extraordinary device for transporting men through the space-time continuum," said McGinley. "You could take us to your time where, perhaps, we could solve your problem. You would not be alone. If you do not wish to come along, send us. Tell us what has to be done. Otherwise…"

"Otherwise we're stuck here on this disappearing cliff, on who knows what God-forsaken world," said Wayland.

"I cannot believe," added Mac Conmara, "that your philosophy is so rigid that it cannot allow for actions that might save the universe from the malfeasance of mankind. I would have agreed with you once upon a time, but now…I see no other solution but to go to the significant time and place where a simple action could divert the arrow of time…just enough…"

"It is not that simple," replied Viktorov. "When you change something that has already happened, you create a duplicate reality. If the change is minor, the alternate remains local. If the change is major, the effect may extend across the entire universe. You create another phase of the multiverse."

"But if this is so," replied McGinley, "and your future people do cause the death of Time, then would not an alternate of the space-time continuum be created? You could not kill Time completely."

"Unfortunately, that cannot happen. You see, Time only exists because of the phenomenon you call Light. We all are only pieces of light slowed down enough to solidify, as are the planets and the stars and therefore, the reality we call Space. In the natural order of things, the universe will expand and its energy will be used up until it has to stop expanding. Then it will be drawn back onto itself, attracted by the dark mass of its center…the great opposite force it left behind. It will begin to accelerate as it nears this center and when it reaches it…"

"Another Big Bang!" said McGinley. "But with the death of Time…"

"Energy is the movement of Light which is propelled by Time. No Time, no movement, thus no energy, and no return. This kind of death is final."

"So what you're saying," said Wayland, "is that time and light are part of the same thing."

"Very good, Wayland," said McGinley. "We'll make a scientist out of you yet."

"But what then would cause the death of Time?" Wayland asked.

"The people of my time have developed a way of traveling through space…not through time, except for my own effort of course, but to travel faster than the speed of light. Your scientists think this is impossible, but I assure you it is quite possible. If this was coupled with the technology which I developed it would allow them to approach the final stages of the Big Bang. This would prove to be disastrous!"

"But why would they want to do that?"

"To harvest the most elemental aspects of existence. To give themselves riches and power beyond imagining."

"So how do we stop them?"

"First, by never allowing them to find me. Second by stopping you from traveling through time and changing things such that they might notice. They must never believe that time travel is possible."

"And what if they develop time travel independently from you? We thought of it…why could not some future scientist do the same?"

"I am monitoring them. Not only can I travel through time and send things and people back and forth through time, I can also see alternate worlds by virtue of this device."

Viktorov pointed to a flat screen that was mounted on one of the laboratory tables. As he did this, the screen began to flicker, then images appeared on it of a number of red-robed men clamoring about an odd-looking piece of apparatus. Rapidly blinking characters, which the others took to be lettering of some foreign language, began to move across the screen.

"Oh no!" said Viktorov. "Oh no…it has happened!"

Somewhere in Virginia, 2024

Melanie was tired and ready to give the job of driving over to Judo. It was time once again to stop for gas. They were not about to make the next big town along the interstate, Johnson City, on their rapidly dwindling ten gallons of gasoline, so they exited onto I581 toward Roanoke, Virginia. Near the first cluster of Quality Inn, Super 8, and Motel 6 establishments they located a filling station. The automatic pump rejected their stolen credit card.

They drove back up Peters Creek Road to the Waffle House. Roanoke, it seemed, had not devolved into a citadel of doom as had other burgs since the upheaval that had started in Washington. It was as normal as banana cream pie. A smiling waitress showed them to a booth by the window and asked if they wanted coffee. Judo ordered pecan waffles and Melanie asked for an omelet with ham, cheese, tomatoes, and jalapeños—hold the onions.

"This place reminds me of the one back in Oak Ridge. We used to hang out there after high school sometimes," said Melanie. "Sometimes *during* high school."

"We need money, don't we?" asked Judo.

"Yes, and we'd better dump the car. Anyway, it's about out of gas. Maybe we can find a nice pick-up truck. Not better mileage, but a bigger gas tank."

After the meal and a slice of banana cream pie apiece, the pair of wayward fugitives looked up and down the parking lot which the restaurant shared with a motel for a car or truck they could steal. Just in back of the Waffle House they saw a school bus. At first, the sight of the big yellow vehicle failed to elicit curiosity. Then:

"Look what it says on that bus, Melanie," said Judo. "Long Island School District 204. Doesn't that sound familiar?"

"It looks just like the one that *She* took us for a ride in back in Egypt, or wherever that was. But it can't be, can it?"

But it was. The door opened and out stepped Dr. Madison James McGinley. "Oh good…we found you," he said. "Quickly now, get on the bus."

"I guess we're either on the bus or we're off the bus," said Melanie. "Let's be on it."

On the bus, besides Dr. McGinley, were Lorcan Mac Conmara the alchemist, Riordan Éamon Ó Ciardha the alchemist's apprentice, Wayland Delany, and an Irish Wolfhound named Teige. Missing from the congregation was Grisha Viktorov, known to the time-travelers as The Dweller in the Mist. Viktorov was, nonetheless, at the controls; he was back in his laboratory on that strange alternate planet in the distant past where once the group had stood on a cliff, facing a wall of mist.

"I imagine," said McGinley to Melanie and Judo, "that you two would like an explanation. We convinced the Dweller to allow us to retrieve you from this time period so that you could assist us on what will be a most important undertaking. He set us up with this bus and can send us anywhere in time and space. We are going to attempt to prevent the death of Time itself! Are you game?"

"Say, Mel," Judo said, "look out the window. There's a state trooper looking at the VW. I think I'd vote to go along with the Professor."

Melanie nodded in the affirmative. McGinley sent Wayland to the Waffle House for a big box of cheese burgers and fries and a couple of liter bottles of Coke. Once Wayland returned, McGinley sat down at what would be the driver's seat, if the bus had actually been drivable, and spoke into a microphone. "We are ready now, Grisha," he said.

1779, Louisenlund Castle at Güby, Germany

Comte de Saint Germain and Prince Charles of Hesse-Kassel stood watching a clay bowl in which a certain substance had been set aflame. Already the Count had exorcized the Creature of Fire that leaped therein. Now the special incense, having been blessed, was poured into the fire and the four lamps set in a circle surrounding the flaming bowl were lit. The Count began to chant:

"Notamargatet, bless this circle. Yanoda, Milole, Alag, Aothio, bless this circle…"

The Prince had witnessed this ritual before, but it always enchanted him. He, like the Count, had placed the purple Sacred cloth on top of his head. The mystical symbols embroidered there were powerful. Soon the flames would die and a magnificent diamond would appear in the bowl, liquified at first, then becoming solid and translucent. The Prince had made the right decision in providing the alchemist with this isolated laboratory; riches beyond imagining would follow. The chanting continued:

"We invoke ye, Yalantina and Lemirot. Come forth, Lesiab and Telar. I call you, Elana, Ustael, Thaerrub and Badora…"

Something unusual was happening. Never before during the gem making ritual had the Prince seen the kind of thick mist that was forming in the room. As the mist swirled like a miniature cyclone and moved toward the alchemist, Prince Charles ran from the room, screaming. Count Germain stood stoically as he was swallowed. Moments later he was standing in front of a raised platform on which were seated ten men dressed in crimson colored robes.

"Are you spirits?" the Count stammered. "Have I actually been called into the company of the Holy of Holies? Am I to be judged for my sins? Or to be rewarded for my devotion?"

One of the men spoke: "You are le Comte de Saint Germain?" The Count replied that he was. "You know one who calls himself The Dweller?" Again, the affirmative. "This man we would find and bring to justice. His real name is Grisha Leontiy Viktorov, a rogue scientist who has stolen important technology from us. You know where, and when, to find him, do you not?"

"I…I don't know. I'm not sure. I was taken there by…another seeker like myself. Hermes. He…she would know. Find Hermes."

"Our ability to penetrate Time is limited. You will go to this Hermes for us. Return and help us to find Viktorov. You will be rewarded if you are successful. If you fail…"

25

The Magical Yellow School Bus

The table hadn't been dusted in a while. A ceramic bowl sat dead center; within it drooping flowers were evidence that watering had also been forgotten or simply ignored by the chamber's resident. A cube the size of a man's hand was set near the table's edge. It appeared to be made of fine crystal, but an internal glow indicated some purpose other than decoration. Occasionally, the glow would brighten and sometimes flicker. On this occasion, a ray of light shot out from the cube, setting the mites of dust in the chamber's dim atmosphere to dancing like an animated cluster of stars in a swirling miniature galaxy.

An image appeared, floating, an eerie apparition resolving incompletely. A soft buzzing sounded. The man, a short pudge of a man who had been relaxing on a spongey and formless piece of furniture, answered the call of the cube with a clap of palm on palm. The image solidified into that of another man, this one tall, lanky, and robed in folds of crimson material that shimmered, even as the image undulated. The image raised an arm in a sharp salute which the man returned, although lazily.

Unseen by the man was another object which occupied a place on the table just behind the ceramic bowl. The object was invisible because it didn't exist in the same space-time as the man of the chamber or the projected image with which he now spoke. Its size, relative to the bowl, the table, and the man, was incongruent for the object was a full-size yellow school bus lately from the Twentieth Century of the planet Earth. But as this was not Earth, nor the Twentieth Century, and as the school bus still remained in its own space-time bubble, it had not expanded to what would be its proper dimensions in this one.

Grisha Leontiy Viktorov, also known as the Dweller in the Mist, had explained to the scientists and their companions who now sat inside the yellow school bus looking out the windows, that because the universe was expanding, not only did the distance between stars and planets increase over time, the space (thought of as empty by some but composed of "ether" by others)—the space between the most minute objects that made up atoms (such as protons and neutrons and quarks and so forth)—that space also expanded. Thus any object that traveled through time would expand, and conversely, any object, like the school bus, which visited another time within a bubble of its own space-time, would not.

Inside the bus a fascination with the new scale of things prevailed. They watched and listened to the conversation between the man and the image, but also marveled at ordinary objects, their details and their sizes. The ceramic bowl seemed monumental. The cube was monstrous. And the insect that approached their invisible bubble was…

"Holy shit!" said Wayland. "Look at the size of that thing!"

"Can it sense us?" asked Melanie.

"I should think not," answered McGinley.

"I sure hope not," added Judo.

"What species do you think that is?" asked Mac Conmara.

"I should think it is something that evolved from one of our Earth's own cock roaches," said McGinley.

The bug came closer and closer to the school bus. Suddenly, a huge hand descended upon the bug, squashing it rather efficiently. Juice and particles of exoskeleton splattered the space-time bubble containing the school bus. "Yuck!" uttered Melanie. For a brief moment, the outlines of the bubble became visible. The man saw, but shook his head at the obvious illusion, then returned to addressing the image.

"Yes," the man was saying to the red-robed image, "we can be ready within the week. As soon as the location of Viktorov is discovered, we can retrieve him. Once we have the renegade back we can force him to reveal the final refinements for the machine!"

So, thought McGinley, it is just as the Dweller said. They have part of the time travel machine built. Once they have Viktorov's technology they can couple it with their faster-than-light device and…

"Soon," the man told the image, "we will travel to the origin of the universe…the time and place of the Big Bang. Very soon. Then, what wonders we will behold!"

"And what wondrous dark energy we will collect," answered the image.

Karnak, Egypt, in the year 1346 BC

Hermes Trismegistus, who was called She, had reverted to his original sex and now was known as Thutmose, presumptively the son of the god, Thoth. Thutmose was acting as an adviser for the Pharaoh Akhenaten and his wife, Nefertiti. Today Thutmose was engaged in a game of Senet with Nefertiti. Two of her children, 2-year-old Meketaten, and 1-year-old Ankhesenpaaten (who would one day marry her brother, Tutankhamun), played on the floor beside them. Nefertiti threw the four two-sided throw sticks to determine how many of the squares on the board she could move. The game was symbolic of passing into the afterlife and Nefertiti was usually very lucky at it. She counted out the recessed square ceramic tiles with a tap of her cone-shaped piece in each, but came to a square where one of Thutmose's pieces blocked her advance. She was displeased.

"Oh," said Thutmose, "did I put that there? I think it was back over here." He promptly, with the political acumen which had sustained him in good favor with the queen up to now, moved his piece out of her way.

"Ha!" she exclaimed. "I have reached the afterlife. Now I will be with Aten and Amun-Ra."

Only if you get past Anubis in the realm of Amenti, thought Thutmose. He will weigh your heart against a feather and no doubt find you wanting in worthiness. Of course, he said none of this.

"Come children," said Nefertiti. "It is time for your bath."

After the queen and the children had left, Thutmose sat

contemplating the Senet board. A mist formed next to him and a man stepped out of it. Thutmose/Hermes was astounded to see Comte de Saint Germain standing there. "How did you…why are you here?" he asked.

"I'm glad to see you too, Hermes. Say, who is that guy I see in the next chamber? What is wrong with his head? It looks all elongated."

"That is the Pharaoh. He came out of his mother feet first. Got stuck, they say. Pulled his head out of shape. But you haven't answered my question."

"I need to find the Dweller. I got to ask him to give me permission to time-travel again. I can ask him to let you go, too."

"First of all," replied Hermes, "I'm pretty happy right here. The Queen is quite enchanting, and eager, if you know what I mean. The Pharaoh has his other wives, so he's too busy to care. Secondly, if you're here, that means you *are* time-traveling. Besides, why should I tell you anything?"

"There is a reason. There are a group of people in the far future that want to find the Dweller. They are very powerful and we could benefit fabulously from their good favor. Think of the wealth, the prestige, the glory of it all…"

"This sounds dangerous. Let me think it over. You…I'll have to present you as a foreigner visiting from…maybe the East. Your clothing is too unusual otherwise. Have you anything on you like a trinket that you could give to the Pharaoh?"

Count Saint Germain rifled through his pockets. "I've got this," he said, pulling out a gold pocket watch.

"That'll do."

"Wait until they dig this up in the Pharaoh's tomb several hundred years from now. I only hope to be there to see it."

The Dweller's Planet

The Dweller had brought the magical yellow school bus back to the improbable planet in the impossible past for strategical planning. He listened to the time-travelers report of the conversation between the man in the chamber and the floating image projected from the crystal cube. He explained:

"The man was Nikolai Borisov. You might think of him as the evil scientist in a horror film. He is a brilliant man, but twisted. He gives no heed to the dangers of his endeavor to reach the Big Bang. The projected image was most likely Chang Jin Chong, one of the Counsel. It is under his direction and with his support that the quest for ultimate time-travel continues. If they find me, they will torture me until I reveal what they want to know, then they will kill me. There is only one solution to this dread future, I fear…"

"Kill yourself first?" asked Wayland.

"Unacceptable, Wayland!" admonished McGinley.

"Of course, the lad is correct in his thinking," continued Viktorov, aka the Dweller. "But they will persist in their research and eventually may come up with the answer anyway."

"Then we need to kill all of them," Wayland blurted.

"Why are you so blood-thirsty?" McGinley wanted to know. "No, there must be another way."

"I have an idea," said Lorcan Mac Conmara. "Why don't we give them what they want, but with a hidden flaw that will defeat them permanently. There is an old alchemist's trick of misdirection. Layers of encrypted text are used to disguise the true meaning of any tome describing the practice. Legitimate alchemists did this just as much as the charlatans did."

"Excellent," said McGinley. "We could produce a document purporting to be the Dweller's notes. But it would have to actually work, wouldn't it?"

"It would work, but it would send them in the wrong direction," said Viktorov. "Instead of taking them back to the Big Bang, it would hurl them toward the other end of time…the death of the universe when the expansion stops. But…"

"But they would have to run out of gas, so to speak," offered Judo, who had been unusually silent lately. In truth, with this new and treacherous adventure afoot, Judo would have preferred to have taken his chances with the State Police back in Virginia.

"What worries me though," said McGinley, "is how they are accomplishing this search for the Dweller. They appear to believe they will find him, and soon!"

"There is only one person who knows how to find me," said Viktorov. "Hermes."

From ancient Egypt to the distant future

Hermes and Count Saint Germain stood before the Pharaoh Akhenaten in the temple to Aten-Ra at Karnak. The Count had just gifted his gold pocket watch to the Pharaoh. The Beloved of Aten, Strong Bull of the Double Plumes, ruler of Upper and Lower Egypt, the former Amenhotep IV, the man who would erase all images of the god now out of favor called Amun, whose own images would be erased by those who followed, whose mysterious life would be at the center of future scholarship and occult speculation: the Pharaoh Akhenaten turned the strange object over in his hands. There were two slender wands upon its circular face which moved, and mysterious symbols unlike any hieroglyphs he had ever seen. And there was a soft ticking noise issuing from the object. Pharaoh was astounded, but could not react as such in public; he who was the Eternal Son of the Sun-Disc, could not appear ignorant.

"It is a fitting tribute," he said. "I shall give it to Kiya, my beloved second wife. Its resemblance to the golden sun will remind her of Him who we exalt."

Just at that moment, the mist formed around Hermes and the Count. It shimmered as it swallowed the two men. Then they were gone. When they materialized, it was not in the antechamber of the future rulers as those rulers had expected. The adjustments were faulty; the coordinates were slightly skewed. Hermes and the Count found themselves face to…face?…with a creature resembling an old Earth octopus but standing on two human-like legs, with short tentacles dripping down from a frowning jaw. There were other things: translucent things not unlike jellyfish, floating in the air or darting about. It took the men a minute to realize they were not under water.

The creature before them blinked its two bulging eyes. The Count instinctively cowered behind Hermes. "What is that? Where are we?" he stammered.

"Somebody snatched us and dropped us into this space-time," Hermes said. "Either the Dweller, or your people. This is all your fault!"

"Do you think it can talk?"

"I don't see a mouth…oh, wait a minute…"

The creature did indeed have a mouth: one lined with rows of thin, sharp teeth. It opened its mouth very wide as it advanced toward Hermes and the Count.

Meanwhile, in the laboratory on the far-flung future home of humanity, Counselman Chang Jin Chong stood before the scientist, Nikolai Borisov, and demanded, "Well? Where are they?"

"I'm sorry, your eminence, but we seem to have lost them. I told you, our time-travel technology has a few glitches. If only we could transport the whole machine with an operator inside, maybe we would have better control."

"And the irony is, our chance to improve that technology is now lost in time!" said the angry Counselman. "You must find them and retrieve them. Your own well-being depends upon it."

"I've set a program to search. But it is a time-consuming process and there is no guarantee. The location indicator we implanted in the Count seems not to be functioning. No wait…"

The time machine was flashing. Something had appeared inside the transition chamber. The something was not the Count, nor was it Hermes—at least not in the form one would have expected. The something was large, it had writhing tentacles through which a gapping jaw could be seen. The most horrible aspect of the something was the red puss-like gore that dripped from the jaw and ran out onto the floor.

Borisov assessed the situation quickly, for that was his wont. A brilliant theoretician, he usually hesitated to jump to conclusions, but in this case, the conclusions were obvious. He slammed the time machine into reverse—well, he set the temporal direction indicator back to zero, revved up the auxiliary power, and gently pressed a button that sent the creature back where it came from.

"Now what?" asked Counselman Chang.

"Now we try for an earlier moment in the same space-time that thing came from. If we can retrieve our objectives before they get eaten…"

The magical yellow school bus materialized at the back of the Temple of Aten-Ra at Karnak. McGinley checked the sensor board. "Oh, oh," he said. "Our quarry seems to have flown the coop. Hermes was in the temple a moment ago, but a time rift has appeared and he's gone!"

"Can we follow him?" asked Mac Conmara.

McGinley spoke through the bus communication panel to Viktorov, explaining the problem. Viktorov spent a moment or two fiddling with dials and gauges and finally answered that Hermes no longer existed in any space-time he could find. He postulated that the man was probably dead. But then…

"He's back. I find him now in the laboratory on my home planet. They have successfully retrieved him. I can't explain the momentary voiding of his being…perhaps a glitch…but he is definitely in the grasp of our enemies."

"What will you do?"

"I'm going to have to relocate. All of this equipment…it is too cumbersome to move. I'll take only the controlling aspects of the space-time device. I'm bringing the bus back. We'll put the machine into the bus and try to hide somewhere in time."

"The notebook? The one you altered with the fake data?"

"That I will leave for them to find. Unless they are more clever than I believe them to be, they won't find the flaws in it. If they implement the technology, they will find themselves up…what is your time period's expression? Up shit's creek without a paddle."

26

Goodbye, Goodluck, and Don't Forget to Write

It was a nice little planet, no mammals yet, just a variety of slug-like creepy-crawlers and a flying lizard or two or three to break the monotony. The plants were edible and the water clear and refreshing. They could have stayed there throughout eternity—the end of which seemed more imminent now that the Dweller's people had the Dweller's notebook. Would they see through the misdirection in the almost cryptic notes? Or would they be tricked into traveling to the wrong end of time, to perish as the universe squatted down for the big leap back to its origins, the Big Crunch?

The Dweller, according to Wayland, was chicken shit scared of his own people. So scared he couldn't conjure up a modicum of confrontational courage to fight back. The eons of evolution between the Dweller and the rest of them must have dimmed the human spirit. Not so with the McGinley, Mac Conmara, Ó Ciardha, Delaney, Washington, Langford company. Even Teige was snarling his displeasure at the inaction of hiding out. Even if it was a nice little planet.

The inevitable confab confirmed a course of action; they all agreed to commandeer the school bus with its newly installed time machine and attack the problem frontally. It would mean stranding the Dweller on the planet, creating a Robinson Crusoe sans Friday.

But if successful, they would come back for him. If not…

Surreptitiously they entered the bus. One by one. Wayland had been assigned to distract the Dweller while McGinley started the countdown. There was a characteristic hum to the thing as it warmed up and the Dweller noticed. Wayland hadn't wanted to resort to physical force but now he held the man back with an extended arm while he tried to explain.

"We have to do this," Wayland said. "It's in our nature."

"You must not interfere," said the Dweller. "Not now."

"We must. I gotta go now. Sorry about this." And Wayland landed a haymaker on the Dweller's jaw. The man crumbled; Wayland ran for the bus.

The planet. Well into the future, as the human race considered elapsed time. Distant from Earth, as the human race could measure the enormity of galactic space. Evolved humanity, as even this humanity of disintegrating spiritual integrity might interpret itself. The planet of the advanced humans, where one such human, Nikolai Borisov, having interrogated the captured Hermes Trismegistus, having leaned where to look for the elusive Grisha Leontiy Viktorov, known as the Dweller, having scoured said location finding nothing living, having brought back through time and space from the Dweller's lair the copious notebook containing secrets sought, now consulted that notebook one final time for confirmation.

"It does not seem logical," he said to Chang Jin Chong, the counselman overseeing the scientist's work on the time machine. "This last equation…I wonder."

"Does it not answer the question? Does it not complete the theory? Can it not be implemented?"

"It will work, of course. I have already ordered the necessary elements to finish the machine. We will test it, but…"

As the scientist explained his concerns, a yellow school bus materialized just outside of the laboratory building. It was, by virtue of having arrived one day before this current time, enclosed in a space-time bubble, which made it invisible to anyone in this time. Inside the bus, McGinley explained his own concerns, and began to formulate a plan.

"We don't entirely know what is happening inside the lab," he told the others, "but we think they are getting ready to test the time machine using the Dweller's false notes. My concern is that they will discover the deception and reverse engineer the proper patches to the theory, with the result that all our hard work will have been in vain."

"Can we just rush in there and stop it?" asked Wayland, ever the loose cannon.

"I can see security guards that would surely overpower us should we try. However, I think I can build a portable time bubble which would allow one or two of us to enter invisibly. Once inside, I could deactivate the bubble and you would be entering their current time. Give me an hour or so to work on it. Meanwhile, relax and get ready for our success…or the end of the universe!"

"I should go, of course," said Lorcan Mac Conmara. "You need to be here at the console to control things."

"I want to go," said Wayland. "I have had some experience with hand to hand combat. I wish we had some weapons, though. Do you think they might have ray guns?"

"Perhaps," answered McGinley. "You had better look around here for some kind of blunt instruments. Take the bus apart if you have to."

"And I will go also," said Riordan Ó Ciardha. "Where my master goes, I go."

Developing a portable time bubble took longer than expected. Meanwhile, the scientist, Nikolai Borisov, had run a preliminary test with the new time machine coupled to his faster-than-light device. It worked, but…

"I sent a test box a few light years into the past, but the test results show that it traveled into the future instead!" Borisov told Chang.

"It doesn't work then," said Chang.

"Oh, it works all right. It is as I suspected. The Dweller left his notes for us to find and altered them with a faulty algorithm. He has outsmarted himself, however. I now understand how to correct the formula. We will be successful after all!"

The time bubble extended from the door of the bus like a tentacle of protoplasm. The adventurers were able to walk into it and break off individual bubbles for each. Maneuvering across the landscape was a little like sloshing through thickening mud, but they learned as they sloshed, every footstep like pulling that foot from sucking mud. McGinley made a few adjustments at his console and now they almost floated as they moved into the compound.

They communicated using hand signals since any sounds they made would be heard by the security guards. They had passed by those guards that stood around the exterior, but now they encountered a small army of them inside, blocking their way to the lab in which the time machine was getting its final refinements. Earlier, Wayland had dismantled some of the bench seats in the bus. They were now all armed with pieces of metal which could be used as clubs. This would work, but only if they were released from the bubbles into the current time.

Mac Conmara motioned Wayland and Riordan into positions behind the guards. They would each be attacking two guards, and this would leave one guard unengaged. The alchemist raised his hand and counted down by a show of fingers: one, two, three...now! McGinley, back in the bus, had been watching them closely on a viewer on his console. He released the time bubble and the three materialized behind the guards. Long pieces of steel arched and connected with the first three guards. They went down. The remaining guards were now aware of the attack. Hands went to weapons holstered on belts. Again the steel bludgeons bounced upon the heads of the guards. Again three more fell.

"Shoulda worn helmets," quipped Wayland.

The last standing guard now pointed a handgun at Mac Conmara. Just at the instant that he fired, McGinley engaged the time bubble again. The projectile issuing from the weapon struck the opposite wall and nothing else. The guard, dumbfounded, looked at the inert bodies of his six companions, dropped his weapon and fled from the building yelling, "Ghosts! Ghosts!" His exit was followed by the impossible sound of disembodied laughter.

Once in the lab they waited and observed. The scientist, Nikolai Borisov, was making last minute adjustments to a control panel; a series of wires ran from this to a large black sphere, open on one side and, for the moment, containing only a duplicate control panel. McGinley's ability to monitor them was obstructed by shielding that surrounded the lab. He could only guess at the moment when he should again deactivate the time bubble. Then for a fraction of a second, the shield wavered and he caught a glimpse of the lab. Of course, the shield would need to be lifted if the altered time machine were to venture forth. Forth to where? Would the faulty algorithm be in place?

Borisov finished his work at the control panel in the lab. One last lifting of a lever and the time machine began to energize. Vibrations shook the lab and could be felt even in the yellow school bus. Now the shielding lifted. Now McGinley knew it was the last chance they would have to stop the machine. He deactivated the time bubble and Mac Conmara, Riordan, and Wayland entered the time and space of the scientist.

At first, Borisov was not aware of the intruders. He was apparently satisfied with the settings he had made on the control panel, flipping switches and twisting dials until a crisp chirping issued from the spherical machine. Next he disconnected the many wires and tubes that stretched from the machine to the panel and other devices inside the lab. The newly updated time machine was ready for its voyage to the beginnings of existence. He stood in the doorway of the sphere, paused for a moment to turn and survey the lab he would be leaving, and it was then that he saw the intruders.

Three things happened almost simultaneously. Borisov ran back to the control panel and slammed his palm down upon a large button, sounding an alarm that would surely bring the guards. Wayland jumped at the scientist and began struggling with him. Riordan ran to the laboratory door and pulled it shut, fastening it with a latch against the guards.

Mac Conmara, curious as to the workings of the time machine, and thinking he might deactivate it, entered the sphere. By now, however, Borisov had thrown Wayland to the floor and had given a vicious kick to his head. He now ran to the sphere and entered. There he began to struggle with Mac Conmara. Riordan saw Wayland bleeding on the laboratory floor, saw the scientist and the alchemist wrestling in the time machine, heard the guards banging on the door, and he made a decision: he jumped into the time machine to aid the alchemist.

The lab door burst open. Guards seized Wayland, lifting him to his feet. Consciousness came to him in a rush as did the realization of his predicament. He looked in vain for Riordan and Mac Conmara— had they already been taken away? Then a second realization was thrust upon him by the sound of the time machine as it began to dematerialize: his companions were very probably inside the machine!

"McGinley," Wayland yelled, "bring me back!"

McGinley activated the time bubble once again. Nothing happened. Wayland was still in the future space-time where the guards rough handled him and pelted him with questions. Mac Conmara and Riordan were gone, trapped inside the time machine with the scientist, Borisov. To make matters worse, a group of guards had spotted the yellow school bus and were advancing toward it. McGinley could no longer hide in the time bubble. There was only one thing to do: retreat back in time, back to the past where the Dweller was waiting. Waiting for the death of Time.

The planet had no name; they thought of it as the Dweller's New Planet. It was more desolate and depressing than the Dweller's Old Planet, and it hadn't the advantage of all the Dweller's lab equipment, the devices that would have let them track the progress of Borisov's time machine. The yellow school bus materialized right on target next to where they had last seen the Dweller. The Dweller, however, was nowhere to be seen. They had built a series of hastily constructed huts for shelter when they had first occupied that planet—not so long ago, but it seemed like centuries since they had left. They searched the huts and spread out in all directions, but the Dweller had left no trace of himself. There was no way he could have left this time frame or the planet, for that matter. They feared the worse: predators they had been unaware of might be lurking nearby.

"We should go back and rescue Wayland," Judo told McGinley.

"I can't get the time bubble to work," he replied. "You wouldn't be invisible. And there are too many guards. It would be suicide."

"Speaking of suicide," interjected Melanie, "do you think that mad scientist is heading for the Big Bang? You said there was a chance they had seen through our ruse."

"He *is* mad if that's the case. We are still here, so nothing has happened to time…as yet. If we don't find the Dweller by tomorrow, I think we should go back to his old planet where his laboratory is. The coordinates are still in the school bus's data bank. We could track Borisov and check on Wayland."

"At least we would know what the future…or the past, as it were, might bring," said Judo.

Wayland found himself locked in a small chamber with Hermes Trismegistus. Hermes did not remember him from their past encounter inside the Sphinx, and Wayland did not recognize Hermes, as he had only known him as She. At first neither man said anything to the other. But presently, their situation demanded some reconnaissance and deliberation.

"Escape is futile," said Hermes. "There is no doorknob or other means of opening the door out of here. And even if we got out, what would we do?"

"I'm hoping we can be rescued. The Professor still has control of the time machine in the yellow school bus. He'll find a way. If our captors come into this room again we need to be prepared to overpower them."

"I'm not much for fisticuffs. And why would your professor want to rescue me?"

"Because he's a good man, even if you are not."

Even as Wayland said this, Dr. McGinley was bending over the console of one of the marvelous machines at the Dweller's laboratory back in the space-time of the planet where they had first encountered that scientist. It had taken some time to reconnect the time machine to the assortment of devices in the lab. It was time they had previous little of, but time well spent as finally McGinley brought an image up on a screen. There he saw Wayland and Hermes in their adjunct prison, far in the future.

"At least they are alive," he told the others. "Maybe I can retrieve them, bring them here."

"What about the alchemist and his apprentice?" Melonie asked.

"I don't seem to be able to zero in on them. They are moving too fast…faster than the speed of light. I'll keep trying."

"Can you tell whether they are going forward or backward in time?"

"Not yet. In either case we may have a certain amount of time left before anything catastrophic happens. When and if it does, we won't be aware of it. We will have ceased to exist."

"Judo and I have talked about this," said Melanie. "We want you to send us back to Earth, to the America before the white man came. We were happy there. Life was simple even if brutal at times. We'll live out whatever life is left to us in a world where humans are basically good."

"Native Americans fought wars with each other. They sometimes polluted their environments and depleted their natural resources."

"But they didn't make a religion out of greed and hatred, like Twentieth Century mankind has. Send us back."

"I will. But one thing at a time. First…"

Wayland and Hermes had been retrieved from the planet of the future, and just in the nick, as they say, of time. Guards had thrown open the door and had pointed some decidedly wicked looking weapons at the two hapless prisoners. What might happen next would undoubtedly not be good. Then, in an instant, they found themselves deposited on the floor of the Dweller's lab on the old planet where the Sphinx had been and where they had once stood on a rapidly diminishing cliff face and had the discovered the true nature of the Dweller.

"Thanks, Professor. It was getting a bit hairy back there," said Wayland.

"Hermes," said Dr. McGinley, "what are we going to do with you?"

"Um, I had a nice gig going back in old Egypt, if you know what I mean. Send me back there. I promise I'll be good."

"How about you, Wayland? Any interest in transportation to another time? It seems probable that time and existence as we know it will be ending in the very near future. Judo and Melanie are headed to pre-European America. I'm thinking of going back to the twentieth to be with Scheherazade, my cat who may or may not be alive."

"I guess I'll go with you. What about all this time machine stuff?"

"We just leave it as is. On the outside chance that time does not end, maybe we will come back some day and explore the past and the future once again. Oh, I wish that I could say something genuinely philosophical…something encouraging. Maybe there will be an alternate universe that will arise from the chaos in which humankind will be more enlightened, less likely to destroy everything."

"I'd put my money on dogs and cats. Speaking of dogs, who is going to take Teige with them?" asked Wayland.

"We will," said Melanie.

The decisions made, the logistics worked out, McGinley set their plans in motion. A puff of mist here, a wrinkle of reality there, and it was done. Melanie, Judo, and the dog materialized on the Chesapeake Bay Peninsula during the late 14th century. Hermes Trismegistus appeared in the bed chamber of Nefertiti, Royal Wife to the Pharaoh Akhenaten. Unfortunately for Hermes, Akhenaten just happened to be present. McGinley and Wayland found themselves in the professor's cottage, shortly after the time machine had been destroyed by fire. The duplicates of McGinley and Wayland had been sent to this exact time frame by the Dweller, so now there would be two of each of them once again.

At the reunion of the doppelgangers, McGinley and McGinley flipped a coin to see which of them would take a vacation from the lab. They couldn't be seen together. A nice cabin in the Ozarks, perhaps? As for the two Waylands, they thought a road trip was in order. The Finger Lakes were nice this time of the year. They'd be identical twins to anyone who asked. At least the cat was still alive.

The spherical time machine inside of which were the scientist Nikolai Borisov, the alchemist Loran Mac Conmara, and his apprentice Riordan Éamon Ó Ciardha, continued on its journey toward the beginning...and the possible ending...of Time.

Byron Grush

27

The Death of Time

The stars are scattered all over the sky like shimmering tears, there must be great pain in the eye from which they trickled. —Georg Buchner

Even these stars, which seem so numerous, are as sand, as dust - or less than dust - in the enormity of the space in which there is nothing. —Carl Sagan

I always think of space-time as being the real substance of space, and the galaxies and the stars just like the foam on the ocean. —George Smoot

Nikolai Borisov, Loran Mac Conmara, and Riordan Éamon Ó Ciardha had blacked out from the sudden surge of the time machine now equipped with its faster-than-light drive. One by one they woke and little by little came to the realization that they were hurtling through space and time through a universe that was evolving in the opposite direction. From the outside, the time machine looked like a black sphere. From the inside it appeared to have translucent walls; they could see the occasional galaxy spiraling by like a frisbee tossed for some gigantic cosmic dog to catch.

Mac Conmara considered their plight. Trapped in a time machine piloted by a scientist of the far far far future, whom they characterized as mad, like a hatter, a march hare, and a Cheshire cat all rolled into one, they were headed for the beginning of existence—

the Big Bang. Well, there wouldn't be a bang, for who would be there to hear it? They would, that was true, but that was meaningless because there was nothing to explode, nothing in the sense of something banging, in the sense of sound having a medium in which to travel—even if there were ears to respond to it. There would be nothing to hear. Then, at a precise instance, some hydrogen and some helium would be created and begin to expand. Still nothing would exist like stars or galaxies or planets.

There might be something to see, however. The universe would be immensely hot in that first second. One hundred billion degrees Fahrenheit. That heat wave wouldn't last. The cosmos would begin to cool and those errant particles, electrons and protons and neutrons and positrons and photons and neutrinos and God only knows what else, would jiggle and jangle and collide. And eventually they would form atoms with nuclei and spinning electrons and the photons…the stuff of light…would cease to be scattered aimlessly and they would form the afterglow of the Big Bang. Let there be light!

But there would be nothing to see until about 17 million years had passed. The stuff of life would slowly come into being. Stuff takes a long while to get from a silent bang and an emerging after glow to the origin of pulsating slime in a primordial ocean on a little insignificant planet that would come to be called Earth. About 13.799 ± 0.021 billion years later, humans would be splitting some of those atoms and much later, they would be taking the ultimate road trip backwards from the era of humans to that Primordial Singularity thought to be the origin of the universe.

The road trip was not only daunting, it was time consuming—so to speak. The mad scientist and the alchemist and the apprentice, huddled together in the cramped shell of the time machine, had some time to kill. So to speak. At first the three simply glared at each other. Each was readying a verbal assault: criticism, blame, warning, threats. But the spectacle outside their little world, that drama of absolute nothingness speckled with the occasional spot of light, now surrounded them in a dizzying and inescapable panorama. It awed them, dampened their anger. They became thoughtful, each in his own manner.

The alchemist had only his recent experiences with time travel to aid him in comprehension of this impossible journey. In his pre-time-travel past he had been seeped in the Aristotelian view of the universe as unchangeable, at least until Tycho Brahe's discovery of what he interpreted as a "new star" in the cosmos (which in fact was the ancient light of a supernova finally reaching the Earth). Now, to have flown past constellations no longer identifiable, as the distances between those familiar stars multiplied by many magnitudes, his earlier beliefs were shattered again for one last, and now most permanent time. He was transfixed with wonderment.

Riordan, early educated in all things alchemical, had later studied modern science—mid-twentieth century modern—during his stay with Leona Libby. Hence he knew a little about the Big Bang and his perspective gave him a curiosity unimpeded by the fearful awareness that they were headed toward an ending, albeit at the beginning of Time. All things must pass, and it now seemed that all things might never occur, but he would be there to see it and experience it. He sensed the same strange conflicted anticipation in Borisov, the scientist of the future. He found his voice and addressed the man:

"Professor…may I call you that? Why are you doing this? Isn't there a danger of disrupting the beginnings of the universe? If we materialize in the first few seconds, would we not become a sort of fly in the ointment, a contamination, a bad seed to sprout an adulterated reality? Might we be about to cause the death of Time before it even is born?"

"Young person," answered the scientist, "you ask questions that I have pondered as well. However, we are not going to stop our journey at the point of the Singularity or even near it. We are going farther…back *before* the beginning."

"I don't understand. How is that even possible?"

"The unanswered question about the so-called origin of the universe is whether anything existed before the Big Bang, and if so, what was it? If time only started at the moment of expansion, or as we call it, inflation, then it is possible the universe pre-dated the Big Bang but in some other form. We believe that the expansion of the universe is speeding up, which it should not be as it loses energy and should therefore be slowing down. We think some kind of dark energy is pushing it faster and faster, energy born from dark matter. Dark matter must have existed before the Primordial Singularity you call the Big Bang. That is the treasure that I seek…matter in its most fundamental form."

Riordan and Mac Conmara just stared at each other for a time.

Each felt in his heart of hearts that the scientist was truly mad. But what could they do about it? Although the alchemist had examined the control panel in the time machine, he was unsure as to how it operated or even if it could be operated to slow or reverse their progress. The scientist was bent over the board now, studying various readouts, but he gave no clue to the others as to which were controls and which were just gauges or dials.

"What is this dark matter he spoke of," the alchemist asked his apprentice. "Is it 'dark' in the sense of being 'evil'?"

"I don't know," answered Riordan. "It is a theory that tries to explain why it is that all of the matter in the universe accounts for only about 15 percent of the universe's mass. It is called 'dark' because we can't see it. It behaves differently from regular matter. Some think it is composed of subatomic particles which we haven't yet discovered, and others think it may be an extension of gravity."

"Why does our mad friend think it is so important?"

"I remember reading about this. It may be impossible to repeat what I read exactly, but I'll try." [The apprentice here was too shy to admit to his nearly photographic memory. Perhaps the natural diffidence of youth had come into play, or perhaps his esteem for the alchemist required of him the avoidance of a posture of condescension.] "It was something like this: matter was formed after the Big Bang, of course, but the dominant presence of radiation affected regular matter to the degree that its density was perturbed…that is…washed out. It would not be able to condense into structures such as stars and galaxies. Dark matter, by definition, is unaffected by radiation. Its density could provide a sort of well or conduit to allow regular matter to collapse into the structures we see today…well…we saw back in the day."

"I see. I guess. The existence of a force that we cannot see is well known in alchemy and cosmology. Modern science has merely come up with a name for it. Such is the evolution of the mind of man!"

"What if we rush the control panel and just start pushing buttons and switches. We're probably going to die anyway. At least we could keep the time machine from colliding with the Big Bang."

"Let's watch and wait for a bit. Some opportunity may arise. I don't suppose we can talk him out of his plan, but we might distract him enough…"

"I'll engage him in a debate. You've looked at the control panel.

You should be the one to…"

"End this madness before it ends…everything!"

Stars as "less than dust" appeared and then disappeared like twinkling fireflies in the immensity of the darkness. Black holes were present like indistinguishable inkblots on black paper. Supernova flashed and then were gone. Cosmic dust storms surged and ebbed, icy comets surfing their waves. It was all an illusion for the time travelers. They did not exist in the same time frame, or time plane, as it were, of the celestial carnival through which they passed. They rode on gravity waves that undulated like strings twisted and pulled by some god playing with them in a cat's cradle of unfathomable size.

How was it, thought Riordan, that the light from the distant galaxies was visible given that they traveled at many times the speed of light. Was this not a paradox? Yet that enormous velocity was applied to their passage through Time, not through space. Thus the twinkling cosmos presented itself in little flashes—and, on occasion, great blinding flashes such as when they passed through a star going supernova. One such blinding flash had just occurred as Riordan and Mac Conmara contemplated becoming the first ever space pirates. Yes, the blindness lasted just about long enough to make a move toward the console. But how to predict when the next great flash would come?

As they neared the epicenter and the first moment of time, the universe was denser. Blackholes were attracting infant stars and cosmic dust which would form planets and asteroids. The likelihood of encountering another supernova was probably nil. Riordan attempted to engage Borisov in conversation.

"Professor," Riordan asked Borisov, "will we see God?"

"God? Do you think…? Oh, your primitive culture had its religions, didn't it? It's a wonder science ever developed to the point it did. No, young person, there is no God. No God except the laws of physics, some of which we are about to discover."

"But how did all this start? Who started it? There must have been something…some intelligence. Some plan."

"Many scientists believe the universe is a cyclic system. It started to expand, they think, 14 billion years ago…well, counting from when we left the lab this morning. It will continue to expand until it uses all the energy available, then it will collapse in upon itself, resulting in another so-called Big Bang."

"And you don't subscribe to this theory?"

"The expansion is speeding up. It is unlikely there will be a collapse. Therefore, there was a beginning and there may or may not be an end. I am seeking what was there before the beginning."

"God."

"Humph. Can't shake you of that mythology, eh? Have you heard of the Many Worlds Theory, the Multi-universe? There may be many realities. As we travel through Time we may be touching on some of them."

"And you don't think we'll all die when we reach the Big Bang? And cause the death of Time? Show us how to operate the controls of this thing so we can turn it around before it's too late."

"Impossible. You would not be able to stop or slow the machine before it reaches its goal. The controls are frozen. You are paranoid. I suggest you relax and enjoy the spectacle of the beginning of the universe…and the pre-universe."

In a "cliff-hanger" movie of the Twentieth Century, at this precise moment, a dramatic flash would occur and the alchemist's apprentice would cold cock the mad scientist while the alchemist, contrary to the scientist's bluff, would in fact manipulate the controls, turning the time machine around and back toward the future it originally came from, saving them and preventing the death of Time. But it wasn't a movie.

Light issuing from the particles that swirled freely before combining into the elements that would form stars and plants suddenly disappeared. They had reached a point in time some 300,000 years after the Singularity had begun to expand. With the darkness came the heat. Although insulated by virtue of traveling within a bubble of space-time, still the enormous temperatures affected the time travelers. They felt as if they had fallen asleep beneath a heat lamp.

In the stifling hot blackness the alchemist stumbled over something. He realized that when he had entered the time machine he had been carrying a long piece of metal wrenched from the yellow school bus which he had used as a club, but dropped once inside the sphere. He stooped to retrieve it. His sense of the space around him was acute; he had been inching toward the console while Riordan had engaged the scientist in conversation. He swung the piece of metal down against the console, again, and again, and again. There came a cry from the scientist: "Oh no! Do not…"

Gravity inside the time machine disappeared. They floated within the sphere like goldfish in a bowl. The machine tumbled, still hurtling at an insane speed toward the Singularity. As they approached, the space between things began to shrink: the space inside the space-time bubble constricted around the time machine which, in turn, began to shrink. The space between molecules, the space between atoms, the space between electrons and nuclei all shrank as if in concert with the Singularity which, as time rolled backward, became more and more miniscule. The shrinking of things was not happening all at the same rate. Had the travelers been able to see anything, they would have watched as the walls closed in toward them.

Then—the instant. The instant at which Time began. The beginning of eternity. The Singularity. The matter that existed at that momentous instant was solid, dark, and without parts. The time machine sliced into it like a hot ember into dry wood. By now the time machine was itself a solid ball: time travelers and equipment were fused together and hung like striations in a glass marble—a marble made of dense, black glass. But the instant had no measure; it had no time against which it could be said to exist. The time machine passed through the mass of dark matter and exited out to the other side of eternity—the end that was the beginning. Still, ironically traveling backwards through time (for Time now existed on the other side of the Singularity just as the scientist had imagined it would), the time machine began to expand in a sort of bizarre backwards parody of the Big Bang.

Several hundred thousand years later (before?) but a mere matter of minutes for those inside the time machine, the program that had pushed them to this moment had run its course. Their movement through time ceased. The machine and all those inside had expanded to a functional size and shape and the life which had been snuffed out for an infinitely tiny instant returned to the time travelers. Gravity returned and the three unfortunate floaters fell to the floor.

"Where are we?" asked Riordan.

"Better…*when* are we?" said Mac Conmara.

Borisov answered them: "We are hanging in space as the universe is compressing down toward a Singularity. Don't worry, nothing will happen for many thousands of years. But we are on the other side!

We've proven that the universe is cyclic. Now I can only hope all that banging I heard during the dark period doesn't mean you've damaged the controls."

The scientist examined the control console. Dials and touch screens were shattered, but for the most part, the panel seemed intact. He experimented, programming a short jump through time, backwards—that is, toward the beginning of the collapse of this universe, and farther from the Singularity. This seemed to work, and now the space outside of the time machine was filled with galaxies and clouds of cosmic dust.

"We can return to our own time," said Borisov. "Please, if you value you lives, do not interfere again!"

Borisov worked at the console, programming the time machine to reenter the Singularity and to travel beyond it billions of years into the future where his world, a New Earth for the human race, circled a sun in a distant solar system from that of Old Earth. The alchemist and his apprentice could fend for themselves as far as the scientist was concerned. But something was wrong. The programming took all right, but they were traveling toward a Singularity at the *other end* of the Time that existed in this particular universe. They would not return to their own universe. There was nothing they could do to alter the course.

"Well, my friends," said Borisov somewhat sarcastically, "we are off on a new adventure. We may find new worlds waiting for us. Or we may not. Perhaps you were right after all...we should not have meddled with things beyond our understanding. However, I have no regrets."

"What do you think?" Riordan asked the alchemist.

"What? Oh...I was just thinking. I was trying to remember some old formulas I used to work with. Now if we just had some saltpeter and some pure mercury..."

Afterword

I am a shameless thief: cutting from the pages of history to paste together a collage of improbable construction. Words I clip and rearrange. Imaginings grow then from odd juxtapositions and the gaps that are left need the addition of imagery. I have often said (am I quoting here some more capable author?) that the stories tell themselves…I just do the typing.

I found in literature from the worlds of alchemy and the occult a poetic insight I had not expected. As Lorcan Mac Conmara may have mused, there are parallel explanations of the mysteries of life which are painted in many colors: the dull grays and browns of modern science, the sparkling reds and yellows of astrology, the pale pinks and whites of religion, and the deep blues and purples of alchemy. I was intrigued to find a version of the Many Worlds theory in the writings attributed to Hermes Trismegistus. Count Saint Germain's stories read like pulp literature from the 1930s. I borrowed some of both for dialogue and altered the text very little. Part two has the alchemist's voice, not mine, but it fascinates me and so…there ye be.

This is my second attempt at science fiction, not counting numerous short stories I submitted to Fantasy and Science Fiction Magazine many, many years ago—the rejection slips the magazine sent out were written on the backs of old covers. The concept of time travel gels nicely with my obsession with historical narrative. One can imagine, for instance, the conversation between Albert Einstein and Isaac Newton becoming intense. Time travel also gave me the opportunity to kill off certain key figures of history…and of our own time as well. An indulgence of fantasy versus reality, but not without the consequential outcomes that logic would dictate. Pessimism? Paranoia? Who can say?

Most of the "real" people and places portrayed here are familiar to the readers: Einstein, Newton, Enrico Fermi, of course. Leona

Libby is perhaps not as well known, but her achievements in atomic science are laudable. Count Saint Germain is indeed a historical character although claims that he was 500 years old are part of the myth that followed him through the ages. A twentieth-century occultist, Madam Blavatsky, claims to have met him. Isaac Newton studied and wrote extensively about alchemy although he refrained from publishing his musing about his search for the Philosopher's Stone.

Will we ever travel through Time? Stephen Hawking pointed to Einstein's theory that if one left Earth on a spaceship moving faster than the speed of light, one would return to the Earth in a future time well beyond the time it took for the journey. He suggested that traveling backward in time, however, was probably impossible. If it were, why then had no one from the future ever visited our present? Maybe they have. Maybe they declined to identify themselves in order to not cause a paradox and alter the future.

I owe lot to the adventure fantasy of A. Merritt, Clark Ashton Smith, and H. Rider Haggard, and to the classic time-travel novels of Jack Finney, Clifford Simak, H. G. Wells, and even Mark Twain (*A Connecticut Yankee in King Arthur's Court*). And so many others. Like space travel, which now is a reality, time travel has inspired writers of science fiction from the earliest beginnings. Alternate universes suggest a myriad of plot and character ideas, as well. I hope my humble effort entertains; I have enjoyed the journey of writing it.

When I was young and full of myself I thought I knew a great many things. And often was I prompted to impart such insight as I had accumulated. Now, just a few years short of ancient, I am more prone to be doubtful. My voice is a stammer of uncertainty and I hesitate to attempt to set down any great truths. However. The thread winding through this novel that touches on humankind's greed and intolerance reflects our modern-day experience as much as that of our history. Will we never learn? As the poet said:

> *But time is lost, which never will renew,*
> *While we too far the pleasing Path pursue*

About the Author

Byron Grush was born and raised in Naperville, Illinois, just southwest of Chicago. He is a third generation native of that town. Grush studied art and design at the University of Illinois and filmmaking at the School of the Art Institute of Chicago. At the Art Institute he was a student of Gregory Markopoulos, one of the originators of the New America Cinema movement in the 1960s.

Grush then taught at The School of the Art Institute of Chicago, creating a course in film animation in the mid-seventies. He later became an Associate Professor at the College of Art at Northern Illinois University in Dekalb, Illinois, where he taught in the Electronic Media area. He is the author of a book on hand-drawn animation techniques entitled *The Shoestring Animator*. Becoming interested in genealogy, he wrote a trilogy of historical novels based upon what he had learned about his early ancestors.

He and his wife moved to New Mexico in the late 1990s, and opened an art gallery featuring Outsider and Visionary Art in Santa Fe. They returned to the Midwest to retire in the small town of Delavan, Wisconsin, a place that reminds them of their roots. Grush writes, paints and studies Tai Chi.

Byron Grush

Other fiction by Byron Grush

All The Way By Water

Once Upon a Gold Rush

Road of Stars

Dance Beneath A Diamond Sky

Violet at The Breakers: a novella

The New Unwritten Law: a novella

The Scrapple Eater: a novella

1954 or Just press the I Believe Button

Luncheon at the Dead Rat

Romeo's Revenge and Other Wisconsin Stories

www.ingramcontent.com/pod-product-compliance
Lightning Source LLC
Chambersburg PA
CBHW071128260626
47162CB00003B/701